Also by Molly Parkin in Sphere Books:

WRITE UP

Full Up

MOLLY PARKIN

SPHERE POPULAR CLASSICS

SPHERE BOOKS LIMITED

First published in Great Britain by Michael Joseph Ltd 1976
Copyright © Molly Parkin 1976
First Sphere Books edition 1977
27 Wrights Lane, London W8 5TZ
Reprinted 1979, 1981, 1983, 1984, 1985 (twice), 1987

To Sarah
The Shiniest Star

Publisher's Note

This novel is a work of fiction. Names, characters, places and
incidents are either the product of the author's imagination
or are used fictitiously, and any resemblance to actual persons,
living or dead, events, or locales is entirely coincidental.

TRADE
MARK

Set in Intertype Lectura

Printed and bound in Great Britain by
Collins, Glasgow

I was branded on both buttocks with the sure indentation of a whole row of gas taps, each outlined in a faint film of grease.

'You've impressed me,' I said.

He smiled, knowing he had. Who would have thought that this Savile Row suiting, its lines so smooth and self-disciplined, contained such a wild and impertinent weapon. What wisdom, what vigour – what width!

When he unplugged me, the noise was like a soft cork coming out of a bottle. 'Care for a Cuban?' he produced from his waistcoat a moulded, fine leather cigar case. Why not, yes, why not smoke his cigar – celebrate Castro together.

We stood, still half-dressed, companionably smoking – my skirts hitched high on my small shoulder straps, my filmy pants snagged on one shoe. His immaculate trousers, less immaculate now, hung at half-mast from their mooring. 'The occasion, surely,' he said it first, though I had meant to for the last few moments, 'calls for champagne.'

'On the house,' I was able to answer.

We shuffled together towards the large fridge, standard catering model, reserved strictly for drinks. 'Well stocked with champagne, Moët Chandon, I'm afraid, not Dom Perignon. And not even Vintage.' I said all that to hide my shame, to side-track his attention away from the hideous contents that some indolent slob had chosen to stow in the fridge. A battered blancmange, its turreted peaks bruised like a child's badly made sandcastle. The flaky remains of some badly burnt rissoles mixed up with some stale mashed potato. A glutinous glob of spilt greying gravy hung like an icicled finger, almost touching the crazily stacked champagne bottles. 'Stacked by a cretin,' I added, 'as you can see.'

He turned with new interest at my words. 'Really! A mental defective? You employ handicapped persons as part of your staff? That's certainly rare in a restaurant – a high risk I believe. The danger, I mean, from hot flying fat and the degree of high temperature generally. They're like children, you see, the same curiosity and the same unawareness of danger. It's as if that warning device were turned off, its mechanism underdeveloped. And, of course, this being so, the resulting breakages and inevitable losses in food fuck up the fine Samaritan urge to afford work opportunities to these unfortunates: altruism defeated by sheer economics. Nevertheless, I commend you on your humanity. No wonder this small restaurant of yours exudes such irrepressible warmth. It must have taken a very long time—'

'Two days. We've been open two days.'

A sense of surprise shivered through me, or was it my bum getting cold? Two days, was that all? Had it taken two days to disrupt my whole life to this point?

'Though, of course, we'd thought of it – Vincent and I, my partner, I don't think you met – we thought of it long before this. I say "long", though it was actually last week—'

'Wouldn't it be nice to have one's own restaurant, and not have to fuss over food. Just go there with the kids, and Auntie of course, then come home without paying – Vince, are you listening?'

I watched Vincent combing his hair carefully over his scalp. It was blowy outside and he'd walked from Sloane Square, holding his hair in place with his left hand and having to skulk through the side streets because of it, instead of cutting a fine figure on the King's Road.

'I'm surprised you don't go in for a wig, Vince. They do wonderful ones these days. You can't tell the difference, they don't come off in bed—' A Gentleman Caller of mine, a dear love, wore a Crown Topper. Should I spill the beans and say which? Or would that be dreadfully disloyal of me? Yes, it would. Vincent shuddered. 'A toupée, oh, it's not that bad yet! Is it, darling?'

'No, of course not,' I lied. 'Only joking.'

I looked around. A layer of dusty fluff stirred slowly under the sofa, imprisoned beneath the Heal's black leather which I'd bought as a sign of mourning when The Old Man had died. I'd bought lots of black things that year, I remembered. Black lipstick, which I'd had to give up, it made my teeth look too yellow. Black plates which the children disliked. Black pillows and sheets which showed all too clearly afterwards if I'd not slept alone. And I'd taken a black boy as a lover. Just the once, a sweet student who'd come searching for digs. He'd enrolled at the Commonwealth Institute that morning, and was already missing his mother. Above the sofa, the Francis Bacon hung skew-whiff against the wall. It had been hanging that way for over a week.

'Isn't it glorious,' I said to Vincent, 'not to have someone cleaning. Coming in and clearing up, restoring terrible order – though no doubt,' I sighed, 'it will soon get me down. The kids took it upon themselves to do the laundry list last week; it was completely indecipherable. All chewing gum and chocolate bickies.' Vincent turned from the mirror, his follicles now facing immaculately one way. With order restored and his vulnerable scalp thus thatched and hidden from sight, he was able to give me his full attention. 'You'll have to put an ad in the *Chelsea Post*, or on one of the Sloane Square shop boards. That reminds me, I saw a tart's card in the pet shop window, advertising her pussy. "PUSSY FOR SALE", there was no mistaking – rather ingenious I thought.'

'Pussy for sale.' I repeated his words. 'Yes, that's good. You know, I've always thought that I wouldn't mind that, with my own little clientele. It could be quite cosy, if you gave cups of tea and took time off for chats in between. I think where lots of girls go wrong, and don't enjoy job satisfaction, is in not making the service personal enough—'

'That's why you'd be so bad on the game, it's not meant to be personal in that sense. No involvement emotionally – you wouldn't survive for a week. Though it might make sense, my darling, I must say, if instead of being open-house here continually supplying every Tom, Dick and Harry not including

7

your Gentlemen Callers – if there were some way to convert your generous spirit into terms of hard cash in the hand.'

Hard cash in the hand was an obsession with Vincent, who'd been on and off the dole since his first days in Rep. His two bitterest disappointments, professionally, were that he'd failed to play the film roles, firstly, as the homosexual friend of Rita Tushingham in *A Taste of Honey*, and, secondly, as the homosexual friend of Julie Christie in *Darling*. Our relationship, his and mine, was played out with these parts still in mind. As if a third similar role might present itself and he'd be able to audition well-prepared. Which was why one was left with the feeling of having been rehearsed. Even badly rehearsed, the hysteria pitched a little too high.

'I'm starving!' he exclaimed now, one hand on his stomach. Like Hamlet denouncing his sanity. Then, 'What have you got?' 'That's just what I've said, Vince, I've got nothing. It all seems to have gone! Where and how, God only knows, but different people keep popping in and the kids bring back half the school – you're right, it is like open-house. I'd be better off with a restaurant.'

Vincent had taken the few steps to the kitchen and proudly returned with some cheese. A soft triangular piece of Dairylea processed squashed beyond recognition but still safely edible in its silver paper. 'I found this,' he said tearing it off. He shut his eyes as he ate and composed a fine profile, his chin high like Ivor Novello. Or that other famous profile actor, John Barrymore. Senior or Junior? No, wasn't that the Fairbanks, Father and Son? Vincent would know right away. I watched him poised in pure delight, sucking down Dairylea. Could almost see the yellow denseness sliding through his throat, as thick and as creamy as catarrh. And probably as comforting.

'How divine!' he murmured. Divine? Dairylea? Not as nice as the Brie I'd bought yesterday, or the Boursin Fine Herbes, for that matter I thought. What bugger had eaten both those then? Vincent opened his eyes. 'A brainwave! Of course!' What, the processing process at Kraft? Vincent's theatricality could get on one's nerves if he weren't such a friend, fond and true.

'It's only just sunk in — the restaurant. A restaurant! Our restaurant! Why not — run between us — partners, my pet! Oh, yes, what a brilliant idea!'

I looked at my watch, the kids were due back, and Auntie. 'We'll be eating out tonight, Vince — you'll come, do, my treat. It's seven now—'

Vincent was clearly over-excited. He clasped his slim frame with both arms, until his fingers almost met at the back. He managed to look quite epileptic, the body so warped and the face so intent. I'd noticed before — this physical buckling of Vincent's body when his mind seemed caught in a spin. The limbs reflected the mental tension.

'Yes, it's seven o'clock now.' I spoke extra normally in an effort to calm him. 'They should all be back here by now. Auntie's taken them out, over to Battersea Funfair. Perhaps I should cruise over the bridge in the car, in case they can't find a taxi. It's pretty bad on Saturday nights. And Bogey's too small to walk back by himself, which means the girls will keep taking turns giving piggy-backs. It's very dangerous that, in pre-pubescence, giving piggybacks, so I've read. Almost been medically proved already as the root cause of prolapsed wombs in menopause—'

Vincent shuddered. I'd broken the spell of his intensity. 'How riveting, darling. I didn't know that.'

I laughed. A pleasant evening lay ahead, all eating out together. The only question was: out where? Which restaurant? With our own, we'd have no need to wonder.

We sat around a comfortable table for four, all six of us, especially laid in the window of 235, a bistro-type restaurant on the King's Road. The sort that might suit Vincent and me. I'd chosen it in fact for that very purpose, intending a surreptitious study. A glance on the quiet at their organization, at their service and mainly their menu. Vincent, as yet, was not much concerned with the practical running details. He seemed not quite convinced of my participating, not even when I pointed out that the two were linked. The ability, or the will — and the wish.

9

'Oh, but I can see it all so well, can't you! Together, you as Earth Mother, Mummy to all – and me as the gracious Mine Host! Ooh!' He shrilled and drew his breath. 'Ooh, dearie me, I say!'

Auntie blinked, and smiled at me. 'What's Vincent saying?'

'Yes, what is he, Mum? What is he talking about?' Tallulah, my oldest, blinked at me too. Blindly behind her glasses. Zsa-Zsa, her sister, was pouting; as usual looking uncommonly like a young camel. Everyone had warned us, The Old Man and I, that we invited disaster with such a choice of names. So exotic, so hard to live up to. But I had no doubts that my ugly ducklings would emerge much later as swans – as I had, by one means and another. Bogey my two-year-old beauty, was less handicapped it seemed by his name. Everyone wrongly assumed him to be named after Humphrey Bogart; in actual fact Bogey merely referred to a slight blockage of one nostril. An irregularity at birth causing an abundance of snotballs. I might have wondered if his condition was hereditary, but there was no way of checking on this since I'd never known who might be his father. It's true that for the one whole winter following his birth I did pay additional attention to those Gentlemen Callers of mine with uncommonly severe sinus trouble, and signs of sustained coughs and colds. But since that season was particularly harsh, and all seemed to fall in the grip of the weather with more or less similar suffering, I relinquished my fruitless quest.

A waiter came to take our order, as I was about to explain our restaurant idea. He was young, with hair like Christ, wearing a Habitat apron: navy blue with wide butcher-boy stripes. Vincent simpered, 'I like your pinny.' The boy tossed his mane and ignored us.

'There now, she's taken offence! I must mind my p's and q's! Naughty Vince – smack his pandy and ask for more.' Vincent rapped himself over his knuckles. The children dissolved into wild paroxysms of mirth. The waiter walked away. Vincent pursed his mouth exaggeratedly and stared deliberately at the boy's backside. 'Oh my, with a neat little botty like hers, you'd think she'd try to be nicer.'

Bogey sneezed and showered the surface of the table with mud-toned mucus. Vincent winced and held a delicate hand to his eyes. 'Darling,' he said to me. 'The little chap's condition would appear to be worsening. Oh dear,' he peered in horror through his fingers. 'Someone please mop him before I vomit.'

Nobody had a hankie. Auntie leant forward obligingly. 'Shall I use this clean serviette then, on little boyo's nose? Or am I to leave it on my lap? It don't do much good down there.'

Bogey put out a tongue to catch the flow and smacked his small lips in delight. It was just as well, I sometimes thought, he enjoyed himself so much. Come famine and flood, this son of mine would probably survive us all, a cycle of self sufficiency.

Vincent's handkerchief was from Turnbull & Asser and was tied silkily around his neck. 'Sorry, I'm sure, but no, it's not for sacrifice. I'd have to burn it afterwards. Here, have my napkin.' And he threw it in Bogey's face, who, thinking it was a game, promptly threw it back glistening on one side. It landed on Vincent's hand. 'Ye gods,' he screamed. 'How disgusting!', and jumped violently to his feet knocking, in so doing, his chair back into the legs of a passing waitress. She dropped the carafe that she was carrying. The contents splashed Vincent right up to his crotch, all over his new Oxford Bags. The first time on. I looked at him and then at them. He burst into violent tears.

The Honourable Hannibal Knutt was waiting by the time we finally got back. We walked home. The children ran ahead, while I followed slowly behind with Auntie on my arm. Battersea Funfair had done her bunions in. She'd insisted on coming out in her bedroom slippers, but was now complaining of the pavement's chill striking right clean through the soles. 'That's why people wear shoes, Auntie,' I patiently tried to explain. She didn't like shoes, but favoured wellington boots instead, as being much more comfortable. But those were for winter and we were now in spring. Her slippers were usually from Woolworth's, mauve whenever possible, mock satin, quilted. They looked hideously out of place, even in the streets of Chelsea, at the bottom of her dark lisle stockings (to hide her elastic supports, worn for varicose veins). But Vincent found them very camp. 'Oh yes! The height of chic!'

He gave a despairing groan. 'Oh Christ – look. Look who's there. He'll wake up half the street.' Nutty had sighted us as soon as we rounded the corner. He was outside my house sitting in the middle of a heap of scrap metal, honking his horn as a welcome. Vincent spun round. 'I can't stand it, darling, not today. Nutty would be the last straw. That car of his is a positive disgrace, it's a wonder your neighbours don't register a formal complaint. Or apply for a reduction of their rates. What is it meant to be, anyway?'

'It started life as a Land Rover. Very suitable for scouring his estates. It's a country car—' I could smell the manure from where I was. 'I quite like it myself. It's quite relaxing. You don't have to worry about the kids. Spoiling the upholstery, I mean. I much perfer it to a smart saloon. I find they give claustrophobia.'

Nutty suffered from claustrophobia. Which was why all his cars were open. The one he'd given me was open too, a Morgan Sports, bright yellow to match my front door. And soon, in fact, to match the entire frontage of the house. 'The painters are coming tomorrow – they'll be painting the brickwork bright yellow.' The children could hardly wait. Vincent held his hands to his shoulders in horror, palms facing outwards, fingers lightly curled. I thought how much cleaner his nails were than mine. But mine were painted Biba Black so no one ever knew. 'Yolk yellow?' he said sarcastically. 'Canary? Cowslip? Or urine?'

Auntie suddenly fell on one ankle, snagging my Ossie Clark sleeve. 'Dew, dew. There's clumsy I am. Oh, there now – see what I've done. Your lovely frock, all ruined.'

'It's all right, Auntie,' I soothed. 'It's ever so old, this one—'

Vincent arched an eyebrow. 'One *week* old! I know Ossie's latest things.' He stopped in the street at an extra-loud hoot from Nutty. 'I can't come on, I simply can't. He's so ghastly.

No. honestly – but before I depart, my darling, do, please do, consider our restaurant. Its not as daft an idea as you think—'

'Isn't it?' I said. 'P'raps not.'

Nutty's normal eye bulged, bull-like, at the thought. His other swivelled wildly, like a bright ball bearing released from a magnetic base. The children loved that eye of his. Tallulah was banking on it rolling right out of its socket one day and bouncing down over his bones. They looked at it now and all laughed – Bogey, the loudest of all, clapping his pudgy little hands together in delight. Auntie shooed them out of the room. 'Say good night now to your mam.'

Nutty smiled benignly at the scene. 'A credit to you, the team. Only wish, m'dear, they belonged to me. Any thoughts in that direction?'

'No, Nutty. Not about that. What do you think of the restaurant idea?'

He glanced at his watch. 'Which one? Well, it's up to you. I've eaten myself, but I'm eager to oblige. How about Greek or Chinese?'

I gave an exaggerated sigh of utmost exasperation. Of course he didn't notice. 'No, Nutty. I'm not talking about eating now. I mean the restaurant *idea*. Having my own. I mentioned it just now. Three minutes ago, remember?'

You had to be brutal with poor old Nuts. Though he'd managed to scrape into Eton, they'd only kept him there because of family connections. Or as an example of vacuity due to determined inbreeding.

His eye began to bulge again, and his left leg started to shake. 'Sit down, Nutty, you'll spill your drink. Well, what do you think of the notion?' I stood before him smiling kindly. He was still, without doubt, a handsome man, though gone to seed now somewhat, mentally. Bats in the belfry and given to bluster. 'Oh I say! What fun! And who shall finance this splendid endeavour? Might I be allowed in as a partner?'

Lionel Striving was coming for lunch, I changed the sheets in readiness. His masculinity was so abrasive, you could almost graze yourself on it. Sometimes after we'd been together, I'd feel the need of a bath, and a big swill round with lanolin. Bogey's Johnson's Baby Lotion. Why did I keep seeing him then? Because I couldn't say no. And in any case despite his bull-like loving, his cock was incredibly short. I'd nearly laughed the first time I saw it and would have asked what had happened, but I thought it cruel to make anybody mind about mere lack of inches down there and I wanted him to know, to understand someone warm like me, that there were some women in the world to whom that sort of thing was not important. I put his lunch on a tray and carried it up to the bedroom. Cornflakes, and the top of the milk straight from the fridge, nice and cold. He arrived on the dot, as per usual. I accepted his brief-case and brolly and passed him his usual hanger – a birthday present from me.

We kissed with cheeks, he spoke at once. He liked to speak, non-stop. In that way I quite enjoyed our meetings, it meant I could lie back and listen. Or not, or think of other things against the sweet companionship of another human voice. 'Feel this,' he said, and drew my fingers to his flies. 'I've had this huge erection all the way from Eaton Square. It leapt into life at the traffic lights. Simply from thinking of you.' I could feel nothing. 'quite an embarrassment, paying off the fare. Had to hold my brief-case in a pertinent position in case the chap should see—'

'How sexy,' I murmured, still searching.

'Yes. Shows something, eh? About the state of me. Stallion stuff, I'd say. It's either that or love. Come on then, let's put it to good use. Knickers down, knees up! You riveting, randy whore!'

He lay heavily on top of me, rubbing himself up and down. Good old-fashioned missionary style. 'The only way for me. The fair sex down under, in their place, all proper.' I'd tried to introduce a string of variations. 'Look here,' he'd said. 'This isn't some sort of novelty act. We're not touring the Halls, you know. The fact that missionary is the most used way of doing

14

it, from here to Timbuctoo, is simply because it's been tried and tested and found to be simply the best.' I didn't agree, and in any case, it wasn't true, what he said about Timbuctoo. I'd read somewhere they did it there like dogs, with the woman's face shoved hard in a bush.

A layer of sweat was forming between us, his rib cage pressed hard on my nipples. I thought of the plans for our restaurant. When this was over and Lionel had eaten his cornflakes, I'd walk up the road to the Estate Agents. Giddy and Giddy & Son. Would the son be Giddy too? Lionel erupted and roared. I took it he must have come off by the crashing crescendo and shouting. My twatty was starting to ache. My pubic mound, the bone down there, was feeling extremely sore. It usually did, with Lionel. The fact of his foreshortened dick, no doubt, caused our frames to come that much closer.

He'd flopped, spread-eagled on my body. Panting and winded with his tongue lying pink and glistening on his lower lip. I wished he'd move, but knew better than to suggest it. My skin was starting to prickle and itch. 'Excuse me,' I said carefully. 'But I think I've got to scratch—'

He didn't answer. I tried to lift his head as gently as I could. 'Lionel?' Nothing. 'Lionel?' He took no notice. 'Lionel. Your milk is getting warm.'

'Oh hell, is it?' he lifted himself at last. 'Mmm. I needed that. I really did.' He tweaked my cheek and stretched. 'How are you feeling? In the pink? We certainly do make music, eh!'

'A very pretty tune.' I smiled at him. He stood and flexed his muscles. 'Look at that. Look. Feel. Go on, just have a feel. Not bad for forty-odd would you say?'

'Not bad at all, Lionel. Must be the cornflakes.' It occurred to me that if there was such a thing as purple flakes, he could combine his favourite food and his favourite colour. It was quite fortunate that cornflakes were his favourite, a fact we stumbled on at our first meeting – which led directly to the luncheon invitation which was now a regular weekly event.

He peeled the silver foil from the mouth of the bottle, and tilted the contents carefully, making certain that the creamy top should stay intact. The top was half the enticement of the feast. He caught me watching him and, unconsciously almost, straightened his shoulders and sucked in his stomach.

'Another birthday soon,' I said. Ours fell within days of each other.

'I know. I shan't be here.'

'Oh dear. Why not? Where will you be?'

'New York, I think, on that date. Or possibly Washington, one of the two.'

'That's a shame. I was going to combine it with opening a restaurant. Celebrate the two together.'

He stopped, mid spoon. I watched a soggy flake fall on the sheet.

'You what?'

'You heard.'

'I know. But let's get this straight. You say you're opening a restaurant? And you'd like to do so on my birthday? How sweet. But I shan't be here.'

I let him go on thinking it. 'Well, in that case, I'd best open it on mine—'

'Now, wait a minute. Hold on there. What's made you think of a restaurant?'

'To get something decent to eat. For me,' I said. 'And the family. Quite simple really. I don't know why I didn't think of it before. Though I didn't think of it this time, if it comes to that. Vincent did. We're doing it together.'

'You're not! That great big poof and you!'

'That's right. The two of us.'

'You're mad. You're daft. You're crackers!'

'Oh yes. That's nice.'

'You are. Who'll run it then? Who'll do the work? Who'll organize it all?'

'Who'll cook?'

'What?'

'I said, who's going to do the cooking. You must have a cook in a restaurant. Mustn't you?'

'Well yes, darling, I suppose you must. I quite honestly hadn't thought of that. Had you?'

'No Vince. I've only just thought of it now. Who do we know?'

'Who's keen on cooking?'

'And who's good at it too, I suppose.'

'Rufus Justice. What about him? You always talk of his dinners. Those parties of his. He does all the food, for as many guests as a restaurant.'

'That's different though. It takes him weeks—'

'Too slow you think—'

'Yes. Much. In any case, he's got a job. A barrister, remember? That keeps him pretty occupied. He wouldn't have time, shouldn't think. He'd like it though, I'm sure.'

'Well why not ask him? He'd do it for you. You know he would.'

'I know. It wouldn't be fair though, would it. To ask him to swap Chambers for our kitchen. Though he has said I can count on his support.'

'You've told him then, already?'

'Oh yes. I've told them all.'

'Oh, what did Brad say? And Ulysses Stuffy Uphill?'

'Oh, sweet they were, the both of them. Of course several may be wanting special measures—'

'Their drinks you mean? There'll be none of that. No swigging our profits away. No special anything for anyone. They're all going to have to pay. Oh yes dear. That's understood. Everyone darling, all the same. We must make that a rule.'

'What, even the children?'

'Well, p'raps not them.'

'And surely not poor old Auntie?'

'Well, that's what I mean, you see. The list could start getting endless – really, darling, I'm not exaggerating. We have to draw the line.'

'We'll draw it after Auntie. And you and me of course. And whoever'll be helping out. Who will be helping out?'

'With what?'

17

'Well, with waiting on tables. And washing up. And taking tips and things.'

'Bags me, the taking tips. I am qualified, after all. The greatest tip-taker in Notting Hill Gate. By the way, how are things regarding premises?'

'Oh yes, I meant to say. They called me up from Giddy's. There is a place not far away that's just come on the market. Hold on a sec, I've got it written down. Yes, here. In Holbein Place—'

'Where's that?'

'Let's look it up in the A to Z. H, h, h. Holbein. Got it. Ooh, nice, around the corner from the Royal Court. See, here, it leads off from Sloane Square. That's good, I'd say. Let's look at it.'

'What, now?'

'Why not.'

We'd taken it on sight. 'Oh darling, isn't it *us*!' Vincent was over-excited. 'Just look at this dear little hatch which goes up and down from the kitchen—'

'Dumb Waiter—'

Vincent looked shocked. 'Oh dear, is he?'

'The hatch,' I said. 'That's what it's called. A Dumb Waiter.'

He smiled in obvious relief. 'Really? How simply divine. You're knowledgeable I must say. A mine of information.' He leant forward and whispered to me. 'Isn't it ghastly – the smell of the grease. Don't let's stay too long. It will start to seep into our clothes.'

'We'll open the windows when we have it. Or install some sort of air conditioning.'

I agreed with him, it was pretty ghastly. Much like the present owner. We'd shaken hands, but his had slipped from mine like a fish straight out of the sea, coated in a stinking film of oil from where he'd been cooking a fry-up. It amazed me to see how full the place was with people actually eating. My stomach heaved at the sight of the stuff, not helped by the skin condition of the so-called chef, who seemed to be suffering from a particularly scaly form of eczema. He'd have to go for certain. And so would the washer-up, the surface of whose person was similarly affected. It was obviously contagious. They both smiled at me. And at Vincent. 'God Almighty!' he'd murmured and clutched on to my arm, backing discreetly away. 'Mutt and Jeff,' I'd murmured back, but tried to give an answering smile and put up a good show on both our behalfs.

'The kitchen staff?' The owner accompanied us out of the kitchen. 'Do they, um, I mean—' I floundered, but Vincent continued. 'I think my partner is wishing to know if the kitchen staff come, as it were, with the place. Since we have staff of our own, you understand.'

The owner shrugged. 'It's up to you. You're lucky to find anyone these days. These two have been with me a week. That's how it is – they come and go in the catering trade. You've probably found that yourself though.'

We nodded, each disinclined to reveal our amateur status. 'I'm leaving for precisely that reason – it's a bloody dog's life, I tell you. I'm taking up tailoring with my son, he's teaching me how to do it. Nothing could have persuaded him to come into business with me. Bloody shrewd too. There's more profit in a pair of pants than bacon and eggs, believe me!'

'We may not be serving bacon and eggs. Ours may be more haute cuisine,' Vincent said loftily. I stared at him, impressed by his confidence. I hadn't thought what we'd be serving. Just food was as far as I'd got. The owner made a face at 'haute cuisine'. 'That's a fool's game for a start. Even assuming you can find the bloody chef. They tried that lark, the previous people here. And left in the end with not so much as a how's-your-father.'

'How's your father?'

'He's fine, and how's yours?' The owner laughed. 'Don't mind me. I'm known for my sense of humour, though I've nearly lost it in here—' I looked around at the clientele, a strangely mixed bag as far as I could tell. Halfway between a workman's café and a straight suburban teashop. Several little old ladies sat on their own, pecking away like genteel birds. The price must obviously please their pockets, living on restricted incomes. The owner caught me looking and nodded in their direction. 'Pain up the arse, that lot. Try to get away without paying, half of them. Do you know what one of them did the other week? Brought a dead fly in her handbag and stuck it there, right in her salad! I saw the old bitch do it, with my own bloody eyes, God'strewth! I waited out of curiosity to see what she would do. Of course she ate it all up, didn't she first – then called me to look at the fly! "Very nice too," I said to her, "would you care to eat it for afters, madam? I'll call down to Cook for some custard."'

Vincent shuddered. 'What repartee.'

'It's my sense of humour, I told you. Yes, they come in here,' he looked around. 'All walks of life, I tell you. After a week, you lose all faith in the human race. Just animals, they are, you'll see—'

'How long,' I asked politely, 'have you been here, then, Mr – er?'

'Bummer.'

'Beg pardon?'

'Yes. Bummer. Bummer's the name. Sydney Bummer. Let's say Syd though, it's Syd to my friends, which of course is what I hope we'll be. If you see your way clear to buying the business, you can study the books – they're all here.'

'Books?' Vincent echoed vaguely.

'They tell all about the turnover,' I said. I'd heard about books before. They were something you showed to accountants, though there was no reason why we need be bothered.

'I'm throwing the goodwill in for nothing—'

'How sweet of you, really, too kind. Isn't it darling?' Vincent smiled and turned to me. I nodded.

The owner beamed. 'I thought it might be an incentive, to speed up the deal, so to speak. If you were wanting to, you know, you could take the place over tomorrow—'

'Tomorrow! Hear that?' Vincent turned, eyes shining, to me. 'Mr Bummer said tomorrow!'

'I heard him, Vince,' I said.

'Tomorrow's too soon. Next week would be more like.'

'Oh no – throw caution to the winds! Live dangerously, darling!'

'No, Vince,' I said. 'Be serious. I'm not having Scabs in the kitchen, nor his sidekick, not stirring my gravy—'

'I quite agree, a ghastly crew. They can go, though, at a moment's notice, that's what Sydney Bummer said. We don't have to open tomorrow, not business as usual, not that. But I see no reason, darling, none at all, not to start clearing the place and redecorating. The sooner the better, I'd say.'

I had to break off at 12 o'clock to meet up in bed with Brad.

'Can't you ring him and put him off?' Vincent said. 'And help me finish this ceiling?' He'd wrenched his neck at the start of the job and had been in a bad mood ever since. It was my idea that we should paint the restaurant ourselves. Not simply because of the saving, but as much because I liked to see the look of things change beneath my brush. A labour of love is how I saw it. Vincent had been all for bringing in professionals. 'Oh no,' I'd said. 'They'd never get it done. Look how long those are taking to paint my front, not to mention to to-ing and fro-ing. Auntie claims that one of them has bladder trouble. He's in and out of the lav all the time.'

'Wanking probably dear.'

'Over Auntie? I very much doubt it.'

'Or you.'

'Or even you, Vincent.'

'Everything's possible. I shall look with more interest, which is he?'

'The sandy one.'

Vincent screamed and curled his lip. 'Ooh no! Not him! Oh well, we'd best forget it.'

I'd cadged a can of colour from them. 'It'll be lovely, this yellow, for us, Vincent. Be like walking into an egg. Rather appropriate for a restaurant—'

'Should we paint the outside White Eggshell?'

'Nice idea, but no, better red. Red and yellow.'

'Well, you're the expert. I'll leave all the colour to you, darling.'

'Don't sound so dubious. You have to be bold. It'll be beautiful, honest, I promise. A home from home. That's the point, isn't it?'

'I suppose so,' he said grudgingly.

It was a larger job than I'd imagined and even I was beginning to be daunted. This was our second day. 'Take a break then, Vince. Have a drink, go on, the pubs are open. I shan't be that long anyway.'

A drip of emulsion fell on his upturned face. 'Oh shit. I'm fed up with this! Right then, that's it. I will, I'll go for a drink, and I'll time how long you will have been gone—'

'Yes, I don't mind. Why should you do more than me. Give me an hour, that's all. I could put him off, but I can't. He's so gorgeous – you know how it is—'

'Oh, all right. How long then?'

'An hour. I've just said.'

'I've only got an hour, I'm afraid, today Brad.'

'Come on sweetheart then. Let's get started. Don't waste it.'

'What's it to be?'

'As starters?'

'Mmm.' I watched him getting undressed. The youngest of all my Gentlemen, with legs that went up to his ear lobes and a body like Michelangelo's David. Good at any age, of course, but better at twenty-two. 'Hung like a horse,' I'd said to Vince. 'I could tell by the bulge in his jeans, dear!' Not that size had meant that much to me, or did now, for that matter – it was just that having had Brad—

'Sixty-nine?' He flashed perfect teeth.

'Why not?'

He guided his upright equipment within inches of my nose. I sniffed at it. 'Mm. Smell of rubber. Have you been elsewhere, sir?' 'What thoughts!' he scolded. 'Suspicious girl! What, me with another?' I laughed. His gross infidelities were a running joke between us, as indeed were mine. A friendship lacking possessiveness, which was why it has lasted so long. Nineteen, he'd been. Driving a minicab, in those days, one of his many jobs.

I opened my mouth as wide as I could. I had to, to get his dick in, and nearly gagged as it hit my throat. I began breathing through my nose. Poor Bogey would have a job with sixty-nine in future years, I thought, unless they managed to unblock him.

Auntie came knocking at the door. 'You in there, love? Would you like some nice tea? I got the kettle on the boil—'

'Not now, Auntie! Perhaps a bit later.'

'That's it then, love. Mind to come after then, is it.' I heard her humming down the stairs. Perpetually cheerful. Brad was her favourite of my Gentlemen Callers. 'There's good-looking, he is – like a film star.'

He'd removed his cock at her knocking. ''Nother way? Eh, sweetheart? Say which.'

'Well, what's the time? Oh dear, not long. Side by side? Me on top? I don't mind.'

We did it both ways and finished laughing, on the dot. No time for tea with Auntie. 'I'll stay, you go,' he said. 'It'll give her a thrill, poor old girl.'

'You're sweet,' I said. 'Same time, next week?'

'Sure thing. Be good.'

I was still smiling when I got back to Vincent. 'It's easy to see you've been screwed.'

'Of course,' I answered. 'That's the point of poking – that people should see. Cause and effect—'

'Get this in your hand, you horny bitch.' He passed me a brush. 'And try cause and effect on this ceiling.'

Vincent knocked off at six o'clock. 'I'm knackered! In any case, darling, I do have a date—'

'Oh, do you? Anyone I know?' I doubted that it would be.

Vincent's preference tended towards rough trade, rather than people one might meet socially.

'Well,' he said vaguely. There was a silence, neither of us spoke.

'You must be careful, Vince,' I said at last. 'Remember poor old Pokestrong—' Arnold Pokestrong had been found, six months or so before, in more than mysterious circumstances. An Inspector Nark from Scotland Yard had called on me soon after. 'A routine visit, Miss, that's all. We're visiting all Mr Pokestrong's friends. I take it you were a friend of the deceased? We found your name in his address book.'

'Oh yes. A friend, of course. I was always very fond of old Arnold. Though I hadn't seen as much of him lately—'

'You wouldn't have cared for the sight I had of him then, Miss. Not being a friend I can assure you. Even I as a total stranger was, how can I say, deeply shocked—'

'Oh dear, don't tell me.'

'I wouldn't dream of it. The state he was in. You know of course, you're familiar with the case I take it, that a revolver held that closely to the head would cause it – the head I mean – to be blown to smithereens. Which was exactly what happened to your friend, Mr Pokestrong. Can you credit it, can you envisage the scene! We found one of his eyeballs lodged high up in the curtain pelmet, and the other underneath the settee! Both surprisingly intact, one even complete with lid—'

Vincent sniffed. 'My trade's not that rough, darling. In any case, poor old Arnold invited disaster. And I'm far from being a masochist. Though,' he straightened his back with a groan and massaged the side of his neck, 'no one would believe it looking at me today. I leave you to it, sweetie.'

I didn't mind him leaving me. In fact I even preferred it. I'd brought the portable gramophone with me and my newest Barbra Streisand record, 'The Way We Were'. Not one of Vincent's favourites. Now I could play it all night.

'I'll stay on and see it through now. Finish the whole bloody thing, after I've seen to the kids, that is.'

I rang them, Tallulah answered. 'Yes?' she shouted into the

phone. I could hear Bogey sneeze in the background.

'It's me.'

'Oh, hi there Mumsy! Zsa-Zsa's just burning the toast!'
Almost everything Tallulah ever said went with an exclamation
mark. A sense of drama.

'Is Auntie there, chicken?'

'Yes, somewhere. I think she's taking a bath.'

'What, now? It's a funny time to take a bath—'

Tallulah started to giggle. 'She tripped on a pot of paint! It
spilt all down the garden path! And splashed all up Auntie's
leg! Right the way up to her knickers!'

It wouldn't have need to go very far. Auntie's knickers began
at her knees with good old-fashioned modesty and the rein-
forcement of sturdy elastic.

'Is she all right though?'

Tallulah was not noted for kindness. She continued to
giggle. 'Oh yes. Except that her botty's all yellow! We saw it,
she showed us. She did! The path looks ever so pretty. Like the
one in *The Wizard of Oz!*'

'Oh yes,' I said. 'The Yellow Brick Road. Follow the Yellow
Brick Road.' I sang it.

She squealed at the other end of the phone. 'Oh Mummy!
Don't! Your voice is so horrible!'

'Thank you,' I said. 'See you in a minute. I'll bring home
something nice to eat.'

'Oh goody! I'll have Kit-Kats — two of them! And don't forget Bogey's bananas. He's eaten all the ones that were here!'

'What, seven since yesterday?'

'Yes! And he's pooping a lot!'

'That's not the bananas then. They'd have the opposite
effect. He must have been eating something else as well—'

'Zsa Zsa can't find her new plasticine!'

'That sounds much more like it then. Well it's better out
than in.'

I stopped off at Safeway's on the way back and shopped
somewhat haphazardly, but in the end the queue was so daunt-
ingly long that I left my wire trolley where it was with every-

thing still in it. I could take the kids out to eat, and Auntie and her nice clean botty. To The Great American Disaster, that was their favourite these days, though not necessarily Auntie's. Or mine for that matter, I thought. Not relaxed enough for me. Too frenzied, and not enough elbow room. Not that there'd be that much elbow room in our place. An intimate setting.

Zsa-Zsa opened the door. 'Nutty's inside,' she announced. That would save a tenner or so. 'Might I make this meal my treat, m'dear?' 'Thank you, Nutty, how nice.'

He greeted me as usual with exaggerated formality, his cock eye on the move. The children gathered round to watch it bounce. 'Hullo Nutty. How are you?' I bent to pick Bogey up, hoping to show the question needed no answer. The bore who bored for England, someone had brutally said of Nutty. Bogey's nose was on the run, he buried it in my neck. 'Oh Bogey baby, just hold on. Quick someone, pass a hanky.' Tallulah threw over a dishcloth. Zsa-Zsa uncrumpled an envelope. I sighed. 'Oh Christ! For goodness' sake!' Auntie came into the room.

'Auntie,' I implored. 'Bogey's nose. Have you got a paper hanky?' She picked up the bottom of her pinafore. 'There's my pinny for little boyo's nose.' I gave up.

Nutty had come in a taxi. His old heap had eventually given up the ghost. 'Been a stout old fellow, the Land Rover. Tried and trusted for many years. Coughed his last though now. Couldn't get it to budge, not an inch.'

'It will be joining the others then eh, Nutty?'

''Fraid so.' Nutty had a cemetery of deceased cars on his estate, given over now to the chickens. The children loved it, collecting eggs amongst gear levers and steering wheels.

'What will you do, get a new one?'

''Nother Land Rover, no doubt, know of one not far from me. By the way, old girl, that same chappie is selling a vintage Rolls. Thirty-two or thereabouts, been in his garage since forty-five. Interested?'

'What? Who, me?'

'It's your birthday, isn't it, next week?'

I laughed. 'Oh don't be daft, Nutty! What would I do with

a Rolls!' I stared at his one good eye, the other spun feverishly round. Auntie smiled at him innocently. 'Rolls-Royce is it, then? There's posh. I'd like to ride round in that, indeed I would.'

Nutty bowed. 'Then, Madam,' he said, 'you shall.'

Rufus Justice rang as we were leaving for The Great American Disaster. I could barely hear him above the general clatter. Bogey had broken Tallulah's straw hat, a fragile affair dating back to the previous century and only just bought in a jumble sale. She'd delivered a blow to the back of his head which caused him to lose his balance. He lay now bubbling at my feet whilst Zsa-Zsa, springing to his defence, had tugged the sleeve of Tallulah's frock so hard that it had ripped right out of its socket. Tallulah screamed with outrage. And Auntie joined in for good measure.

'Is everything all right your end?' Rufus Justice sounded anxious.

'Oh yes. The same as usual.' I managed to make myself heard. 'Not a frightfully good time, not just at this moment though, Rufus. Why not ring me later at this number?' And I gave him the number of our restaurant.

He rang just as I'd finished the ceiling, I stood with the brush in my hand. 'Hold on, Rufus, I'd better put this brush in water – it'll dry hard otherwise.'

'What brush? What is going on? And where am I ringing you anyway?' He hadn't believed me, Rufus, not about running a restaurant. 'But why? What's the reasoning, dear? I've known you long enough to understand how attracted you are to hare-brained schemes, but a restaurant is frankly ridiculous. You have no understanding of food. It's an art which has somehow by-passed you. Unfortunate but, even so, true. Have I managed to make myself understood?'

'Oh perfectly. An admirable presentation of your case.' That was the trouble with Rufus, he conducted all conversation as if he were still in court. 'It hasn't influenced my decision though, not in any way, Rufus. I'm sorry.'

'I'm sorry too,' he sighed heavily. 'I'm far too fond of you to wish to see you make a spectacle of yourself and a scapegoat of those of us who will undoubtedly be required to grace your emporium.'

'Oh Rufus, I shan't mind if you don't eat there. I hadn't expected it, quite frankly. Your standards I'm sure would be far too exacting for amateurs like Vincent and me.'

'What brush? Well Rufus, a paint brush — I'm here painting up our restaurant of course. That's the number I've given you—'

I heard him groan. 'Oh God, you've not gone ahead?'

'Despite your good advice. 'Fraid so, Rufus, never mind we'll communicate after hours.'

'Now is after hours isn't it?' he managed a note of pure misery. 'I'd rather hoped we'd get together at some point or other this evening.'

I looked around, there was still a lot to do. The restaurant occupied two floors, ground and below stairs, where the kitchen was. And, come to that, the lavatory. The only lavatory in fact, intended as unisex, and only able to be reached by walking through the kitchen. Hardly hygienic, that. And hardly convenient either. What if a queue should happen to form between boiling fat and the frying pan?

I'd brought in a fresh stock of yellow emulsion, and had covered almost everything in sight, but only on the ground floor. Now I was half way down the stairs. I'd never really done stairs before, not all the banister bits, which were taking amazingly long.

'Well Rufus, I'm only half way down the stairs — though you could come and give me a hand. Vincent was here until earlier, but now he's pursuing his private life.'

He grunted. 'And by so doing, is displaying remarkable sense. What on earth possesses you to venture into the tedious province of painting and decorating! Surely to God you could afford to give that task to some small firm or other?'

'Labour of love,' I said briefly. 'I don't for a minute expect you to understand.'

He sighed and remained quite silent. Oh dear, now he'd sulk for days.

At four o'clock the telephone rang. Auntie was still waiting up. 'The kettle's boiling dry back here, and I'm getting a little bit sleepy, love.' I managed to persuade her to give up the vigil by promising a prompt return. And in any case, by that time I could barely lift my brush. One wall remained – and the outside lav, which I couldn't have faced tonight. The cistern dripped rusted moisture on to the head of whoever performed at the bowl. We'd be in trouble over toilet facilities, according to Rufus. In big trouble with sanitary inspectors and health authorities. He could see it coming. Such trouble indeed that it might result in the closure and condemnation of the entire property in its present state. I chose not to believe him, but he was adamant, quoting certain bye-laws, recently reinforced, appertaining to this very problem.

I thought about it now, driving in my open Morgan through the empty streets of Chelsea. Up a deserted King's Road, past the Town Hall on my left and Chelsea Registry on my right. A party was ending in Carlisle Square, two girls puking up on the pavement. My puking days were long since passed; I'd learned now to encompass drink. Though not drink and pot put together. 'Smoke this' – Brad had offered me his joint only the other day and after only three puffs I'd passed my breakfast all over his brand new suede boots.

The light was still on in the hallway and on the top landing too, but that was always left on all night for the children to go to their lavatory. I supposed we could replace ours in the restaurant of course, put in a new bowl and cistern, to render it slightly more appetizing. Though unisex it would have to remain, simply through sheer lack of space. People didn't have separate loos for men and women in their homes, I thought, why should we?

I went upstairs to check on the kids. Bogey had kicked off his blanket; the girls slept beneath duvets, but the condition of Bogey's breathing had suggested that a duvet for him might be dangerous. He sneezed in his sleep as I bent to kiss him and

29

he woke up with a satisfied chuckle. Next door another child cried out, still dreaming, but when I went in there was no sound at all, only regular steady breathing. Auntie was fast asleep as well, her false teeth soaking in Steradent and her head covered completely in curlers. She was wearing a warm winceyette from British Home Stores and a Fair Isle cardigan for extra warmth, despite the central heating. She'd knitted it herself; it had taken her six years during which time she'd gained so much weight that now it no longer fitted, but suited a treat for sleeping in. I left her door ajar as I had found it. She liked to see to the children at night, in case I was entertaining. This arrangement suited everyone. I went to bed myself, too tired to take off whatever make-up may still have been on my face, and fell asleep with yellow emulsion in my hair and a streak of it all down one cheek.

In the morning I drove the girls to school, and dropped Bogey at his nursery. 'When can we come and see our restaurant?' Tallulah squinted at me. I leant forward to polish a spot of scrambled egg from her spectacles. Those eyes of hers needed attention, extra attention I thought. Though the optician had claimed that eventually the eye would right itself. The one was looking now past my shoulder, as the other fixed on my nose. Zsa-Zsa gave a hideous grin and displayed her unfortunate gums. Of course she could have those cut back later on. A twinge of discomfort pulsed somewhere in me at the thought of the knife and the chisel.

'What's that, pet?' I said with extra sympathy to Zsa-Zsa to make up for planning her pain.

'I'm telling them all at school,' she grinned even wider, 'that the ones I like can come and have free food. And the ones that I don't won't get nothing!'

'Anything.' Tallulah corrected. 'Not nothing.'

'Nothing.' Zsa-Zsa looked mutinous.

Tallulah continued. 'When? You haven't said. When can we come and see? Tonight?'

'Oh yes! Tonight, can we, Mum?'

'And bring some friends if we like?'

We'd reached their school; they climbed over the side and jumped safely on to the pavement, both of them shouting at once. Bogey gurgled by my side licking his wet upper lip. I wiped it with the handkerchief I'd pinned on to the shoulder of his dungarees. Why hadn't we thought of that before?

'Tonight? Well yes, perhaps you can all come and see the place then. Have to be careful, though, of the paint. It's still pretty wet, I expect. So best to bring no friends, I think. Just us, until it's ready.'

Vincent arrived at the restaurant with a big black eye and a very bad hangover, and slumped himself into a seat.

'Watch out,' I said. 'Still wet! Ye Gods – what's up with your eye? Did you end up fighting for your honour?'

'Oh darling, no jokes. Not this morning. As you can see I'm not in the mood. Jesus, any chance of a cup of coffee? Or a cold beer or something? My throat's like the bottom of a baby's pram – all piss and biscuits, I tell you!'

I sympathized and popped over to the off-licence for his beer whilst waiting for the kettle to boil. That's something we'd have to reapply for, the existing licence to serve alcoholic beverages. According to Rufus it wasn't as simple as it sounded. 'You'll have to present yourself in a court of law and prove that you're both sober citizens, for a start, my dear!' Nobody, in a court of law or out of it would have accepted Vincent as such this morning. I reflected when I brought his coffee. He'd aged overnight.

'You look about eighty this morning, Vince!'

'And you're going bald,' he said bitchily. I laughed.

'Poor old Vin! Well then, what happened?'

'He hit me.'

'What with—'

'Well darling, not his handbag.'

'Oh dear, did you put butter on it?'

'Butter?'

'Yes, butter. The best thing for bruising—'

'What, *Last Tango* butter you mean!' We both laughed then; he was feeling better. I decided against pursuing things. Vincent was never one for indulging in details.

'What do you think then' – I waved my arms around – 'of the decor?'

He followed my actions with his eyes. 'It's a curious effect – all the yellow. It mostly makes me feel sick. One can only pray it won't effect the same response from others.' I could see what he meant in fact. Now, here in the light of the day with shadows cast and weak sunlight slanting over everything, there was a certain biliousness about it.

'Perhaps it's you,' I said accusingly. 'The sight of yourself has put you off. It's putting me off to be quite frank. Can't you turn your back or something, just for today.'

He hunched a huffy shoulder, and pursed his mouth to a prune. We neither of us spoke, but the silence, though lasting almost till lunch time, was of a friendly nature. I couldn't remember a time, not a single one, when relations with Vincent were other than cordial, in fact. I spoke first, that was usually the way of things, to protect his pride.

'I hope things won't get on top of us, Vince.'

'Things, darling?'

'Yes, you know, make us nervy and irritable. With each other I mean, running this.'

He laid his brush down on the draining board and yawned, then winced with the pain. 'Oh dear, I ache in every orifice—'

'Every?' I raised my eye brows suggestively. He'd never actually made that clear to me, Vincent, who did what and to whom with him. I would like to have known in fact, very much. I felt he might have several tips for me as to comfort. It was difficult to tell with Vincent which way would be to his liking. The preference for rough trade indicated that he felt himself feminine, in which case he'd presumably have it up his bum, playing the passive partner. Though on the other hand he sometimes came on so strong with me, and bossy to boot, that I suspected he was in fact butch. It would have been nice to ask outright, though the fabric of our friendship resisted such familiarity.

'You're a coarse old cow,' he said now. 'Shall we push off for something to eat?'

Shepherd's Pie was what we decided on, up at the Queen's Elm pub, which enabled me to call in at Old Church Street and pay off the painters there.

'Oh darling,' Vincent was whining now, desperate for a hair of the dog. 'Don't you think if they've finished painting your front you could send them down to finish off the restaurant? There's still the outside all to do. I simply couldn't face it darling, honestly!'

I'd forgotten about the outside. Christ, yes, there was that to do! But I was disinclined to look as if I was giving in that easily. We played those games, cat and mouse.

'Well, I don't know—' I drew the words out reluctantly, although I'd made up my mind.

'Dearest heart, my darling child—' he put on his pleading face.

'All right, you've talked me into it. Though they may not be free, of course.'

'They'll be free if you pay them enough,' Vince said. A good point that, regarding paying. So far I'd forked out everything and with things standing as they were – with Vincent almost insolvent as actors of questionable talent usually are – it looked as though this would continue to be the case. Not that it mattered to me. The money was there to be spent.

Auntie came up to the pub. She liked a nice drink, midday, and enjoyed sleeping it off afterwards. In bed with her telly on, fully dressed, but with her hefty corsets undone. Gossard these days, instead of Spirella. In two pieces, instead of the one. So that somewhere in the region of her heart there hung a pouch of flesh, as soft and white as pastry. Bogey was extra fond of kneading it, pushing his tiny fingers in until he lost them there, all ten. Oh yes, she served her purpose well, in every way acting as substitute Granny. As indeed she had been a substitute mother to me for so many years in childhood.

'Dubonnet and Pernod, please for me.' Auntie's latest alcoholic enthusiasm.

Vincent was ordering. 'Christ,' he said, 'I'm sorry, Auntie, I can't say it! You'll have to ask, I don't trust my stomach!'

'I shall,' she answered him happily.

We sat by the window, just behind the door, watching people come in. Vincent went white when his drink hit his stomach. 'Oh hold on to me, darling, do.' I put my arm around his shoulder, and he leant his head against mine.

'There's a black eye he's got! Where did he get it from?'

'From Sainsbury's, Auntie,' he answered.

Zoë Knickerbocker arrived half-way through, hot on the heels of Ulysses Uphill; Stuffy we called him – though not to his face. He was one of my Gentlemen Callers – a fact of which Zoë was unaware. She possessed a curious penchant for pursuing my admirers. I didn't mind – Christ, I had enough to spare after all. And as far as I could tell she hadn't any, apart from the blotto bastards who occasionally fell out of the Queen's Elm into the nearest free bed. She kept hers double in case. Fingers crossed and knees wide for anything that came her way. Three abortions, I'd seen her through. One indeed, I'd even been called upon to pay for, though I obviously wasn't the father. She'd promised faithfully to pay me back, but I didn't expect to see a farthing, knowing farthings no longer existed. Instead I'd sent her to be fitted with a coil, like mine. Though lately I'd taken to reconsidering my coil after I bumped into somebody who's had herself satisfactorily sterilized. 'Why not?' she'd shrugged, stirring the spoon in her coffee, 'after all, let's face it, at our age, we're not looking to have any more.' 'What sex, or babies?' I'd asked respectfully. She was sixty, but still having periods. Not a medical phenomenon, though worthy for inclusion in the *Lancet*, I would have thought. Or at least as an item on the Woman's Page in the local paper.

'Oh, babies of course, my dear. You won't see me giving up sex! Hell, no. Sex goes on till you reach the coffin! And for some—' she leant forward confidingly, exuding a drift of Calèche '—and for some I've heard of – the coffin is where it continues.'

She'd caught my interest, I'd never known a necrophiliac.

Two holes, she'd claimed, they'd punched in her stomach to

34

sterilize her. One to pinch up the tubes, and the other for the torch to see what they were doing. 'Were you conscious throughout, then?' I said. Suddenly squeamish for no reason at all, except feeling I might make a fool of myself if they did all that to me, by shouting out when the scalpel hit my stomach. Though of course they'd obviously use a local anaesthetic, or so one would hope. And it would give a good chance of a read. I'd been meaning to get on with the latest *Guinness Book of Records* for some months. Studying that, a book that size, meant my eyes mightn't wander round to see what they were doing down below. I'd ask my gynaecologist what he thought. He'd never been that keen on my coil, but refused to give me the Pill, simply because of some varicose veins that developed whilst carrying Bogey. And the last time I'd gone to have a nice, new, clean one put in because the old one was looking so battered, he'd taken it upon himself to scrape around my womb. He'd claimed several small strong barnacles, as if he'd been deep-sea diving in a Mediterranean lagoon. 'Not a bad trip then,' I'd said crisply, when at last I'd surfaced to consciousness. That was the trouble with inner workings, like taking a car to the garage. The medical profession prospered on mystique. Women weren't in a position to query, but were forced back into the foetal position, gaping at both ends. I'd gaped when he'd given me the bill. And I did more than gape, I ground my teeth in discomfort and at the humiliation of having to walk round for a full week afterwards, looking like Donald Duck: my spine at the angle of a diving board, bum out, knees bent like Max Wall doing his professor's walk. Like a very bad period pain. What had he scraped my inner linings with, a razor blade! And all this pain because of the fear of procreation.

'I'm thinking of having my fallopian tubes cauterized, Zoë. Why don't you?'

Zoë smoothed her hair, and tugged her sweater tight. 'Why, do you think it would suit me?' she turned, addressing the table.

Auntie smiled and nodded, 'Nice'. She'd switched over to port and pints to go with her peanuts. 'Three Ps, see,' she'd explained. Like Philosophy, Psychology and Politics.

Vincent's attention had been wandering. 'What! Suit you? Oh yes, without question, Zoë darling!'

'But isn't it painful?' Zoë placed her hands protectively over her nipples. A solitary drinker sitting nearby dropped cigarette ash into his Scotch. 'I'm frightfully sensitive there,' she continued. 'But I do suffer badly from sinus.' We all stared at her, was she drunk or what?

'What the hell are you talking about?' The real object of Vincent's attention had swayed his way out of the pub. I was surprised that someone quite as gay as that, so overtly lashed and lip-sticked, had been allowed into the place. And it was interesting as well that Vincent had found him so riveting. Still, his judgement, so normally scathing of 'drag', might be swayed by the loss of his eyesight. The black eye now was closing up. He focused on Zoë with the other. She turned his attention to me. 'Fallopian tubes! Her suggestion not mine—'

Vincent frowned 'Well! Oh, I lose patience! Sort it out for yourselves. I shall go and relieve myself downstairs—'

He returned with Ulysses Uphill. 'Look what I found in the bog! Zoë spun round, 'So that's where you'd got to, is it. I thought you'd deserted us all.' She spoke accusingly, almost demanding his presence. A mistake. That wasn't the way through to Stuffy, I knew. He needed a great deal of air.

We smiled at each other, he and I. 'How's the Thesis going, then, Ulysses?'

He nodded and pulled out a pipe from the pocket of his Harris tweed jacket. 'It's going, it's going,' he mumbled. 'I shall soon bring some more for a Reading,' he ended vaguely, filling his pipe.

The smell of tobacco was pleasant. Zoë scowled and looked from me to him, then back again at both of us. 'A Reading,' she said sharply, 'what Reading? Will I be invited?'

Ulysses pulled on his pipe and stared over Old Church Street, ignoring her. His silence spoke louder than words.

Vincent was feeling more himself, despite the dramatic eye. The present silence, started off by Ulysses, hadn't seeped through to him. Auntie started on another bag of peanuts.

'Nuts?' she waved them in front of Vincent's nose. 'Oh, thanks Auntie. Do for my afters!'

We'd all finished our Shepherd's Pie. All except Zoë. Ulysses wasn't eating, he wasn't much for food. Vincent turned and looked at him. 'Still taking care of your figure, Ulysses – my, what I'd do for your waist line!' Vincent was just as thin in fact, but his was the outcome of rigorous slimming. Another of his continuing obsessions. 'It went, no, truthfully it did – my body. Around about twenty-seven! The whole lot, I swear, from ankles to earlobes just absolutely sort of *caved* in! Difficult to explain – but all the tautness, darling – you remember taut! There's nothing quite like teenage taut! You know what I mean, it went!'

Oh yes, I remembered 'teenage taut', when my budding breasts were as firm as my buttocks. Hard to believe, but true! I could have sat on them, if someone had turned me upside down and wished to address my knees. But 'teenage taut' develops into something else with women, equally nice, only different. With men like Vincent though, in his emotional line of business, when outline could be said to be all – age obviously meant a turn for the worse. He spoke now, cutting abruptly across that very thought. 'What do you think then, Ulysses, about our restaurant plans?'

Zoë still held the scowl she'd assumed over the subject of the Reading. And Ulysses continued to ignore her. The reading of his Thesis was something between him and me. A private procedure. A privilege which he bestowed on me. One in fact which I wished he wouldn't. My leanings were not in any way towards Medieval Literary Anarchy In Verse, but I understood that it might well be, his Thesis when finished, an extremely valuable work. To scholars.

He took off his glasses and polished them, steel-rimmed National Health, the sort that John Lennon once wore. But Stuffy, in his, looked more like Stanley Spencer, with the same sort of haircut and fringe. Actually fashioned, so he led me to believe, with a pudding basin placed on his head, the hair beneath being shaved off with his razor. Like a medieval warrior in fact, well in keeping with his Thesis. He polished the glasses with Auntie's unused paper napkin (she liked to save napkins for Bogey's nose). I watched them moving methodically round, much in the manner he used for my nipples. One of the most arousing of my Gentlemen Callers on those – though you wouldn't have guessed it from looking at him. Except that Zoë for instance, who did have a nose for these things, she must have sensed it somehow – his low-keyed, though humming, sensuality. He looked so attainable, that was the trouble. Not being obviously attractive, physically. Well, not like Brad, let's say. But appearances in these matters can be hugely misleading – something Zoë had yet to learn. Nobody spoke; we waited for Ulysses. And that was another of his things. The ability to make you wait, although on reflection, what he actually said – when he chose to say it – was never that pertinent anyway. But Zoë couldn't be bothered to wait – 'Restaurant! What restaurant is this? You've said nothing to me about restaurants.'

Ulysses blinked. Auntie shut her eyes and smiled – I'd have to take her home soon. Zoë turned her face to me, and then spun round to Vincent. The light caught her nose, just where she'd had it bobbed, high up on the bridge of the bone. We'd all told her she was crackers, last year when she'd had it done. It had changed a haughty, noble nose into a small pig's snout. In summer time, it caused no end of trouble, keeping it out of the rays of the sun. A complicated business involving a transparent plastic shield tied round her head with elastic. Her friends refused to lie on the beach with her like that, let alone walk along the street. But I didn't mind, not brought up with Auntie's excesses. Ridicule didn't affect me any more. It was true, now I came to think of it, we hadn't as yet told Zoë about our restaurant. I'd been too busy breaking the news and testing the temperature with my various Gentlemen Callers to concern myself with anyone else. Apart from the immediate family. It seemed to me that those two separate groups would be the most affected – the principal beneficiaries in this changing life style of mine. And in any case Zoë had only just returned from wherever it was she'd been. Researcher cum glorified secretary on a series for television, I think it was this time. Person to Person. Or Heart to Heart. Just like John Freeman's Face to Face. What exactly Researching involved was vague, but it meant that she wasn't completely broke. And now that the job was finished, she was on the look-out for another. I tried to remember if she'd ever cooked for me, actually offered me food that she'd prepared herself in the various rooms she'd lived in. But nothing came to mind at all, no memory except of mildewed bread and crusted cheese much as I might have offered myself before the kids had forced me into a more bountiful order. We still needed a cook, for sure. And not *only* a cook for that matter. I glanced at her surreptitiously. What about waitress? Or would her now unfortunate profile tend to put patrons off. Someone should have put a ruler to her nose, the original one that is, and then given instructions exactly how much to take off. The proportions in a person's face ought not to be tampered with lightly. In Zoë's case, I considered the excessive millimetre of that inch removed to be as serious indeed as rape.

What was the lighting like in our restaurant? Lighting made all the difference. If we had the sort which started at a standing person's chin, Zoë might be in the clear. And I believed in fact that's what we did have. Each table was lit individually with an evil and unflattering light which struck those seated straight between the eyes. Not only blinding them momentarily, when they bent to examine the menu, but also pinpointing pimples, open pores and pendulous pouches beneath eyes, noses and chins. We ought perhaps to see to it. It wasn't the sort of lighting that even I, with less than average vanity, would care to subject myself to.

Auntie slumped on to my shoulder. She seemed to be falling asleep. 'I'll have to go, I think,' I said, 'and put old Auntie to bed.'

Ulysses stopped polishing and put his glasses back on. 'I'll give you a hand with the old girl—'

'Oh, that's sweet, Ulysses. How kind.' His hand brushed

against mine under Auntie's arm. 'I'll leave you then, Vincent, to enlighten Zoë all about the restaurant. Perhaps we could think of recruiting her in some capacity or other?'

Auntie's eating and drinking habits were beginning to make themselves felt. I'd have to wean her away from port and peanuts, I reflected, as I heaved her up the stairs. Something more sensible like Slimline tonic and a spirit perhaps, something like vodka might help to correct the balance. We paused on the first landing; one more flight of stairs. 'Oh thank you, Ulysses,' I said. 'I think I can manage from now on. I'll just pop her in the loo. I'm sure she wants to go.'

That wasn't as simple as it sounded. I struggled with her back suspenders as she stood waiting, docile, for the signal that she could start. The corset was new and the mechanics seemed particularly stiff. 'Hold on, Auntie,' I said anxiously. 'Don't go ahead until I say when!' I peeled it all back just in time. She flopped, a radiant smile upon her face. 'That's better,' she said, 'thank you, love.'

I left her back suspenders dangling down, the stockings supported by those in front. She pulled her bloomers up herself and wavered towards the door. 'I can manage now, on my own, I think. You go and see to Stuffy—'

I saw him waiting down in the hall. Had he heard her calling him Stuffy? She'd never quite grasped the Ulysses part. That was our fault, Vincent's and mine, for always referring to him as Stuffy in her presence. He probably wouldn't have minded that much, though humour was hardly his bag. She clung like a child to the banisters and eventually arrived at her room. 'Have a nice snooze, Auntie – see you later.'

'And you too, love.' She gave a sly wink.

Vincent allowed us half an hour and wisely left Zoë behind. 'She's still up there, in the Queen's Elm if you want to chat. She's terribly keen on the restaurant. Were you thinking of her as a waitress?'

Stuffy had left me still floating. I could in fact have just done with a little snooze myself, like Auntie upstairs. But Vincent was all for action. 'You've sent the painters then I see,' he said.

'Yes, with full instructions, but I'd better go down, just to supervise and make sure they've got the right place—'

'They're not that daft, surely, darling.'

'Oh I don't know. I wouldn't say that. I've told them bright red for all the outside. And the lavvy, oh yes, I've said that.'

'What, red! It'll look more of an abortion than it does already, painted red—'

It did. They'd done it already by the time we got down there, brilliant pillar-box red, like a spectacular street accident. Very shiny. 'Gloss?' I was appalled. 'Why use gloss? Why not emulsion? Gloss takes so long to dry.'

They were using it, gloss, on the outside too. And had chosen of their own accord to pick out various wooden features inside the restaurant for some reason. 'Seemed to look better,' they announced with pride. 'More finished, if you know what we mean.'

'That will put the Opening off for up to a week, waiting for this lot to dry!' Vincent wailed.

'No it won't,' I comforted, 'contemporary paints dry much quicker – it's to do with the chemical balance. They've gone into it scientifically. Ultra Fast Dry – or Polyurethene, that sort of thing, you've seen it on the telly.' The painters looked bewildered. That wasn't what they'd been using, but I couldn't have stood a scene with either them or Vincent. The session with Stuffy had left me lacking the necessary edge. We crossed the road, Vincent and I, to gauge the effect from the other side.

'It stands out, Vince, you have to say that.' I felt a squiggle of pride. 'Owners of all we survey!' We'd made that arrangement between us, though I had supplied the money for what remained of the lease. A snip, they'd said at Giddy & Giddy, with five more years to go. But Vincent was the one who'd be running it. Seeing to the food and such-like, throwing out undesirables, engaging staff . . . Which made us, in my view, perfectly equal partners. The biggest part of my day, though admittedly not non-stop, was after all committed first and foremost to the children. I looked at my watch.

'I'll have to be getting along, they'll all be back from school pretty soon. Why not come with me? Let's leave this lot here, they can hardly do further damage and we've got loads of things still to discuss.'

Sydney Bummer had left a message to ring him. Auntie was wide awake and full of beans, like a baby, all fresh from her nap. 'We had a bit of a chat, me and Mr Bummer. He was saying what a nasty old job it was – running that restaurant. Yes, yours. I wouldn't have it though. I said he was wrong. "Well we'll see, Gran," he said. I told him no, I was Auntie—' She was full of it.

I dialled Sydney Bummer's number. It was purely a friendly call from him, just to see how we were doing. I passed the telephone to Vince.

'Oh, great!' he enthused, 'almost opening! A chef? Well no, not yet, but almost. That's just what we're going into. Oh, thank you. That's very helpful, yes. Hirastaff, Soho. I see. And Catering Employment, I've got it. Both in the phone book, right-o. Thank you so much Mr Bu–, sorry, Sydney – you're being a tremendous help—'

'Ask,' I mouthed to Vincent, 'how the tailoring is going.'

'Oh yes,' he said into the telephone, 'my partner here is enquiring, Sydney, as to how the tailoring is going.' I could hear the laugh from the other end: 'Tailoring, sailoring! Oh, I'm doing none of that, not yet, no! I've told my boy, I've got to have a rest, a little break after the bloody restaurant game! You'll see! I'll check in a month, O.K.?'

'More like a year,' Vince said primly.

We looked through the Yellow Pages together. Vincent took Classified (Central) and I took Classified (South West).

'Catering. Quality Caterers. Private Catering Service,' I read out. 'There's one here called Winterhalter Gastronom Ltd. And another called Huseyin Yakup!'

'Yakup! Yak-up! Instant returns! Hardly English, I don't think, darling. What about this one? These are Catering Contractors – High Table—'

'Sounds like the Last Supper. Is that what they serve, d'you suppose—'

'Another one here, Prêt-à-Manger. Or Ye Mecca. Or Harold Passmore. Passmore, we'd like a second helping please—'

'I've got one. The Whynot Outdoor. Or the Kookarama Caterers; I expect they supply poached parrots, that's what it sounds like to me.'

'You're thinking of La Cucuracha, darling.'

I sat back, exhausted. We'd been searching for something suitable for over an hour. 'I don't know why we don't take Sydney Bummer's advice and get on to those two he said. After all, he must have tried everyone in his time. And he didn't get Scabs from there, not either of those places. He said Scabs just walked in off the street. Perhaps he didn't have scabs then, they might have come up in the steam.' I was feeling very discouraged. Rufus had refused point blank on the phone to have anything whatsoever to do with the cooking. I hadn't in my heart expected that he would, not ever, so his attitude came as no surprise. It was just that he was by far the most knowledgeable of my Gentlemen Callers on food. Then, having refused, he asked me, as I told Vince afterwards, what sort of food we were serving—

'Well, edible, I hope you replied.'

'No, he meant what nationality! I know, I was as astonished as you are now! He said what was the restaurant going to be – French, Italian or straightforward British. British meaning, so he explained, a place like The Hungry Horse. You know, Yorkshire Pud, and Steak and Kidney. And Treacle Tart and Roly Poly and Spotted Dick for afters—'

Vincent shuddered: 'Christ, consider the number of calories!'

'I had to say I didn't know—'

'Well, sweetie, we're not having pasta, that's for sure!' Vincent smoothed his hand-span waist and stamped an elegantly shod foot. 'It'll have to be French of those three.'

'If we can get the chef though, Vince—'

'I'm sure it's quite simple, you'll see.'

*   *   *

43

Catering Employment was right out of chefs; plenty of washers-up. Renta Staff wanted some French chefs themselves; all they could offer were cooks. Two in fact they had, just put on their books today, who'd double up with other kitchen duties too. All-rounders, both of them, brothers-in-law, who preferred to work as a team. 'Perfect!' I mouthed at Vincent, I could hear the man's voice quite distinctly. Vince put his hand on the mouthpiece for a moment.

'Not French, you didn't hear that part—'

'So what, not French?'

He raised an eyebow 'No, Greek Cypriot,' he whispered. 'What sort of food do Greek Cypriots cook?'

Socrates Parthenou and Aristotle Papadopoulos arrived the following morning. They laughed as soon as I let them in, each short and dark and swarthy. 'You boss? Yes, missus?' They looked from me to each other, grinning from ear to ear and nudging delightedly. 'She boss lady!' And then they broke into their native tongue. Was it Greek? Or Cypriot? Or both? I wasn't au fait, I hadn't an ear for much beyond Paris or Rome. They might have been speaking Swahili or uttering oaths in Egyptian for all that I'd have known. I stood there awkwardly with them, trying to play the Grand Dame, praying that Vince would come soon. He'd know what sort of things to ask them. 'Shall I show you the kitchen?' I said politely, after I'd twice cleared my throat. They nudged each other again at the question and burst into a wild bout of laughter. Possibly nerves. A new job and all that. I smiled and offered my hand. 'But first of course, you must tell me which is which of you—'

'How on earth do we tell them apart, darling?' Vincent was struggling to cope. I felt more confident myself, having watched them working together, assessing the kitchen equipment. They seemed more efficient than one might have guessed.

'The shorter one is Soc and the thinner one is Ari.'

'Soc and Ari! You're joking! You must be!'

'Soc and Ari. They're brothers-in-law. Socs married to Ari's sister. He's got seven and three-quarter children. The three-quarter is due in June. They live not too far from you, Vince, somewhere off Ladbroke Grove. You could come to work together, think of that!'

'Why?'

'Well it's nice, the thought of a team.'

Soc slithered around the kitchen door, smiling from ear to ear. They'd laughed out loud when I'd introduced Vincent, looking him up and down, obviously finding the end result hilarious. His Persil-white pants were terribly tight, he'd just had them back from the laundry. And he'd chosen to wear them with a very white shrunken sweat shirt. The two together pin-pointed the blackness of his bruised eye. 'He boss,' I said firmly to Soc and Ari, attempting to restore some order and soothe away the mortified expression on poor old Vincent's face. The announcement caused further hysteria. 'He boss? No! He no boss! You boss lady!'

'We both boss.' Vincent announced loudly. I looked at him. It sounded like a calypso. He boss. She boss. We both boss, man! He obviously had the same thought, we caught each other's eyes. I couldn't help it, I burst out laughing too and thank God Vincent joined in. It helped at least to break the ice between the four of us.

They were very impressed with the decor. "S'good, no? S'nice, is the colour of the sun in our country!'

'Oh, in our country too.' I was leaning over backwards. A fraction more and I could justifiably be accused of being patronizing. All we needed were porcelain teacups, with the little finger held at a genteel angle.

Ari, the slim one, ventured a tentative finger towards a scarlet shelf. The painters had run amok after we'd left them that day, using up the rest of their paint, so that now alternate tables blazed pillar box red above the rest, as shiny as polished pimentoes.

'Is sticky, no? Look, is wet I think still!' Ari leant forward to wipe his finger tip on Vincent's pristine trousers, taking them to be his painter's dungarees. Vincent leapt back in alarm with a strangled noise in his throat. He'd purchased those pants in

St Tropez; they held many happy memories. 'Watch out,' I warned. But just too late, he'd backed straight into a table. 'Don't speak—' he ground through tightly clenched teeth. 'Don't say a word, that's all!'

But it wasn't as bad as we feared in fact, more staccato, like a morse code in red ballpoint. And only on one buttock too. Soc. rubbed at it lightly with the turps I'd run to buy. Vincent stood by in his briefs. *Eminence*, white as well, but the paint hadn't quite seeped through. 'Lucky that, Vince. It might have looked as if you'd started menstruating. Having red on your knickers!'

An unfortunate start to the day, it might be said, but in the end it made no difference. It had given an air of activity and established some sort of relationship between Soc and Ari and ourselves. The beginnings of a staff at least. And the most important of the staff to boot. 'You cook?' I'd asked the question diffidently, gesturing over the gas stoves which ran down the length of one wall. They'd both nodded over-vigorously. 'He cook!' 'No he!' 'Yes me!' I was satisfied one of them could, at least. And which one made very little difference.

'They seem extraordinarily familiar with the utensils at any rate, Vince,' I said to him when we were upstairs. We could hear the sound of Soc and Ari laughing as it drifted up the Dumb Waiter. The Dumb Waiter was giving us trouble, the pulleys were splattered with paint, and the whole thing was sticking half-way.

'We could cut a hole in the side of it, and serve half-way up the stairs—'

'What, bring the tables down you mean! One on each step I suppose!'

Vincent was getting irritable. The turps had left a stain. Nothing that Extra Strength Daz won't see to, I kept trying to tell him. But he had lesser faith than me in the latest miracles of science.

An acrid smell of steaming fat seemed to be surfacing from somewhere. Subtle at first, like someone passing wind. I'd thought it was Vince and would normally have joked and drawn attention to it, but due to his irritability had refrained.

Now it was unmistakable. 'Oh! Ugh! What's that?' I exclaimed. We both inhaled together. 'Open the door, quick!' he said. 'Those two are stewing plimsoll soup or boiling boot blancmange!'

Soc had discovered a whiskery saucepan of solid grease, which he felt might well be useable. 'Is nice! Is good, yes? Have flavour I think. Plenty old and many meats—' He'd bent to sniff it. 'No, is wrong. Is fish, not meat. I taste.' I turned away and watched Vincent pale a little by my side as Soc enthusiastically plunged a thumb around the rim of the saucepan. It was hot but it seemed to make no difference to the leathery surface of his skin. Acclimatization to conditions, like Arctic explorers and such. A childish joy suffused his face, he gave a little hop. 'Is fat for chip!' He smacked his chops. 'For chips,' I echoed. Vincent put a trembling hand against his stomach. I turned to address him, to tell him of Socrates Parthenou's culinary discovery. But the fumes got there before me. We watched whilst Vincent's slightly pink, turp-stained posterior fled in the direction of our unisex privy.

I managed to persuade Soc to relinquish his find; it followed fast in Vincent's wake and mingled with his own offering to Sloane Estate Sewers. Soc poured it down with a flourish. 'Vamoosh!' he cried looking at me. 'Vamoosh,' I echoed, with feeling. It was touch and go as to whether I'd make my own contribution too. I swallowed hard and smiled as he pulled the chain. Danger averted.

Ari was going over the contents of the cutlery drawer with Vincent. There was, so he claimed, 'mucha missing' – chef's essentials, such as sharpened knives. Ari slid his index finger across his Adam's apple to indicate just how sharp. And skewers which should have been there, were now not present any longer. And all manner of general cooking utensils like cork-screws, a lemon squeezer, a fish slice, the kitchen scissors, palette knives, perforated spoons and a two-pronged fork – for instance.

Soc returned from the outhouse, having chosen to sit at the plumbing. Obviously, by the state of his trousers which he held unselfconsciously at half mast, 'Is no paper!' It took me several seconds to grasp the significance of the statement. Many of my Gentlemen Callers enjoyed a read when they went. But Soc was referring, I could see by the general pointing action, to something a little more basic. It was as well I'd been married myself. I gave him a page of the *Guardian*. The Arts page. He took his time in taking it, caught by a moody, photographic study of Sheila Hancock. 'Is Melina Mercouri!' he scowled and spat on it. A political animal then. And healthy internally too. Not everyone I knew would risk wandering that way before wiping. I remembered that there was no soap out there and passed him the Fairy Liquid. And no towel either come to that. What a shopping list was accumulating!

Vincent had started making notes of all that seemed to be missing. Not only from the cutlery drawer. Whole mincers and blenders, a pressure cooker and both electric kettles! 'Both?' I said. 'Well that's not right. We used one ourselves – when – on Monday.'

'Ah,' Vincent said darkly, 'before the painters came—'

'Oh, don't be daft, I don't think they'd have taken things.'

'Why not? They are all who've been here. Unless you've been leaving the door wide open for people to walk in off the road.'

I hadn't, as he well knew. We'd both kept it tightly shut, simply to keep all previous clientele out. RE-OPENING SHORTLY. SHUT FOR DECORATIONS – we'd had to hang those notices in the window. Not that it made much difference. 'When?' was everyone's question. When indeed!

Sydney Bummer's inventory could well have been inaccurate; I might have reminded Vincent that neither of us had checked it. I'd found it confusing, sorting out pedal garbage bins from piping bags and nozzles. And Vince had been impatient: 'Oh let's just get on with it and open, instead of all this gawping, checking and cross-checking on ghastly little lists. It's too depressing isn't it – as if we were both bloody bank clerks!' I had to admit I agreed.

I looked over his shoulder now, at his notes. 'Should I go out with Soc or Ari? Take one of them with me at any rate, they know more than you or me, over to Mence Smith's or –

better still — around the corner. You know who's there?'

'Who?' Vince sounded cross. Not in the mood for guessing.

'Elizabeth David, of course. Her shop, she sells all sorts of wonderful things for the kitchen. *Bain-maries* and so on—'

'What the hell are bloody *bain-maries*?'

'Double saucepans, one fits in the other. So's sauces don't get all that skin on them. The bottom saucepan's full of boiling water. That's the principle of it anyway. *Bain-marie* just sounds more exotic.'

'More expensive too, old darling. Perhaps you and I should forage first. It's time that these two had a break. Hey, how do you think it works with them?' Vince lowered his voice to a whisper. 'Are they counting this day as employment?'

The thought had occurred to me as well. They were putting in all they'd got. What reason, except to be paid? And what would they do now at midday? How long would they take for their lunch?

They answered without being asked. Each held up their wrists simultaneously and pointed towards open mouths. There was no food at all in the place. Not anything in fact, except water flowing from the tap and a bag of Tetley tea bags that I had brought from home. Soc seized a thick glass-handled tankard from its hook: 'We go pub!' He held the tankard to his lolling tongue and rolled his eyes to the ceiling, like a dog at the end of a walk. 'Got big thirst! Soc and Ari go for Guinness!' So say Tarzan. He speak. To his Jane.

Ari whooped with excitement and jigged a few steps. Soc fell in heavily with the rhythm, the tankard still clutched in his hand. We left them together, Vince and I, singing, engulfed in wild laughter. And walked soberly round to 46, Bourne Street to suss out Elizabeth David.

We left a pile of purchases too heavy to carry ourselves, arranging to pick them up later with the car. 'Are you, sure darling, these are all right? You know what you're doing, you think?'

'Everyone needs a *Bocal*, Vince. It's a straightforward preserving jar. And we need a *Bassine à friture* as well, it's just a

49

deep fryer, that's all. And a *Cercle à flan,* a *Chassenoyau,* a *Chinois, Cocotte* and *Couperet.* And Ari has underlined on your list at least one *Couteau à découper—*'

Vincent exploded. 'What do you mean "everyone needs a Bocal"! The only thing we'll be preserving is our sanity! And as for a *Chinois, Cocotte* and a *Couperet—*'

I took the chance to interrupt during that speechless second. I was quite enjoying myself, airing my French. 'Yes, and in addition to the *Couteau à découper,* Ari also underlined the *Couteau à désosser—*'

Vincent was dangerously quiet. I took his arm and squeezed it.

'– carving knife, and boning knife, specifically in that order. But I'll stop now, Vince. You can relax.' I could see I was starting to jar – or *Bocal* as we say in French.

But something else, it seemed, was on his mind. Not just my purchases, but more the manner in which they'd been purchased. He felt that now we were in the trade ourselves, we surely ought to be buying Wholesale. Direct from Wholesalers in fact, instead of over the counter like the rest of the general public, 'Ordinary Retail' as he called it. That hadn't occurred to me, but now he'd mentioned it I saw it might make sense.

'Not just equipment you mean to say – but actual food as well?'

'Of course my pet, otherwise where's the profit?'

'Where indeed?' I echoed. But what would it entail? Tracking down warehouses? Where though? Around Wapping, Whitechapel, Wembley, Wimbledon, Waterloo?

'It's difficult to know where to start though, Vince—'

'What do you mean, start?' Tetchy. Testy. No wonder life found him in his thirties and still single. Many would-be partners must have been put off by this tone of his. I decided to overlook it.

'Looking for Wholesale, Vince.'

He tutted, impatiently on edge, and we hadn't opened yet. 'You speak of it, Wholesale, as if it's an abstract quality of life! Like Pride—'

'Or Prejudice?' I offered to help him out. He ignored it. 'Wholesale doesn't exist in Timbuctoo you know. Look I'll illustrate what I mean. We're going to be needing vegetables, right?'

I nodded eagerly, 'Oh I agree. For the meals you mean. I think so don't you? It's usual, isn't it, in restaurants – Meat and Two Veg. on the menu. Unless you think otherwise of course. I mean we could just be serving Chop Suey, or Fish and Chips, or Ham 'n' Eggs. Or Tea 'n' Toast—'

'Please. Now you're being silly.'

I was. Yes. Shot through with this gaiety. 'Anyway, go on. Vegetables, yes we'll be needing them, so?'

'Follow me. And just listen. This is what Wholesale buying is all about.' We were almost back to our restaurant, just one more corner to round, on which, as it happened, was situated our nearest greengrocer's. A sizeable shop, a thriving business, to judge by the varied selection. As good as you'd find anywhere in fact, which said much for the neighbourhood tastes. Though not as good perhaps as Kirkwood's used to be, when it thrived on the King's Road near me. It was from Kirkwood's that I'd tasted my very first avocado. 'Four pears please,' I'd said there one day, years ago now of course. 'What, William, Comice or avocado, miss?' 'Whichever's ripest,' I'd floundered. And so started a taste and enthusiasm. But Kirkwood's had long since, several years at any rate, been bought out by the boutique belt, its footage encompassed into the current Antique Market there.

This greengrocer was even keener on display than Kirkwood's used to be, with oranges, apples, bananas, melons and grapes all arranged in a rococo abundance of colour. I was quite keen on the imaginative setting out of stuffs. In that way Mence Smith's was my favourite, but that's because they always used the pavement space as well. And were helped immeasurably these days by the advances in shades of plastic. Even the primary range of straightforward blues and reds and yellows had latterly become much more intense. So that ordinary objects like buckets and brooms and dustpans assumed a special magic. The spirit of the Mardi Gras.

A shirt-sleeved assistant came forward. Vince simpered and

picked up a plum. The assistant gazed stonily back at him. 'Yes guv?' Strange that, what animosity Vince's charm aroused. But it never put him off at all. 'The chap in charge?' he delivered it like Laurence Olivier. 'Yussir!' A new voice joined in from the back; behind us in fact stood the owner, a cigarette packet in his hand. 'My poison!' he announced cheerily, a cigarette already in his mouth. He took it out and waved it in the air. 'I'm of service, what's it to be?'

The transaction took all of twenty minutes, and two quick Scotches round at the pub. It was agreed that Twiddles, Tom Twiddle himself, should supply us with all our vegetables. He'd encompass our order in his own each morning at Covent Garden. Wholesale, with just a bit on the side for him. Almost Wholesale.

'Well done, Vince! How terribly clever!' We stayed on in the pub for another. He smiled, relaxed for the first time it seemed to me since I'd met up with him this morning. 'That's all right, darling. By the end of the day, we'll have tied up the meat the same way, and fish as well, and dairy produce – milk and eggs and butter. Bread—'

'And wine,' I finished for him. He turned, malevolently? no surely not, and said, 'Wine. Well, we'll leave wine to you.'

Nutty would know where to go for wine. 'Play your cards right, and he'll pay for it, darling.'

'No, Vincent. That's not the way we should run things. And in any case, if Nutty feels he can get a financial foothold, he'll be round here all the time. Driving us all mad.'

We waited at the side of the kerb to cross the road. Vincent, suddenly excited, sighted an approaching milk float, an Express Dairy one. He stepped recklessly off the pavement, and hailed it with a flourish. I could see the driver was in two minds whether to stop or not. My partner drowned in the top of the milk, before we'd even opened! The vehicle slowed down; the driver a wizened, weatherbeaten man with a nose like W. C. Fields, remained in his seat without moving. Vincent gushed, and swayed to the offside of the float. 'Do you deliver in this street?' He indicated our restaurant frontage up the road with a further flourish. The driver stared at him sourly. 'No, I don't, I'm just taking a short cut on my way back to the Battersea Depot.' Vincent stared at him nonplussed. 'But that simply doesn't make sense. What are you doing this side of the Bridge?' The driver started his engine up. 'Mind your own bleeding business.' Vincent just managed to leap aside in time. 'Charming!' he shouted. 'You turd!'

Soc and Ari were sitting, waiting benignly for our return. Up in the window, with their noses and kitchen aprons pressed hard against the pane for the amusement of passing people. One or two glanced curiously over their shoulder. There was, three doors away, a very small Voluntary Contribution Centre to Aid the Mentally Handicapped. Soc and Ari and their antics appeared to emphasize the poignant need for such a charity.

'They hardly engender confidence, those two.' Vincent sounded anxious.

'Oh, I don't know. I find them quite cheeky chappies. Cheerful little sods, that's what you want in the kitchen.'

'We'll probably have to ban them then, from contact with the customers—'

I didn't answer; he glanced at me. 'Oh Christ, I'd forgotten the toilet!'

'It'll all be all right on the day, Vince. Honestly, love, just don't worry.' And actually when we entered it afresh after the gap of several hours, I began to feel reassured. Apart from Soc and Ari, the place did seem to possess a certain gaiety. A clumsy gaiety, true, wrought by the amateur application of the paint; but probably due to the glistening red, it had the air of a children's playroom. An atmosphere, already. I left them there and took my car round to Elizabeth David to collect my culinary booty. They, all three of them, rushed enthusiastically, even Vincent, to bring it in on my return.

'Is nice, no, yes? I like! I use!' Soc had unwrapped the meat cleaver. 'Is chop, chop, chopper! I chop off the head of Ari—' He swung it perilously close, not only to the head of Ari, but to the head of Vincent, and also the head of myself. I'd only just seen the latest Sam Peckinpah film *Bring Me The Head Of Alfredo Garcia*. I must remember to tell Vincent after, how a head looked when lacking a body.

Soc was reluctant to part with his find, he tucked it well under one arm. Silly, it was certainly sharp enough to split a hair. Perhaps what he was doing was shaving. Underarm. It would have to have a good wash if that was indeed what he planned.

Ari, meanwhile, had discovered the couteau à découper, and had already cut open his thumb. I'd watched it happen, helplessly unable to stop him in time. They'd warned, at Elizabeth David, how sharp the carving knife was. But Ari had run his thumb along the blade, from the handle to the furthermost tip. Blood dripped from his bitten nail, giving the torn serrated edge a strangely surrealist quality. We stared at it, all of us, dumbly. I moved first and turned on the tap. Oh God, did this mean everything on the menu now might turn out red? None of my Gentlemen Callers much liked ketchup. Or eating shredded Elastoplast.

The telephone rang as I managed to stem the gaudy flow; we all of us watched it dwindling under the cold tap, until the merest hint of crimson combined with the icy water and then gave up completely. The cut itself was long and deep; I privately thought it could do with a stitch, but couldn't face the palaver. Ari gazed at it, a Hamlet air of tragedy to his stance. Soc could hardly stop laughing. I wrapped a Kleenex Man Size tissue round the wound, folding it carefully first to hide one of Bogey's bogeys, and sent Vincent off for Elastoplast. When he came back with it I was talking on the telephone, with Soc and Ari standing either side of me, mesmerized, as if believing that Alexander Graham Bell might have only just invented it. Either that, or something in the lilt of Auntie's always-loud voice at the other end was striking some spiritual strain in each of them. Perfectly possible. She had that effect on the children. Soothing. She wasn't soothing me though now. 'They've just rung up from Boyo's nursery. Waiting for someone to fetch him. Shall I go in my bedroom slippers? I'm all ready, love, if you are too busy. I can catch a bus along the Fulham Road. Won't take a minute. I'll ask them to put Bogey out on the pavement. The girl said they want to shut up and go home themselves. He's a good little boy, he won't move. He'll sit there tidy on the kerb. They can give him a little sweetie to keep him going—'

'No Auntie,' I said with some urgency. 'I'll go for him now, right away.' She could be forgiven, Auntie, for suffering from kerb confusion. Much of my own childhood, and certainly all of hers, had been spent on the curve of a kerb along with other children up and down the street. What she couldn't quite grasp was that the safety factor of kerbs in tight Welsh communities couldn't be compared with those of the Finborough Road, where Bogey's nursery school was situated. A direct route thundering with juggernauts and articulated lorries hell bent towards the motorways and arterial links of London.

I put the phone down, breaking the spell on Soc and Ari. They looked at each other sheepishly. 'Sorry Vince, I have to go. Poor Bogey's being abandoned – I'd forgotten completely about him—'

Vincent passed the tin of Elastoplast over to Soc and Ari. Neither managed to open it. 'Is shut!' Ari said in surprise. 'Is not possible to open,' Soc added, agreeing. I could hear the sigh start up in Vincent's stomach. 'Here's a coin,' I said quickly. 'They're always hard to open, those tins.' I had seen Soc look at the chopper. That would have opened it all right, in one fell swoop. Split in two, straight down the middle, spoiling at least several plasters.

My words had just sunk in to Vincent. 'You're going!' He looked wildly around him, lost at the thought of being left alone with Soc and Ari. No need to be, they'd all three be quite safe.

'But what shall I do while you're gone?' Vincent's voice rose in panic. 'While you're gone?' I hadn't in fact intended returning!

'Oh well,' I said uncertainly. 'There's lots to do, I'm sure. Like make a list of what there is to do,' I ended lamely.

He saw me up to the door and into the car. We both watched from our side of the road a traffic warden smartly slipping a parking ticket underneath my windscreen wiper. 'Fine,' I said mechanically.

'Is fine?' Soc had followed us up and now was standing behind me, squinting up at the sky. He nodded. 'Yes, is fine. Was raining a little. But now, is fine.'

'God preserve me and my sanity, darling. These two will finish me,' Vince murmured in my ear. Soc laughed delightedly and pointed at our heads so close together. 'Boss man, he love Boss Lady! Is good. Is fine, like the sky!' Looking in my rear view mirror as I left, I could see Vincent still on the pavement gazing beseechingly after me, with Soc prancing monkey fashion by his side.

Bogey was sitting in a plastic bucket with another one upside down on his head, behind the door, asleep. It took the girl in charge and me almost five minutes to find him. She thought she'd seen him in the garden last under the gooseberry bush, where Auntie was always telling him he'd first been found. When she wasn't pointing out storks in story books, that is, and trying to explain some sort of link up with our chimneys.

He'd sneezed, that's what gave us the clue. And then he'd sneezed again. When I lifted him out, he was still asleep and snuggled himself up in my arms. The girl smiled in relief at the thought of going. 'I'd have stayed, I'm sorry I had to phone – but I've got a date with a dentist—' she explained apologetically. 'Oh, not too painful I trust,' I said. She looked surprised. 'I trust not either. We've only just got engaged.'

Bogey woke up when I lowered him gently into the car, and crowed with joy at my face. I tickled him softly under his chin. He dissolved into giggling hysteria and widdled all over the seat, slapping his little plump hands delightedly into the spreading puddle. 'Oh Bogey, now look what you've done!' All my fault; tickling small children, I should have learnt by now, ought only to be done immediately after visitations. He sat in it smiling happily and I left him there in the warmth. I worked it out that by the time we'd driven home, he might just start to feel uncomfortable.

We turned into the top of Old Church Street; there was just time to drop Bogey off, sponge down the seat, swill his botty, change his clothes, and whizz back for Tallulah and Zsa-Zsa. Not that I did that every day. We had a rota of mothers who collected in their cars. And another rota which applied to delivery in the mornings. But I had blotted my copybook some time past on the morning delivery. The headmistress had complained of my lateness and unreliability to a fellow parent, one noted for her fanatically correct qualities in these two very areas. It occurred to me now that with the running of the restaurant and the need that Vincent seemed to be displaying over my physical presence, it might be advisable to belong again to the delivery and collecting arrangements. I slowed down and signalled to turn right and park outside our house. Not something I would normally do for any length of time these days. Not in springtime, nor in autumn either, with the open Morgan. The chestnut tree extended from the front garden, casting branches entirely over, not only the pavement, but almost half the road itself. Its buds secreted a strangely sticky substance directly on to the seats of the car. It had taken me several seasons to realize that it was the tree and not someone with a perversely childish sense of humour wiping toffee papers overnight.

I waited some moments before being able to steer over and park. Bogey began wriggling by my side. I looked at him. We smiled happily at each other. Were Tallulah and Zsa-Zsa ever quite as equable as him? Or did the youngest child in a family benefit from all the experience of bringing up the first few. The road was clear, but not the space immediately before the house. An unfamiliar car occupied what I had come to claim as mine. My Residents Only Spot. A large, unwieldy vehicle, with haunches as big as a bridge from behind. But beautiful. Brilliant yellow, exactly the same as my Morgan. And now exactly the same as the entire frontage of the house. The realization slowly dawned as I pushed my gear into neutral, hugging the side of the kerb. I switched the engine off and simply sat there staring. A 1932 Vintage Rolls, Hollywood style. Sunset Boulevard. That's what Nutty had said. My God, and now here it was. A present from him to me. I opened my door and got out. Bogey lifted dripping fists, and faintly steaming sleeves in my direction. I picked him up and placed him on the pavement, then holding one of his tiny hands, walked round to the front of the Rolls. Oh yes, there was no mistaking it was mine. Auntie, complete with curlers, a floral pinafore covering her frock, sat proudly in the front seat obviously awaiting the owner's arrival. Me! Nutty was nowhere to be seen, he'd simply left it and gone.

'Shy, poor thing, I expect it was – a beautiful present then, isn't it – oh, hello Bogey boyo. Come up and sit on Auntie's lap.' Auntie was in her element.

'I shouldn't, if I were you, Auntie. He's sopping wet. Spoil your pinny.'

But she took no notice at all, just swung one heavy leg aside, catching Bogey on the shoulders with both hands and lifting him, dripping, through the door of the Rolls. For some reason she had chosen to sit at the wheel. In the complicated process of leaning out, her elbow caught on what looked like a klaxon horn. Is that how they signalled in thirty-two? Whatever it was she'd started off it now refused to stop. A raucous, piercing sound ripped through the peace of Old Church Street. It sounded like a non-stop cross between a stuck pig and a raped giraffe. Bogey began squealing in joyful sympathy and, as far as I could see, was surreptitiously leaking again all down Auntie's leg. What the hell had they been feeding him all day? Piped lemonade by the look of things. Passing traffic began slowing up, with smiling drivers and passengers. Windows were opening up along the street. Neighbours were watching, some waving. Auntie looked around happily. 'There's nice it is, this noise.'

I grabbed the horn tightly by the bulb. The sound of it ceased immediately. 'Dew, dew, you've stopped it now, you have. Leave it, there's a good girl – everyone likes it, look.' Auntie was seldom cross, but did suffer from disappointment on a simple scale. Both she and Bogey looked at me reproachfully. I removed my hand. The mechanical screeching started again. God Almighty, what had Nutty given us now! Auntie's elbow had obviously triggered something off; put a spanner, so to speak, in the works of the vintage Rolls. 'Give me Bogey, Auntie,' I said, driven by desperation. 'And do what you did just now, again – just lean like you did on the horn. Perhaps that will shut the thing up, since that's what started it off—'

She did as she was told, obedient as a child. It worked until she went to pull away, when it started up again. 'It seems to need the weight on it, love. Do you want me to sit on here?'

Bogey's bottom was icy cold, Auntie's leg would be soon. She suffered already from stabbing arthritis. 'I'll sit there and see to it, Auntie. You take Bogey in and change him. And dry off your leg at the same time. I'll try and turn this bloody noise off. Tallulah and Zsa-Zsa will get home somehow, when they see that I haven't turned up.'

They did precisely that, arriving about twenty minutes later, dropped off at the top of the road. I could see them dawdling all the way down, deep in conversation. Probably about periods, the latest favourite theme. An Indian girl in Zsa-Zsa's class had started hers already. 'What, at nine?' I'd said in some surprise. 'Are you sure, Zsa-Zsa? Perhaps she's just saying—' But she'd pressed her elongated upper lip hard down on her generous lower, and had shaken her head in a positive way. 'We've all seen her bleeding,' she announced darkly. The image of the bright and virgin blood flowing between the dark child's limbs had been at the time strangely moving. I thought of it now, seeing my girls. And the thought led me straight back to Ari and his split thumb. Hell, they'd all flown straight from my mind, Soc and Ari; and Vincent, awaiting my return.

I twisted viciously on the complicated wiring of the horn, having managed at last to locate what looked like the source of something pertinent. The dashboard was incredibly involved, with many knobs, push buttons and protruding screws that I couldn't make head or tail of. Typical of Nutty to have chosen this very time to disappear, having first placed poor Auntie at the controls. He could well be gone for a week, from some misplaced stab at self-effacement. Gifts, so he felt, should be given without fuss. And certainly without the expectation of thanks and gratitude.

The girls drew parallel to me now, with whoops of surprise at the sight. 'Is this ours?' Tallulah kicked the nearest tyre.

'Don't do that. Don't do anything, please,' I begged.

Zsa-Zsa looked in. 'Why not, Ma? Why not to do anything?'

My index finger was caught up in a fine link of wire. The other hand still firmly clenched the horn. The two, I prayed, led straight to each other in some way. 'Shush,' I said closing my eyes. 'I'm trying to stop this bloody horn from blowing. Now wish, both of you, now, together!' I opened my eyes to see that they'd both shut theirs, and were holding their fingers crossed for wishing. Slowly I eased the pressure of one hand, whilst increasing the pull on the other. I held my breath, it seemed to be working at last. Then, gingerly, I removed my grasp completely from both. 'Silence reigns. Whew!' I gasped. 'Thank you girls!'

They beamed at me. I kissed them both. 'Was it us? Did we do it, Mummy? Did we help?'

'Help? I'll say you helped. Do you know how long I've been stuck here? Half an hour, with my hand on the horn—'

They looked at each other and burst out laughing, then chorused together to me: 'As the actress said to the bishop, you mean! Can we have a ride round in the car? Oh please, Mums! Can't you drive us all down to the restaurant? You said you would – you've been promising – you know you have! Is Vincent there? Let's go and see him now—'

'A quick visit then, before tea. Go and call Auntie and Bogey. I'll wait here, working out what's what and how to start this thing—'

I only prayed that nothing untoward would happen, no crashing spectacularly on the King's Road, not knowing the ins and outs of Nutty's insurance arrangements.

The girls arranged themselves in the back behind the dividing glass panel. Electrically operated, as they soon discovered. Auntie sat next to me in the front with Bogey, now dry, on her knee. She'd put her chapel hat on for the occasion. A dusty straw affair with quite unsuitable Union Jack streamers hanging on one shoulder. The glances of amazement from the amused and chic coterie on the King's Road had as much to do with her chapeau as the car, I felt. She thrived, as usual, on the attention. And by the time we'd passed the Chelsea Odeon, now closed for alterations, she had taken it into her head to wave her hand in gracious affectation, much in the manner of the Queen Mother herself. Had she worn her Woolworth pearls and her other bonnet, a turquoise toque from C & A, the passing pedestrians might well have mistaken her for that Royal person. A clutch of American tourists clicked excitedly on the corner of Radnor Walk, and one with a whirring cine camera crossed over to our side recording us in a running position all the way down to the opening of Royal Avenue. Auntie was ecstatic. And so were the girls in the back. The first time, to their knowledge, they were on film! They wound down the window and hung out like two unattractive flags. The American, whilst continuing to focus, shouted out 'Say, kids – so what are you called?' And it was only when they readily shouted in return 'Tallulah and Zsa-Zsa!' that he fell back and stopped filming, feeling for the first time that he may have been taken for a ride by two plain and plainly precocious Limey brats.

We majestically rounded the sweep of Sloane Square, where Bogey cooed at the pigeons after Auntie, relaxing her handflapping turn, had lifted his small wrist to wave. Several of the pearl-grey birds fluttered past our expansive windscreen, an indication of just how slowly we were going. It didn't get up much speed, a magnificent vehicle like this. I'd ridden in them before. Many times, with Tallulah's father. They weren't built with excessive motion in mind. They moved instead at a grander pace. Not like my Morgan Sports. I didn't much care myself for this degree of dignity, but it suited Auntie a treat.

It suited Vincent too. And it certainly suited Soc and Ari. They greeted us as we drew up outside the restaurant like the reception committee of a tribal community in the outback of Equatorial Africa, who'd never seen a wheel in their entire existence let alone four of them supporting such a streamlined chunk of machinery. Vincent couldn't get over it. 'Oh darling, it's simply divine—' Soc and Ari echoed the same refrain, but in their own way. 'Is bloody swell! Boss Lady very rich!' They both looked at Auntie with a mixture of rare regard and awe, and down at Bogey as if he were Little Lord Fauntleroy. Then they stood uncharacteristically silent for a moment, rolling the bottom edge of their kitchen aprons nervously in their fingers. I introduced them all round. 'This is Socrates Parthenou, and this is Aristotle Papadopoulos, they are brothers-in-law—' Both the girls burst out laughing. Soc and Ari joined in with relief. 'Is Soc and Ari. Him and me,' Soc explained to Auntie. Ari nodded vigorously and placing a comradely arm around Soc's shoulders, he gave him a smacking kiss on the side of his cheek. Bogey clapped delightedly and blew kisses out to all of us.

'This is it then,' I said to everyone.

'Is this it?' Auntie looked dazed.

'Is it,' Soc and Ari chorused, convulsing the girls even further. Vincent turned impatiently. 'Christ, let's get inside then, shall we. We're all out here like a garden party—'

'Be careful,' I warned, 'of the paint, kids. And Auntie, watch out how you go.' Auntie walked before us all, with her skirts pulled tight to her legs, showing the outline of her back suspenders and the bottom line of her bloomers. Both Soc and Ari had the decency to look away. Of course, where they came from, the women in Auntie's age bracket were held in particularly high regard.

'Do you like it, Tallulah and Zsa-Zsa?'

'Is nice, no, little misses? Is bright. Is nice and bright, yes? Is bright like the sun in our country.' Soc and Ari were anxious to please.

'Aren't they like monkeys?' Zsa-Zsa whispered. 'Look at their legs, they're all bent.'

Tallulah pinched her. 'Don't be so rude.' Zsa-Zsa grimaced back, looking for one split second uncannily like Ari. Pray God the wind wouldn't change.

'If the wind should change, you'll stay like that my little lovey.' You could always rely on Auntie.

'What do you think then, Auntie dear?' Vincent stood, hands on hips.

'Yes,' she said. 'Nice and slim.'

'No, Auntie,' I hastened to explain. 'I think Vincent means what do you think of the restaurant.' She looked around. 'Is this it?'

'Well, yes, and downstairs. That's the kitchen, down there.' I pointed down the Dumb Waiter.

'Is that how you get there, in that?' She looked bewildered.

'No Auntie. That's the Dumb Waiter—'

'Poor thing,' she looked sad. 'There's a pity.'

Tallulah was nudging Zsa-Zsa. 'There's someone who can't speak down there—'

'Where?' Zsa-Zsa was rather keen on the infirmities of others. 'Let's go and have a look. Can we go?' She turned to me. 'Is he deaf as well as dumb?'

Vincent stamped his foot and, groaning, put a petulant wrist against his eyes. 'You're all insane—'

Bogey sneezed six times in rapid succession, showering Soc and Ari. Vincent screamed, 'How disgusting!' as Soc and Ari shook themselves dry, like terriers coming out of the sea.

Tallulah tugged me by the sleeve. 'I want to spend a penny. Where's the place, Mum?'

'Oh, downstairs. Through the kitchen. We're all coming down, I'll show you.'

Soc and Ari led the way. The banister rail was still sticky.

'Sticky. Is sticky. Yes is, is sticky.' Three stickies before they'd even reached step six.

'It's sticky, this paint, isn't it love?' Four stickies.

'It is sticky, yes Auntie. Mind.' Five.

There seemed to be a transformation in the kitchen. A lot of blood about. I quickly looked at Ari's thumb. Had his fountain of blood been reflowing? But no, the pale pink of his Elastoplast shone clear as a baby's scalp. 'What's all this?' I turned to Vince. 'This blood? Not, surely, human?'

Soc and Ari started to grin and open their eyes very wide. They looked at each other and then back at me. 'Is body, Boss

Lady! We kill! We take the chopper and we go choppity, choppity, chop! Chop! Chop, chop!'

'Chop?' Auntie's voice sounded faint.

'Tlop. Tlop, tlop, tlop.' Bogey crooned to himself contentedly.

I saw Zsa-Zsa's mouth about to open. 'Don't,' I said. 'There's a good girl. Your Uncle Vince might lose his marbles. That's true, isn't it Vincent?' He was looking very neurotic. And edgy.

'I've come to a decision. While you were gone. We're—' he cleared his throat. 'I mean to say that what I think – well – we've been hanging around long enough. Let's open the restaurant tomorrow!'

The butcher had been, that's what had galvanized things. And one fridge, the smaller one, was full of meat – hence the gore. But from there in fact, everything else had plopped into place. The greengrocery and fruit would be coming via Twiddles at the crack of dawn. Vincent had rung the local depot of Express Dairy, who'd start delivering tomorrow. And after all of that had been arranged so efficiently in my brief absence, there did seem no valid reason in the world why we shouldn't declare serious intention and open. After all, that was the whole point of the operation. Or had been originally. For the first time a sliver of doubt threaded through me. We hadn't thought much about menus. 'What'll we serve? People to eat, I mean. Food.'

Soc and Ari fully agreed. 'Is nice. Food. In a restaurant. Boss Lady know her onions.' They each of them nodded solemnly.

I looked around at us all. 'What would you like to see on the menu? We should all really just say our favourites and ask Soc and Ari if that's what they can do—'

Vince coughed and cleared his throat. 'Might it not be better done the other way around, darling? One hardly imagines the repertoire to be extensive.'

'Blancmange. Vanilla. In the shape of a rabbit. That's my favourite of all in the world. I'm fonder of afters than befores. I always have been. I like a nice rice pudding. And I like treacle tart and custard. And gooseberry fool and double cream. And

Christmas pudding I like. Oh, and sherry trifle with ice cream. And spotted dick with treacle, and chocolate cake with currants—'

'Currants, Auntie?' Zsa-Zsa asked with interest. The question startled Auntie, lost in her childish reverie.

'Currants, love? Yes, I'll have some. I've always been keen on currants.'

A crash came from the direction of the outside lav, and then a stifled cry from Tallulah. She emerged to the sound of the gurgling cistern, the lavatory chain in her hand and a gout of scarlet paint all down one side.

'It came away when I pulled it and I fell against the door. Look,' I could hear the break of imminent tears in the tone of her voice. 'I'm covered in paint.'

'Never mind. It'll all come off. Don't worry, it couldn't be helped. It's a hell hole, that lav. That's another thing, Vince – don't we have to start getting permissions?'

'It is possible, perfectly possible, to operate proceedings whilst awaiting these various documents. It's a question of Applications to relevant Bodies. Your licence, for instance, to serve alcohol, can be provisional until you and Vincent, as joint proprietors, are authorized. You will, of course, both be required to attend a Court of Law and—'

Rufus' voice droned through my tomato-red telephone. That was one of the very good things about telephones. You could yawn without giving offence. Brad, burrowing down below between my legs, under my orange duvet, bit tenderly on my clitty. That stopped the yawn.

'Oo – ouch!'

'What's that?' said Rufus, surprised to be interrupted. Brad chuckled wickedly into my pubic hair and eased his thumb into my bum.

'Sorry Rufus. Yes, you were saying – the Sanitary Inspection? The placing of what, did you say?'

Brad pulled the duvet down leaving my body bare and, grinning up at me, slowly removed the intrusive thumb and sniffed at it appreciatively. 'Shit,' he mouthed at me silently and blew me a loving kiss. I ruffled his hair with my free hand, and slid one finger over his large hard shoulder, in under the muscled arm. Then I brought it up and smelt it. 'Sweat,' I smiled back at him, mouthing it silently too. He lifted his hand and pointed to the telephone, indicating that he wished me now to cut the crap and get on with it and him. I nodded, and spoke into the mouthpiece. 'Oh dear,' I put a sudden note of urgency into my voice. 'Oh dear, Rufus. I'm sorry, I have to go. I shall see you tomorrow, at the Opening. Come early, about six o'clock. I'm asking loads of people to drinks, first. And then if they'd like to stay on and eat, they can. But it'll be like a normal restaurant – I mean to say, they'll have to pay. Even you – do you think that's too awful?'

I'd thought it was rather awful, asking, actually asking close friends to pay. But Vincent insisted, and I could see his point of view. Best to start as you mean to go on. And after all, they'd be getting drinks free, at least for an hour and a half.

'That's about right, darling, an hour and a half of solid boozing – get them so sozzled and in need of another, they'll gladly pay for the rest.'

'What, food do you mean Vince?'

'No, not just food, don't be foolish – but drinks, I mean, as well. Straightforward drinks, like a bar.'

That was one of the things that Rufus was referring to, the fact that we weren't like a bar, and were strictly not allowed to serve alcohol without food. Our licence didn't run to it. He'd blown me a raspberry, right in my face, Vince, when I'd pointed that out to him.

Brad had popped in unexpectedly, not a habit much to my liking. But this evening, this eve of our Grand Adventure, I was prepared to forgive. He'd dropped a fare around the corner. Someone I knew in fact, a rather neurotic divorcee, who lived in Elm Park Gardens.

'I'm surprised she didn't ask you in—'

'She did.' He'd grinned.

'Well?'

'No!'

'Why not?'

He'd slipped his hand inside my blouse and squeezed a still soft nipple. 'Saving it all for you, honey.'

'Honey yourself.' I'd kissed him. Rufus had rung after the fuck, the first one, that is. We were just now up for our third and Rufus had rung again, having checked on Statutory Regulations appertaining to Restaurant Acts since 1967. Only trying to help, of course. But I'd have to speed things up a bit with Brad, there were still lots of phone calls to make. Lots of people to invite.

'No, I don't think that's too awful at all.' Rufus sounded most loving. Brad pushed a swelling penis hard on the palm of my hand and curled my fingertips around the smooth and circumcized glans. Rufus' voice dropped to a low and lustful pitch. I had better stop him now, before he started to declare himself. Brad believed him to be my trusted lawyer. Which he was, of course. As well.

'Right, I shall see you tomorrow then Rufus. Got to go. Thanks a lot for the phone call.' I could imagine the hurt expression on his face.

'That guy really bugs me, whoever he is. Talking to you in my time.' Brad frowned sulkily and clenched a powerful fist. 'He'll get a mouthful of this, next time. Fucking knuckle sandwich, got it!'

'I have indeed, or so it would seem,' I said, squeezing hard. 'Phew, you're cocky!' I steered it now towards my sticky nest. 'There you are, nice buttered bun—'

'Right, here it is. I'm ramming it in. Jesus Christ, don't let go, I'm slipping. Oo, it gives a funny feeling, kid. Like skating, like losing your balance. I'm mad on your body, you know that? I'm mad on the second and third. All this spunk – you drain me dry, you really do. But I can't get enough. You know after the last time, my balls were so loose, so empty, I mean – they hung right to the back of my knees. I had difficulty driving, I can tell you. Adjusting the set, so to speak.'

'Oh, sorry about that, Brad. You might be better off with

someone your own age, you know. Someone with less of an appetite than me.'

'I love you, you randy old cunt.'

We left it that he would be calling in at the opening Do, fitting around his cab fares. A temporary job this latest, a minicab firm, back to where I'd first met him.

'How much,' I'd said, 'do I owe you?' We'd come to the end of the journey. His driving had been atrocious. He'd stared at me, more at my mouth than anywhere else. I'd always responded to that. A trick of Cary Grant's originally, though Brad would barely know that. 'How much?'

He'd glanced towards my house. 'I'll swap.'

'You'll swap?' I'd said. I liked the way the light caught on his skin, catching the pale, fine golden hairs across his wrist. I guessed his chest to be quite smooth, with no hairs on at all except a halo around each youthful nipple.

He'd winked at me. 'I'll swap,' he'd said again. 'The fare for your telephone number.'

'You cheeky thing!'

'That's me!' And he'd winked again.

After he'd gone, I got on to Vince. 'How's the list going?' I said.

He sighed. 'Oh I don't know,' from the other end of the phone. 'I shan't be asking that many. I expect you, darling, to do most of that. The ones I know, in any case, don't have the money. There wouldn't be that much point. We don't want to get caught napping with a crowd of out-of-work actors. We're running this thing for profit.'

I thought of his black eye. 'What, none of your friends, Vin? Or intimate acquaintances?'

'No, what's the point.' I thought he sounded depressed.

'We'll meet up in the morning. I'll arrange for the kids to be dropped at school. They'll be all right. We'll go to the restaurant together, shall we?' I usually could cajole him out of his intermittent despair.

'No, I'll see to being there in the morning. You go and get all

68

the booze. There's still all that to be seen to. Who did you arrange to get it from in the end?'

'Oh all around, just different people. They seemed to think Soho was best. Nutty said somewhere in St James', of course, but it seemed to be so expensive. I've told him he can supply the champagne for the Opening. That appeared to keep him happy. Apart from that, I'm just getting ordinary things like Red and White, and different spirits like gin, and Scotch and vodka. That's right, isn't it? Oh, and brandy I thought—'

'Crème de menthe, darling. Don't forget crème de menthe!'

'What?'

'Yes. For me.'

'For you?'

'Well,' he sounded impatient. 'After all, if we're going to get launched on this ludicrous venture, we may as well see to ourselves.' I was shocked. I hadn't thought that he was feeling just like me.

'Oh Vince. I quite agree.'

'Well good then, that's settled, isn't it. Crème de menthe for me. And what's going to be your comfort?' My heart sank, I'd half hoped we were going to pull out.

'I'm thinking,' I said. 'I know, darling. What you drink at Mario and Franco's, the stuff they set light to, you know.'

'Zambucca. Yes, that's an idea. With the coffee beans floating on top. Yes, that's what I like. I'll have that.' Strangely enough, the thought cheered me, just as the crème de menthe had cheered Vincent. By the end of the conversation we both were quite looking forward to the morrow and all that the morrow might bring. And by the time we said good night to each other, it was with a sense of suppressed excitement. But I had lots of phone calls still to make and many more people on my list of invitations to make it all go with a swing.

I was the first customer into the Soho wine store. Delmonico's, that's where I'd gone to, parking outside in Old Compton Street. Bang on the double yellow. There was no other way, they didn't deliver. Not the same day, anyway. But the advantage of

Delmonico's at this late stage of the game, until we found another way to do it, was that they did sell at wholesale prices if you paid cash on the nail. I put myself in the hands of the assistant, a sexy Italian man of somewhere around my own age. 'Signora?' Marcello Mastroanni lines around the eyes. And a lower lip a bit like Rossano Brazzi's, as he'd been in *Summer In Venice*, or was it *Holiday In Venice*? *Venetian Holiday*? Oh hell, *A Venetian Summer*? I gave up, attempting instead a spot of Sophia Loren smouldering. He got the message at once. A queue was forming behind me, but we didn't allow it to interfere. Jesus, you never got this in Safeways. Not this tingling you wouldn't say where.

'I'm afraid my order's very big. I'm going to need a lot.'

He held my gaze and murmured his approval, then pounded one foot on the floor like a horse on heat. Though in fact it was merely a signal for extra assistants from below to attend to the growing crowd of customers.

'I give you, signora, my fulla attention. You say to me now whata you want.'

Not always easy to put into words. 'Now, where shall I start?' I said busily. After all, first things first. Poor Vince was back there in a sea of fresh veg whilst I was allowing my fancy—

The whole procedure took under an hour, and several assistants to carry all the cases of intoxicating liquid to the car. I'd somehow managed to miss a ticket. 'You lucky, signora!' they said shaking their heads. 'You crazy to parka that there!'

My one was the last to leave me, checking that all was all right, and that nothing could possibly fall from the open car.

I could barely see over in the rearview mirror, I should have to drive on the side ones. 'You cana see?' he murmured anxiously. How sweet, the Latin solicitude. 'You ·coma again, signora?' I nodded, unsmiling. High passion. Sultry, like – oh well, LLa Lolo. She'd do to be going on with.

'Ah, molto bella!' He spoke so appreciatively, I almost let myself smile, which would have spoilt the whole effect in one fell swoop. 'Bon giorno. You aska for me, Giorgio, when nexta you coma—?' I batted at him heavily with outrageously half-lidded eyes and, with the merest indication of a mature and knowing pout, I let him understand I'd understood.

The restaurant was in an uproar when I reached there. Vincent was near to tears. Soc had just dropped a dozen eggs all the way down the stairs and, in doing so, had slipped and broken his fall on the kitchen door, wrenching it from its sockets. It hung now precariously on one hinge, supported cross-like on the back of Ari, playing the part of Christ trudging up to Calvary. Two Sanitary Inspectors were studying our Arrangements, and looking extremely severe. A very young police constable was drinking a cup of coffee, his open notebook on one knee and a biro behind his ear. I looked at the biro with interest. I wouldn't have put mine there, for fear of it marking my cheek, unlike an inoffensive lead pencil. His cheek, I saw now, was in fact marked. Why hadn't he put the top back on?'

'I've been here since the crack of dawn!' Vincent said accusingly; his lower lip trembled dangerously. 'No point at all. On my own for hours. No deliveries came – Tom Twiddle died in the night—'

'He didn't! Tom Twiddle? I don't believe—'

''Fraid so.'

It was the young constable who'd spoken. I looked at him with surprise. Not only young, police these days, but confident as well.'

'Oh, did you know him? Mr Twiddle?' I asked politely. The Sanitary Inspectors had returned to the Outside Arrangements, and were pulling the chain again.

'Did I know the deceased? Indeed I did. He was married to my cousin's auntie. Not exactly a blood relative – but family even so.'

'Did he supply you with vegetables?' I continued to make a show of interest. This constable was obviously local and might be of great help to us à propos alcohol after hours. I knew myself from long experience that the popularity of many estab-

71

lishments existed solely on this service. And that if we were to adhere, Vince and I, too closely to the licensing laws, our clientele might fall away like flies.

'Not me personally, no. I'm not much a one for a full-scale meal, not since my mother went—'

'Oh dear.' I made a suitably sympathetic face. Death seemed to streak through their family. 'You're on your own then—'

'No. I'm with Dad. Mum went off with the window cleaner. They've settled in Australia.'

A curdled gurgle came from Ari, still wedged underneath the door. He looked so natural in that position, like an ornament on the mantelpiece – one of those plaster ones of long thin girls with salukis – that no one had thought to relieve him. The whole of it in fact, it now occurred to me, might have been from a Joe Orton play, or something by Stoppard. *After Magritte.* Vincent had started to shake, it was clearly time I took control.

'Soc,' I said pleasantly. 'Could you possibly help Ari?'

Soc looked at me and then at Ari in amazement. 'How I help? He have the door to the kitchen on his back. He look like a silly snail.'

'That's as maybe, Soc, but you see it won't be possible to let him stay like that. Not with opening this evening.'

The light dawned, and the penny dropped. Soc knew what had to be done. His brother-in-law must be removed from his present recumbent position. He pushed him hard with both hands, away from himself in a rapid propelling motion straight towards the two emerging Sanitary Inspectors. They watched in astonishment as the kitchen door crashed against the opposite wall, narrowly missing one fridge and a crate of full milk bottles. Vincent burst out crying. At that moment, Auntie arrived.

It was amazing what a difference Auntie always made, bringing her own brand of abstract calm, reducing total chaos to the norm. Soc and Ari were the first to feel the effect, being almost as childlike as she. And next, of course, was Vincent. He always felt better when Auntie was there, always more in the ascendancy with someone to condescend to. Even the three strangers in our midst, though I dealt with the Sanitary Inspectors and the charming young constable.

After the three of them had gone we opened another bottle of champagne, which made, by then, our fourth. Nutty had had three dozen delivered, though he hadn't shown up in person. His telegram had indicated that we might expect him this evening. Soc and Ari were already drunk, sitting each side of Auntie, nestling in like two small birds against the mother hen. She'd tilted her hat at a tipsy angle. 'There's a lovely time we're having!'

'We still haven't got any vegetables then?' It was the first time I'd dared to broach it, but Vincent was now appearing to be more relaxed. He waved his glass in answer. 'Vegetables! Pomegranates, peas, potatoes, parsley, parsnips, pears.' It sounded like spot the odd one out, that you get in children's comics. Two, I'd spotted. Pomegranates and pears.

'Shall I hop out and get some then? Twiddle's, I take it, are shut. As a mark of respect to poor Tom. Not a bad way to go, in your bed—'

Vincent sniffed. 'Depends who you're with, I suppose.'

'Yes, but it has a certain dignity, I mean.'

'As I said, it depends who you're with.'

Twiddle's was shut, with blinds drawn down almost to the bottom of the windows. Almost, but not quite. Just space enough to display a dozen or so bunches of black grapes, which someone had thoughtfully placed there as a tasteful sign of mourning. Would the constable wear a black arm band? Or didn't the Metropolitan Police Force condone such affectations on their uniforms. The public could, after all, construe a stripe of that sort as an extra degree in rank. I looked at my watch. It was Wednesday. 'Early closing,' I said. 'Don't forget.'

Vincent yawned. 'So what,' he said. 'There won't be much eating this evening. People, I'm sure you'll find darling, will be far more interested in drinking—' He yawned again, and stretched his elegant legs. Soc and Ari, watching him closely, immediately did the same. As best they could, with their limited physical frames. They reminded me, in their poses now, of the gonks that the girls used to have. A weakness, the gonks, of Zsa-Zsa's in particular. One hundred and seventeen and a half, she'd managed to collect by the end. The half being the head and shoulders of one that Tallulah had spitefully scissored in two during a quarrel. For a year or more, the amputated lower limbs had rested in the S bend of the lower lavatory, causing a mysterious blockage, such that the cistern would continue flushing for a quarter of an hour. The plumber, who eventually discovered it, had handed me the little legs with quite a suspicious look as if I had dismembered some small foetus of my own, and chosen this as the means of disposal. He was Irish and obviously Catholic. That reminded me.

'Quite hopeful, I thought, the findings of the Sanitary Inspectors. We seem to have just scraped through, Vince. But we have to supply soap and towels, isn't that what they seemed to be saying?'

They'd said a whole lot more, of course, but the champagne had sweetened the outcome. They'd fallen for Extra Brut. We'd made them promise to come back with their wives and have a meal on the house. Vince had proffered that invitation; in fact I felt he'd made a mistake. He seemed to be making more than one mistake this morning. And what's more now didn't mind. Which was all to the good. Vince, when minding, was very tiring. I preferred to carry the can, to that. I looked to left and right. Jesus God, what was it – 'He stood alone when all around had fallen'. That's how I was standing now. But I didn't mind, it was all so amazingly pleasant. And I had a good feeling about tonight. Like a benign producer, who knows he's backing a winner.

'I'll go out then, I think, and get some food. Pity about the Express Dairy, Vince. Didn't they say on the phone?' The Express Dairy had failed to deliver. They needed to have it in writing. Vincent had bought the crate of milk bottles and the doomed eggs, a dozen of which, of course, Soc had done in and now had to be replaced. Yes, Vincent had bought those from the Welsh Dairy up the road. Hardly wholesale, of course.

'Cream. And cheese. Oh, and butter Vince. You didn't think of those—'

'Don't forget Dairylea, for us. Oh, and single cream, not double. Bigger profit margin, I'm sure.'

Would the profit margin ever appear? On paper, there, where we could see it? In any case did it matter that much? We were hardly Heavy Industry. Not likely to affect the National Deficit in any direction. Either way.

I found myself in the Welsh Dairy too. Bowen's. She came from Bridgend. I'd have to bring Auntie in to meet her.

'My auntie, I'll have to bring her in to meet you, her mother's brother used to be a gardener in the Blind School in Bridgend.'

The woman's eyes brightened immediately. 'Oh, who would he be then?' She called her husband. 'Dai, there's a person here whose auntie's mother's brother was a gardener in the Blind School in Bridgend!'

Dai came from Cardiff himself. Clearly the ins and outs of hired help several generations before in an establishment for those without sight was not about to arouse his interest. I could see he considered Bridgend to be one of the arseholes of South Wales. Auntie wouldn't take to him at all.

'Oh I'm not sure you might have known him. I didn't know him myself. Rather unfortunately, in one sense, he went totally blind himself. A direct result of the gardening. Severe sunstroke, they said. One blazing afternoon in August. He fell flat on his face in the fuchsias.'

Mrs Bowen clucked sympathetically. 'The right spot then to do it.'

'Yes, he just stayed on inside.'

On my way out I remembered bread. 'Is this all you've got left?' I said. I'd thought of buying proper bread. Long French loaves, the crusty sort to lend a spot of class. Chop them into little chunks that people could tear with their fingers. The Bowens only had Hovis left, two sliced and one uncut. It would do for toast, of course, with the corners off, with pâté. But perhaps we weren't putting pâté on the menu. I'd have to buy some menus. Christ, what a cock-up already!

'Tell me,' I leant forward attempting to enrol Mrs Bowen as an ally in this hideous mistake of ours. 'Tell me, do you know of anywhere close where I could get French bread at this hour—'

'What's wrong with British?' she frowned. 'These grains, this wholewheat here, they use in Hovis, comes from Carmarthen they say. There's a granary not far from the Great West Road run by Elwyn Hughes. Your auntie might know him – Glamorgan boy—'

'Thank you,' I said and escaped.

The Food Hall in Harrods saw to my needs. I paid a quid to a boy to help me take it all out to the car. The bill gave me awful goosepimples. But at least we were now prepared to do business. The pâté had cost me the earth. Much more than I could remember any of my Gentlemen paying when we'd been out to dinner. Never mind, tonight we could reckon on running at a loss. Tomorrow we'd be starting in earnest.

And I was lucky too with the menu cards. Fluorescent pink from a sweet little place near South Ken. Designed by a student from the Royal College. The size of the *Evening Standard*, with nothing on them at all.

'Are you sure they're menus?' I asked the young man serving.

'Not sure at all, but they might be.'

'It's the colour that's caught my eye.'

'That's what caught mine as well – that and the student, of course. I'd have them dear, if I was you. He'll be delighted to know they've sold.'

I pictured them sitting on our scarlet tables, and warring away with our yellow walls. 'I can't resist, it's a silly buy – but I'll have them anyway.'

Auntie was fast asleep when I got back, stretched out on one of the tables, with her handkerchief across her face and her legs hanging over the side. One slipper had fallen to the floor. I picked it up and fitted it gently to her foot. She woke up with a start.

'Oh, there you are. You're back then. Did you manage to get what you'd gone for?'

'Yes. I did. I got everything, I was lucky. Half day closing, but not at Harrods.' I smiled at her. 'Have a good sleep? You'll need that with the high jinks later on.'

Her face lit up like that of a young girl anticipating her first dance. A fine dew of perspiration lay upon her upper lip and in the crease beneath her chin. She mopped at it now with her hanky.

'Where is everyone?' I looked around, no sign of Soc or Ari. No sign of Vincent either, come to that. They surely hadn't buggered off, with all we had to do!

Auntie blinked. 'They've buggered off.' It sometimes amused her to swear. I laughed.

'Oh, have they then! That's nice. And where have they buggered off to?'

Auntie laughed too at my 'buggered off'. 'Home, they said. To change for tonight. To change for the party, they said—'

'What, Soc and Ari, change? Are you sure? Changing into what?' She must have got it wrong, Auntie. She quite often did, after all. What the hell was their game, Soc and Ari? What on earth would they be coming back as? Maitres d'hôtel or the like? Or dolled up in national costume? Little skirts and skull caps on their heads?

'They've gone,' Auntie said. 'For their whites, which Soc's wife has been busy washing. I think they've gone to help her iron the hats. Those big chef's ones, you know. They've got a lot of tucks in them, and seaming. Very hard to do. I offered, but no, there's nice they are. They said they'd do it themselves. She's not been well you see, she's expecting—'

'Yes, Auntie, I know. Did they say what time they'd be back?'

'Well, they left here a bit after Vincent. Time for him to get to the top of the road—'

'You mean Vincent doesn't know they've gone?'

Auntie looked anxious. 'Oh no, he doesn't. He left them in charge. I promised that I wouldn't say. I didn't do wrong, did I?'

'No, of course not. Everything's lovely. I've got all the food anyway. Enough to do everything cold if we like. That would certainly cut down on cooking.'

'Cold, love? Not very cosy, cold. Can't you manage to heat something up for people? A nice hot gravy?'

'On salad?'

'Oh, it's salad, is it? You count me out.' Auntie pulled a babyish face of dislike. 'Old lettuce leaves and sliced cucumber, ughavee! Cold comfort!'

'A nice vinaigrette, made by Vincent. That's one thing I know he can do—'

Auntie pulled an even longer face. 'A lot of old grease poured all over.' She managed to make it sound like diesel oil. 'Better to serve beetroot sandwiches. There's no one who doesn't like those.' To be followed by banana sandwiches as dessert?

'Oh, by the way, where has Vincent gone? Home to change as well?'

That I would more readily believe to be true. Vincent sometimes changed as many as four or five times in a day, especially when things weren't going well. He actually believed in some superstitious way that what you wore could alter or affect events around you. Auntie confirmed this to be the case.

'I must be thinking of that as well,' she said. 'What frock and hat to wear. My new two-piece from Tesco's, the one I got last week.'

Auntie was terribly keen on Tesco's and took a weekly trip by bus and tube over to Brixton, which boasted the biggest Tesco's in Central London. She claimed their Acrylic range, in fact all their Man Made Fibres, could knock spots off Fortnum & Mason's, which she'd found to be dreadfully disappointing. She didn't care for the colours for a start, and too much of it at Fortnum's was fashioned from old-style stuff like Pure Silk & All Wool and 100 Per Cent Cotton. Auntie was all for progress. Her new two-piece was a violent lime, about the colour of bile. Vincent had shaded his eyes when he'd seen it, and begged her to switch it off.

'With your turquoise toque?'

Auntie considered it carefully. 'I had thought my pink

sequin beret—' My pink sequin beret, she meant. My Biba one with the matching bolero. She unfortunately, or otherwise, couldn't get into the bolero. She had tried, but it barely went past her elbows. 'I can't get it to budge,' she'd complained, still struggling. 'Don't try then, Auntie, that's best. Otherwise it'll only tear.' A shower of glinting sequins had drifted like snow past her knees, coming to rest on the top of her Surplus boot-ees. 'There's pretty,' she'd said. 'I could think to stick them on with glue, in a bit of a pattern, look.' But the beret had not the same problem over fit. She and it had become inseparable.

'Well, you'd match up with the menus anyway. Exactly the same colour, see.' I showed her the fluorescent pink and she clapped her hands like a child.

'Oh, there's lovely, yes, indeed, we'll match up with those a treat. Oh, that's it then. Shall I wear these bedroom slippers with it? These mauve ones, or get some new? Peter Jones have got some pretty primrose, quilted satin in the window. With fluff all around the ankle. A little bit pricey though, that's the trouble. I don't really like paying much—'

'Oh go on, Auntie, treat yourself. You know that you can afford it.' I knew she could. It wasn't the money, it wasn't the price that kept Auntie out of smart stores. She felt much more at home in the chain ones, that was all. More at ease, with fewer glances from astonished assistants and fellow customers. She kept most of her worldly wealth with her at almost all times. She had it hidden in an old envelope at the bottom of her big Mock Croc handbag. A very nice line put out by Marks & Spencer's, but only available in limited outlets. She'd got hers from the Newport branch when she'd gone there for a friend's nephew's wedding. We'd had words, she and I, more than once, over this. But Auntie, when she wished to, could become ex-tremely stubborn. She didn't believe in the validity of banks. Nothing could persuade her that putting money where you couldn't see it was in any way safer than having it here in your hand. Her mother before her had felt the same. She'd put all of hers in a pillow case, and slept on it every night. And when she'd died they divided it up. Auntie still had her share. And stored it in similar fashion after I insisted that she take it out of her handbag. She'd compromised. The bulk of it in her bedding, and a working capital beside her in her bag. Only I knew that it was in there, but how much I could barely guess. Two hundred, two hundred and fifty? Somewhere around that sum.

'I'll come with you Auntie, now if you like. We can walk from here up to Sloane Square. Peter Jones is half day Saturday.'

Auntie shook her head. 'No, love, I think I've decided. The primrose might just be too much. Introducing that extra colour. Best to stick with what I've got. The Tesco two-piece – what about you?'

I had to admit I hadn't given it that much thought. And in any case the issue was complicated by not knowing quite what my function was going to be. Was I expected to waitress? And who would be manning the till? Or seeing to drinks then, come to that?

The telephone rang. 'The Brick Bistro?'

'What's that? Oh, yes!' It was the first time that someone had said it. We hadn't in fact thought much of the name. We were meaning to make up another, Vincent and me. But between us, in our dilatory fashion, we'd neglected to inform the painters. And they, in our absence, had simply repainted the existing sign. It stood in bold raised letters, above the door and windows, picked out by them in yellow. But with the bottom of the B in Brick missing, so that it actually read The Prick Bistro.

'I understand,' the voice continued, 'that you've been closed for redecoration – is it also true there's been a change of ownership?'

'It is,' I said importantly. 'But I'm sure you'll find the welcome just as warm.'

'Mm,' the voice assumed a slightly unpleasant edge. 'Well to be absolutely frank, the Brick was never noted for the warmth of welcome. I'm ringing to enquire if the prices are the same. I happened to drive past the other evening, and the décor appeared to me to be, hmm, rather more, what shall we say – more trendy. One rather hopes that nothing quite as revolutionary has occurred in the kitchen. I happen to have patronized the old

Brick for quite some time – it seemed to be value for money—'

'Oh,' I interrupted eagerly. 'This is exactly what we hope to continue, of course, why not come and try us.'

It was becoming important to convince this man. Our very first customer possibly. I should have liked Vincent to be on a telephone extension and reiterate what I said. There was a silence at the other end. Perhaps I'd come on too strong.

'We're actually opening up tonight, with a celebratory party. Why don't you come, Mr—? I didn't quite catch your name—'

'That's because I didn't give it. I shall think about your invitation. Not much of a party man myself. What I'll probably do is let you get into some running order and pay you a visit next week.'

How sour some people sounded. Was this how it would be? Or did I have the right to refuse entry to the unpleasant? I'd have to ask Vincent about that one. There was no real reason to accept every Tom, Dick and Harry. Not if you didn't like them.

Auntie and I couldn't leave now, of course, I realized that. Who would let in Soc and Ari? I dialled Vincent's number and let it ring for a full five minutes. There was no answer at all. At this rate I'd be opening on my own – well, with Auntie at my side. Though, come to that, it wouldn't matter much. Just like giving a party, but not on home ground. I set about unpacking all my purchases. Auntie attempted to help, bumbling about the kitchen and bumping into me each time I turned round. My menus lay unwritten on, blazing beautifully on their own. It seemed a shame to have to sully them. Perhaps we could ask people just to take pot luck. Was it really necessary to offer a choice? After all, when you went to dinner in a person's home, you had to eat what they gave you. And we'd only have mostly friends having meals here anyway.

Someone was knocking upstairs. Soc and Ari? Vince had his key. Auntie went up to answer the door, and came down with Zoë Knickerbocker. She was wearing black sheer stockings with a seam up the back and a tight black short-sleeved dress.

'I've got my pinny. I bought it in Barker's. A proper waitress apron. Well, more French Maid in a Feydeau farce. And suspenders as well – do you like it?'

Auntie and I both stared at her in amazement as she bent over to show us her bum. Did she think they'd be eating down there on the floor out of dog bowls, or what? She stood up and took a deep breath to show off her breasts to advantage. The pinny was very pretty in fact, frilly and bibbed and made out of nylon organza. Auntie felt the fabric between a critical thumb and finger.

'Artificial,' she said approvingly.

'Oh yes,' Zoë answered. 'Drip dry.'

She seemed so at home I couldn't quite bring myself to ask what she was doing here. We hadn't discussed it as yet, Vincent and I, quite what to do about Zoë. He must have asked her behind my back. It made no odds, we could certainly do with her help.

'Ulysses said you were opening and could probably do with some help. He's coming later, isn't he? To the party I mean—'

'Stuffy? Oh, good old Stuffy. That was nice of him. I was meaning to ask you if you wanted a filling-in job, Zoë.'

'Tell me,' she pirouetted on her platform soles like a ballet dancer whose pumps have strayed into cement. 'Where shall I start? And what would you like me to do? Where's the music in here, anyway? You've got to have sounds for some atmosphere.'

Black Soul was what Zoë said we must have. Records by people like Barry White. And Isaac Hayes. 'You've heard of him, he did Shaft.'

Auntie had pricked her ears up at Shaft. Shaft was her favourite film music. 'We've got Tamla Motown at home. Lovely records done by Diana Ross and different negro boy singers – what's that set of them?' Auntie turned to me. 'Related to each other, brothers, isn't it? Or cousins. You know, there's a little one. Always laughing—'

'Jackson Five.' Tallulah and Zsa-Zsa had been terribly in love with Michael Jackson last year.

Zoë wrinkled what was left of her nose in a look of deep

disgust. 'The Jackson Five! Diana Ross! Oh no. Tamla Motown's old hat – Curtis Mayfield and all those cats, they're the ones you want now.'

Zoë prided herself on knowing the latest 'in', and because of that, she earned Auntie's regard.

'By the way, what I meant to ask was, what sort of food are you serving? French? Italian? What are the cooks? What nationality are they?'

A manic scampering was starting upstairs, a staccato drumbeat on the front door, and a sound of high-pitched excitable squealing, obviously aimed through the letter box. Zoë looked startled and abruptly stopped questioning me. Auntie laughed and sighed with relief.

'They're back, the boyos are back—'

I managed to leave an hour for getting myself ready, after I'd seen to Tallulah and Zsa-Zsa and Bogey. They would be coming, for just a short while. I'd got Vincent at least to agree – but grudgingly.

'It's not a party at your place – it's not the same as home. We have to start remembering, darling, that these premises are actually open to the public. They'll be our eventual patrons. It's hardly conducive for passers-by to peer in and catch a glimpse of what seems the start of a kindergarten—'

But I'd fled before he'd managed to get really into full swing. There was a side to Vincent that was frightfully suburban. It wouldn't have put me off, not at all, to see a lot of children in a restaurant. And certainly not if they were obviously the children of the owner. In fact quite the opposite surely. Wouldn't it show simple faith in the food? After all you wouldn't wish to poison your own family. There were for certain, to my knowledge, at least two restaurants, Italian ones in expensive Beauchamp Place, to which the patrons were proud to go and be hailed by the proprietor's relatives.

But I had to admit that he looked magnificent, Vincent, though still disagreeing with him. He'd arrived, all done up, just before I'd left intending to leave Soc and Ari in doubtful control with Zoë. He'd caught me in the nick of time, as I was settling Auntie in my passenger seat. She was agitated and upset, in an agony of indecision over the primrose satin slippers in Peter Jones. I'd solved it by saying I'd buy them. A small present for all that she'd done. A piddling price for me to pay by any standards, hers or mine, for all that I owed her in fact. But Auntie was proud and misguidedly puritanical about the acceptance of all gifts. As if they were bribes and enticements, which may bring her to deeds she might later regret. I actually felt the same way, though in recent years had been learning to come to terms with it. To accept a little more graciously, understanding what joy giving could give to the giver.

Vincent would have caught my eye and attention even if I hadn't known him.

'My Christ, you look incredible Vince! A Cossack! All cream, how original!'

Not half as original as it seemed apparently, simply a copy of an outfit of Ricci Burns – the hairdresser of Mick and Bianca Jagger. Vince had seen a photo of him wearing it in somewhere like the *Daily Express*, and had had it run up by a boy who made costumes for the Ballet Rambert. Each sleeve umbrella'd down below his knees. He'd have to be careful, stirring even simple stuff like coffee. Let alone the possible complications of soups and suchlike. He'd have to be careful standing, come to that, it also occurred to me. The paint, as I feared, was still tacky to the touch in places.

I bore this in mind, changing now and choosing what to wear myself. One thing, there was plenty of selection. An abundance of old clothes of everything, going right back. To before my mother had been killed. I unfolded the frock I'd been wearing that day, blue cotton with white cuffs and collar. Too small now for even Tallulah or Zsa-Zsa to wear, but still in prime condition. My Best, it had been, I'd only worn it twice before. Each time to Sunday School. But it was Wednesday then, that day they'd put it on – because my mother was coming to see me. There was the hint of darker things than that as well. Snatches of half-conversations. An air of troubled tears and tension mounting up as the day of her visit loomed nearer. Quite ordinary things like having my bath, or being tucked into my bed, or on that very Wednesday morning whilst eating my breakfast – I had the feeling that it might well be the last time I'd be doing it, in that house. It dawned on me eventually that my mother might take me away.

She didn't come. She'd died. She'd gone to Heaven, that's what they said. She'd been killed on her way down. They'd made me say a prayer for her to God, kneeling beside me in the dark. Asking His Everlasting Understanding and Forgiveness for my mother's Waywardness and lapse of Faith. I did obediently as I was told and prayed for my mother's Salvation. I didn't mind at all that she hadn't come. I had no wish to leave where I was living. I liked it there with everyone, and Auntie.

I looked at myself in the mirror, and thought 'How incredibly plain'. As easily plain as poor Zsa-Zsa in this light, taking the features one by one, unassisted by the aid of cosmetics. Nobody knew of course, except myself, how extremely plain I actually was. But they hadn't had to learn to live with the inadequacies of my basic equipment. They only saw what was presented to them – a concoction of subtlety and skill, a combination of many other women like myself who'd made use of their odd looks, almost ugliness. I was big of course, which helped a lot, built on the lines of Earth Mother. Generously endowed everywhere, but still perfectly in proportion with a fine length of leg to balance it all up. I looked at my body critically now, turning sideways to suck in my stomach. Still firm, the flesh. Still there, the breasts and buttocks, not falling yet, surprisingly. I pulled my arms back and jutted my front – as proud as the prow of a ship. Oh yes, a body built for men. To ensnare and enfold. Seductive, but still comfortable. As if Sophia Loren had been put in the mincer with someone like the Queen Mother.

I rubbed my damp hair with a towel, nothing much more was required. It clung uncharacteristically in tight curly tendrils around my skull. The result of my recent perm. Friends had been horrified before I'd had it done, my strong straight hair hanging like shiny metal to my shoulders had seemed such an integral part of my appearance – like Joan Bakewell and hers. And the change of colour from almost black to hennaed red hadn't gone down too well with them either. But I knew best, much better than anyone else on the ways to extend my appeal.

I pinned the drying hair behind my ears and prepared to start work on my face. Auntie chose that precise moment to knock on the door and barge in. 'I can't decide between the two – what do you think?' she said. We stood there looking at each other. Me, tall and nude, still suntanned from last summer. She, short and floury white, corseted from her midriff down, two hefty brassieres in her hand. One peppermint green, the other a ripe rich peach. Her breasts hung down like carrier-bags, the nipples on a level with her navel. Or where her navel must be, nestling secretly behind the corsetiere's armour. We neither of us felt any self-consciousness. I was as familiar with each dear fold of her body as she certainly was with mine. The fact that at some time, in infancy and the ensuing years, her shape had been much like any other, and that only in adulthood and now in old age had it become like this through sheer neglect – that's what struck me as tragic. That this piece of machinery through misuse had not afforded her more pleasure of the sort that I so enjoyed. That to have been through life and die a virgin like Auntie, seemed such a waste.

'That's pretty.' I pointed to the peppermint green.

'Marks and Spencer's. New Line of the Month, it came in on Monday. Women fighting before they sold out!'

I envisaged a sea of sweating, wild-eyed Auntie figures triumphantly waving peppermint-green underwear high above their heads in the direction of the till. Like a lingerie forest, no less, with my own Auntie the indomitable leader.

'What's the trouble then, why don't you wear it?'

Auntie held it close to her skin. 'My blouse though, you see, is see-through. You can see it, you see, showing through. See?'

'I do see. But I don't think that matters, does it? The green will go nicely with your lime-green suit. You'll be wearing that, won't you? With the blouse?'

It was worth putting everything into words with Auntie, I

found. She might well, if she'd taken it into her mind, have just gone out in blouse and bloomers. Like a child of the streets back home.

Her face puckered. 'I'm not sure now at all. I was thinking to wear my Crimplene. The floral I got at the Co-op. The duster-coat.'

'Yes. With what skirt?' I tried not to sound too doubtful.

'Well, a safety-pin? Pinned down the front? No need for a skirt then you see?' Auntie's voice wavered unhappily, knowing that wasn't the answer. She patiently needed me to make the decision for her.

'Oh, I should stick with the original plan. The lime-green's lovely, Auntie. With the see-through blouse and the nice new bra, and the beautiful bedroom slippers – you'll be belle of the ball, believe me!'

I'd convinced her. She turned, humming happily.

Twenty minutes it took to do my face, to transform it from a baldly empty canvas of barely formed major features to a vibrant pool of beauty. Who was it who taught me the tricks of the trade? Sweet Stephen, my husband, as long ago as that. So that even before I was out of my teens I was practising the intricacies of full theatrical make-up. It amused him, it amused us both when he went out dressed as a girl. 'My friend and I,' he used to say, in a high false voice at a chosen cosmetic counter – 'my friend and I would like a spray of Chanel No 5, before we decide to buy.' And I'd be standing there beside him, barely able to control my convulsions.

I left the doing of my mouth till last, to match up with what I would wear, and turned my attention towards my wardrobe. It ran the whole length of one wall, an open-plan fixture custom-made for my clothes. I chose the shoes first, as a start. My highest heels, which brought me now well over the six-foot mark. Like all my other so-called faults, my height I'd decided to emphasize instead of disguise. Like, for instance, having Auntie here to live with me as instant explanation of my origins instead of pretending they were what they weren't. But these decisions, like going ahead and giving birth to Bogey, were ones only I could make. I couldn't have taken them, or made up my mind so definitely if I hadn't been in this blissfully single state.

'Wow! Wowee! Hey, Mums you look ever so nice—' Tallulah and Zsa-Zsa chorused approvingly. They'd been taught to express appreciation instead of holding back in misplaced politeness. Bogey looked up and joined in, dribbling delightedly, one thumb stuck in his mouth. 'Thumb.' I frowned tapping it lightly. 'Tum,' he repeated happily, leaving it where it was. Zsa-Zsa removed it firmly from his face. 'Naughty!' He looked at her openly in surprise, then started giggling again. 'Naughty Bogey! Naughty boy!' Zsa-Zsa greatly enjoyed the role of disciplinarian.

'All ready to go then, are we? Coats on. Come on now. Where's Auntie?'

We waited whilst Tallulah ran up to get Auntie from her room. I adjusted a curl in the mirror. I'd chosen to wear my Zandra Rhodes, a toss-up between that or the Thea Porter, both equally sumptuous and startling as gowns but the Zandra Rhodes won marginally on points for being a one-shouldered affair. It plunged diagonally from directly beneath my left earlobe to barely above my right breast. There was no question of wearing a brassiere, nor of concealing each prominent nipple. The fine material tantalized them into life. I presented a pretty explosive image. Too much? Should I be more subdued? What, and look like everyone else? I adjusted the silvery lily in my hair. One of Zandra Rhodes' signatures, the lily. A recurring motif which ran through many of her designs. Who'd bought me this dress? Was it Nutty? Or one of the others. It was sometimes hard to keep track of. I thought of poor old Nutty now, and of his desperate devotion. A Sir, he'd be, when his brother died. If I chose I could end up a Lady. And if I gave old Nutty a son and heir, I could claim to have mothered a Lord. That might have appealed immensely at one time to me. But not any more. I'd gone past it, something that Nutty, still entrenched in social mores, would never understand.

Auntie was taking her time, it seemed. I despatched Zsa-Zsa now after Tallulah. Bogey leaned against my knee. I resisted the impulse to pick him up. He could have played havoc with my hair. How strange it must seem to be as small as Bogey, on nodding terms with only large shoes and legs. It would be nice for all of us if he could stay that small. Like kittens who seem less lovable when they grow into cats. Someone should patent a shrinking powder to cut everyone back to size.

Now Zsa-Zsa had seemed to have disappeared. What the hell were they up to up there? Bogey crooned contentedly down below. I propped him like a piece of pottery against the wall. 'Stay there, little boy,' I said seriously. He watched, waving, whilst I made my way carefully up the stairs, negotiating one step at a time in my precarious heels and swirling hem.

'Auntie!' I shouted. 'Tallulah! Zsa-Zsa! Where have you all got to? The time is getting on. We really ought to be going.'

'Auntie's broken her bloody zip. It got stuck half-way—' Tallulah's voice floated down. 'We're putting her into something else. We're being as quick as we can. Poor Auntie's upset, we won't be long—' I descended the stairs again. One more up there would hinder rather than help. The phone rang as I reached the hallway.

It was Vincent. 'Where are you?'

'I'm here.'

'Well that's obvious.' He sounded impatient. 'Aren't you coming? There are people arriving. And I don't know what to do.'

'Play host,' I said, trying to calm him down. It didn't bode well for the future that, his constantly rearing panic. No wonder he didn't do well getting parts, producers must find his fusspotting a bit of a pain in the arse.

'That's all very well. Play host, you say! It's you they're all coming to see—'

'Give them a drink. We'll all be along in a minute. Auntie's broken her zip.' And I put down the receiver quickly before he had a chance to reply. There was in me a certain quality that appealed to hysterics. A curious calm, a kind of haven that drew neurotics with a rare magnetic force.

Auntie appeared at the head of the stairs wearing what

looked like a nightie. Which it was, as it turned out. Brushed nylon and highly inflammable. If someone should decide to stub their cigarette out on her, she'd burst into flames without question. Charred Auntie. 'Will this be all right?' she quavered.

'It's lovely.' Too late for a change. 'What a good idea. Who thought of it?'

'Tallulah.' Her sight must be worsening.

We arrived in the Rolls just as Nutty drew up in a jaded Land Rover. The contrast between the two vehicles seemed particularly poignant. It was the first time I'd seen him to say thank you face to face. He squirmed in deep embarrassment, eye-bouncing and turning bright purple. Passers-by paused in curiosity at the scene we must have presented. Me like a Grecian goddess. Auntie attired as if for the boudoir, right down to her bedroom slippers. Tallulah exceptionally squint-eyed with excitement. Zsa-Zsa all teeth, tickling Bogey. Quite safe, he'd only just emptied his bladder. All of us gazing at this stammering, strange-looking person, babbling as one possesed. Nutty's dad had died in the loony-bin, as, some said, his brother would too. And it's true that Nutty himself sustained a loose-screw somewhere. I'd thought so in those early days when he'd prevailed upon me to play games. I'd grown frightened, genuinely in fear when faced with that look of insanity, alone with him there in his house. And it was because of that, the feeling that the line was too fine between life and death, my sanity and his madness, that I'd since refused to participate. Though that in itself was still playing the game, still pandering to his deep masochism. He claimed it was impossible now to even see me without getting an erection. The fact that each time he'd tell me of this, knowing that I'd answer sternly that I wasn't interested, heightened the erotic tension. I wasn't by nature sadistic, he'd forced me to assume the role. My eyes dropped to his private zone. His member indeed did seem swollen. It bulged behind his cavalry twill, pointing towards the pavement. I hoped Auntie hadn't noticed. Not that she'd know what it was. How sad to never have held a cock in the hand. To stroke, to suck, or to stiffen. Though what she hadn't had she didn't miss of course. I'd see to it that my girls didn't suffer a similar fate, though they'd probably see to it themselves, without help from me – the way they were going. All three of my children and their friends exhibited the normal preoccupation with each other's parts, to judge from the number of Hospital Games they played behind locked bedroom doors. Bogey was pigeon-holed as patient. Hovered over, stripped and shivering with pleasure, beneath the hungry curiosity of half a dozen small and serious schoolgirls with Kleenex Tissues tied round their heads like nurses. I sometimes wondered whether this assuming the centre of such a sexual stage so soon might not damage my son in later life. Would he feel drawn to public display of his person? Strip off, strolling, along Oxford Street. Or, more decorously, take to exposing himself on the top seat of double-deckers?

That's where, after all, I had got my first glimpse of Man's Wonderful Trouser Worm. Aged about ten, the same as Tallulah, wedged between it and the window. Very well fed, was my first reaction, if not to say positively plump. Gorged and without doubt moving in my direction! As pale as an uncooked pork chop, with a slit-like eye in the centre of its head. It wasn't shyness, certainly, that prevented our closer acquaintance, but simply the fact that I had to get off. I've always been able to recall its appearance, though not that of its owner.

Now Nutty, from nerves, plunged his hand in his pocket, as if trying to conceal his discomfort, when in fact the jerky action he'd engaged upon only drew our attention even more to that area around his old-fashioned, buttoned flies. His fingers moved feverishly behind the material – was he wanking himself or what! Out here! In the street! A stone's-throw from Sloane Square! How unseemly. And how out of character.

But a final wrench, in full view of spellbound family, soon revealed the source of his struggle. It wasn't his manly mast-head after all, that appeared to be ripped from its roots, but instead the passionless source of the swelling was withdrawn from the confines of his clothing – a long, shiny leather jewel case. He thrust it awkwardly under my arm. 'Ha, happy b-b-birthday!' he stammered. 'For, for you. For ne-next week.'

Pearls. The sort I didn't like. Discreet and perfect. And real. Impossible to wear without worrying. Ones that would have to exist, living most of life unloved and locked up in a vault. Insurance, of course, for the future. Collateral. For all that that word meant. They lay on their bed of crimson velvet, glowing, yellow as ancient teeth in a set of very old gums. Depressing me. I looked at them stonily, saying nothing. Nutty anxiously registered my distaste.

'Do you like them?' He shuddered in agony.

I debated for seconds. Well, why not. 'No. I don't. To be perfectly truthful, I find their obvious costliness offensive. And besides which,' I put on my scolding voice, 'you should never give anyone pearls as a present. "Give pearls. Give sorrow." That's what they say. An old superstition, Nutty. I'm surprised at your insensitivity—'

Despair and delight danced all over his face. In disgrace. He had brought the wrong present. With luck I'd ignore him the entire evening, which ensured his enjoyment already. I watched his surreptitious fingers sneak into his trouser pocket. This time there could be no doubt at all as to what it was they were doing there.

There was hardly anyone in the restaurant after all. I couldn't think what Vincent had been fussing about. Nor could he, now that we'd managed to get there.

'I just panic if you're not around. That's all. Don't be cross, darling.' He looked at me beseechingly, needing my full approval. Funny that, when Nutty needed the opposite.

'Cross?' I answered confidently. 'I'm not cross. There's too much to be pleased at.' I looked around. It was small, our little place. Enough to seat twenty-eight people at most, with a bit of a squeeze, that is. But the proportions, the enclosing quality, only served to make it more intimate. Like walking into a womb. It suited me well. In the winter it would look even better, with the lights and the warmth and the welcome. Better even than it did tonight, when one might have wished to dim the harshness of the clear spring evening outside. Or to reduce the definite fug that was building up in here. There was an air-conditioner, I knew. It was simply a case of locating it, which would have been easier had I not mistakenly painted it out in my purge, in an effort to unify everything. We could go into all that tomorrow though. Tonight wasn't really for serious.

Zoë appeared now from down below, followed by Soc and Ari. She looked tousled, elated, her lipstick all smudged. One bra strap was obviousy loosened. Should I tell her, or not? It took a trained eye like mine to suss out that she dipped sou' sou'westerly. Others would probably not notice. But it would help if she'd clean up her mouth. People would assume we had strawberries on the menu. She smiled dazzlingly in our direction, waving madly like Auntie Mame, as if the honours of playing hostess rested exclusively with her.

'I've a feeling Zoë is drunk!' Vincent muttered in my ear. And continued with greater intensity, 'She must be. She's kissing Soc and Ari!'

Something had certainly put those two in the mood, because now they were all over Auntie. 'Is nice. Is pretty. Is pretty nice!' Soc ran his hands over her nightie, snagging it here and there on the stiff Spirella beneath. Auntie beat at his predatory fingers with her handbag, but ineffectually as she sometimes playfully smacked Bogey. But Soc would not be put off. He'd found the squashy bit of her unsupported midriff, and bending his head he bit it. Not hard, but more with the nuzzling motion of a horse, starting from under one elbow all the way round to the other. He moved in a crab-like fashion on his crooked legs. Auntie seemed dazed. But delighted. Ari pressed close to the two of them and clapping his kitchen-care hands high in the air, began chanting an incomprehensible chorus. It sounded after several repeats like – 'Oh Auntie! Oh Auntie! Can I drink up your Chianti.' So much so that soon Tallulah and Zsa-Zsa, and even Bogey in his lisping fashion had joined in and were chanting it too.

The party had got off to a flying start. Two hours later it was still spinning. But giddily now. Food was called for.

It was a stranger who actually asked for it first, who'd wandered in straight off the street. He was to be forgiven for believing the place to be a bona-fide restaurant after all. By that time most people were sitting, if not exactly with meals and knives and forks, and salt and pepper, at least with plenty of glasses. Zoë had homed in on him first of course. The sight of a strange new man. 'Hello sailor!' she afterwards claimed to have said to the first of our true patrons. The greeting could not have been more inappropriate. He was dressed in the garb of a mourner, an official of death with a face to match, who'd been tying up poor Tom Twiddle's funeral.

Zoë's greeting had set off a strange chain reaction. His death-mask had swiftly disintegrated. It split first in vivacious vertical stripes, then criss-crossed into fey horizontals. The results were quite hideous, revealing such teeth as to make Zsa-Zsa's seem like small pearls. But more was to come – his voice, high falsetto, sopranoed a request for the menu. Zoë fell back in surprise at his words. Seconds later she'd collared Vincent, who in turn had come rushing to me. 'There's someone wanting to EAT!' he'd screamed, wild-eyed. 'The public. A person who'll pay!'

He didn't pay, we wouldn't have it. Nobody paid in the end. Except Nutty of course, who paid for it all – to make up for my discarded pearls. He wrote out a cheque for £500 made payable to The Brick Bistro. Vincent insisted on showing it round and dragging poor Nutty with him to receive all the thanks and back-slapping. But when they arrived together at my side, all I gave was a cold withering glance. I would've preferred to be much warmer and as nice as I felt inside, but Nutty had only just bought my displeasure. It wasn't now mine to withhold.

At half-past eleven, a complaint came down from upstairs. Not serious but tetchy, about the noise, from the occupants of one of the flats.

Rufus Justice had arrived very late. None of the others had come. Not Brad. Not Lionel, who'd said he'd pop in on his way to the airport this evening. And not even Stuffy, which seemed the most strange. Only Rufus, and Nutty of course. It didn't matter, it made no difference, in fact it was very much better. It hadn't occurred to me what might happen if they'd all turned up there together.

As it was, now, Rufus was looking at Nutty with more than a hint of suspicion. He'd been present at the cheque charade and had drawled, 'Chap seems frightfully generous – or is he simply showing off,' raising a cynical eyebrow.

None of my Gentleman Callers could claim that I'd led them to believe that I was theirs alone. I reserved all rights, as it were. But I could see that the reality might be hard to accept if presented too rudely – like a dog's nose, rubbed in its own dirt. In any case, looking facts squarely in the face, Rufus himself was married. True, no one had ever met his wife though she was a minor celebrity. An opera singer who had in the past appeared at Glyndebourne but now pursued her career on the continent. They'd lived apart for many years, but, he claimed, preferred to remain married. If only as a preventive measure against either getting trapped in matrimony again. I'd known him now for almost five years, ever since The Old Man had died. Rufus was one of the executors of his Will, fighting hard for my Claims. It wasn't altogether clear to me just what my Claims and Rights amounted to. Those of a Common Law Wife, legally recognized in law. Especially a Common Law Wife with Issue. The Old Man's filial relatives, those distant family connections flung in all corners of the world, had fought it tooth and nail. But there could be no doubt in anybody's mind or any Court of Law for that matter that Tallulah and Zsa-Zsa were quite obviously The Old Man's kith and kin. You only had to look at them to see in Tallulah his cast of eye, and in Zsa-Zsa the equine gums. We could only cross fingers, he and I together, that having obviously inherited his looks they would not take after me mentally. Instead of the other way round. But as far as I could tell so far, the supposition appeared to be fact – like a famous quip of George Bernard Shaw to the actress. Which one? Was it Ellen Terry?

It had taken a celebratory sherry at the end of that long legal tussle to open my eyes as to how Rufus felt. In his Chambers, near Lincoln's Inn Fields. We'd toasted each other, clinking glasses. Mine slumped and spilt all down my dress.

'Oh God!' I'd groaned. 'Now look what I've done!' I was due at the Hampstead Theatre Club in a little under an hour.

He'd unzipped me before the first drip hit the floor. Taking charge, full control, as he liked to. And had sponged down the silk in seconds. 'This will dry with a press.' And before my astonished eyes, he'd taken a small travelling iron from the top drawer of his filing cabinet. The one labelled A-Appliances.

'Appliances,' I'd read out loud. 'All domestic?'

'Not all.' He'd smiled. 'A toaster—'

'Of course. An electric kettle? A shaver? And a—' I thought hard. 'Um, oh yes, a hairdrier.'

'No, wrong. Not a hairdrier. But everything else. It pays to be organized when leading a bachelor existence like mine.' He'd laid a towel inside my dress, between the two layers of material. 'We'll give it five minutes to absorb excess moisture. Then iron. Take no time at all.' He'd turned and looked at me from head to toe. 'Are you cold? Would you care for my coat?'

The time was high summer, his question was silly. The temperature soared in the seventies. I stood there, pleasantly cool for the first time that day, wearing simply my light bra and pants. Both white, thank God, clean on today. But, 'Oh, thank you' I said, out of modesty. He'd proved himself to be a very good friend. No other thought entered my mind. I harboured no hopes for anything further than that. He was personable and highly impressive in Court, but I couldn't imagine there to be a sensual side to his nature.

He removed his coat and held it towards me. 'Let me help you.' It meant turning my back to slip each wrist into the waiting armholes. As I did so, his hands slid on my shoulders. We stood from necessity, very close. His front firmly up against me, whilst I faced in the other direction. I made as if to move away, to button the coat together, but he tightened the pressure from behind. I could feel his hot breath on my neck.

'I can feel his hot breath on my neck,' I thought. It seemed to quicken. And mine did too. I glanced down, my chest was growing goose-pimples. Two huge ones pointing out of my seamless bra. Now Rufus had found them, his breath had deepened into something else, a steady gasp. It seemed the only sound in the whole of Lincoln's Inn, and it set off a curdling excitement. The River Thames ran through my drawers. My secretions could be used as office adhesive. My eyelids drooped. Through the open window, I could see the roofs of High Holborn. I hoped that they couldn't see me, standing now in the Inns of Court with a member jammed into my knickers. God knows when he'd managed to get it out. Had it burst its own boundaries? Would I turn to witness a gaping hole in Rufus's immaculate suiting – and the floor strewn with stray bits of serge?

But it was out, no doubt about that. Hot-foot on the path to my pussy, keeping to the left of the gusset. I remained where I was, but awkward now, with his aubergine easing inside. There seemed no question of a frontal confrontation. We each preferred to pretend that it wasn't happening. My knickers slipped to above my knees. I bent as if to retrieve them. One breast fell out, the other flowed over. My movement, my forward movement afforded Rufus his opportunity. Insertion. Where each of us wished it.

We fell into a rhythm, my nose on my knees. I hoped that he wouldn't take long. The law of gravity began taking its toll – three tears fell, black with mascara.

The gurgling started in somebody's throat – was it mine, just prior to fainting? No, Rufus's. Gradually becoming a roar, and receding as rapidly as it started.

A rat-a-tat-tat! At the outer office! The return of an Articled Clerk. And the hurried need for each of us to get dressed, and my dress still not ironed. But the bond had been formed, the die had been cast.

It surprised me, the sensual side he displayed. He had an obsession with all forms of underwear. Almost each week he'd present me with something, some satiny, lacy, filmy scrap. He'd brought one along this evening. Had cornered me somewhere between the till and top of the kitchen stairs. 'Here.' He said it with heavy emphasis, a meaningful look in the eyes.

I took the tissued envelope in my hand. It was hard to believe it held anything, it felt as light as a leaf. 'Oh Rufus, how sweet. Not another pair. I can't wait. Shall I open it now?' We always went through that procedure, played the same charade. It excited him, the sight of sexy lingerie in the light of day. And in public. It never ceased to amaze me, his inventive approach as to where to present his offerings. A turquoise petticoat in Trafalgar Square. A satin waist-slip in the Strand. Directoire bloomers by Buckingham Palace. A no-bra bra near a bus queue at the top of Tottenham Court Road. A pair of french knickers at Finchley Road tube – the supply and the settings were endless.

'How naughty!' I said, unwrapping the latest. 'My goodness which way do they go?' The elasticized lace lay looped in my fingers attached to two wisps of sheer nylon. Black and a brilliant violet, looking as if they'd fit Bogey's tiniest teddy bear.

A fine line of sweat formed on Rufus's face, on his upper lip and his forehead. I could tell that his hands must be clammy too by the way he wrung them together. I glanced around; Nutty was glowering on the far side of the room, trapped by a crowded table. I'd sent the children home already, under Auntie's auspices. Vincent was waving his sleeves vivaciously, displaying his actor's training. Six months in Scarborough Rep, he claimed, to teach him all that he needed. Zoë was sucking a stick of celery, legs crossed, leaning on the front door – as if to suggest that whoever might pass, wish to enter or else to go out, would first be required to penetrate her. She looked quite engagingly pretty, flanked in the shadows by Soc and Ari. The lighting was kind to her nose. They'd had a good time here tonight, our resident chefs, Soc and Ari. Accepted as guests along with everyone else. No cooking of course, simply serving my purchases. Tomorrow they'd have to start working.

'They go that way.' Rufus was speaking.

'What, which!' Rufus pressed close with one thigh. He'd startled me; I'd lost the thread, momentarily. With his pressure my attention returned. I must subconsciously have been anticipating his next suggestion. Deducing the lie of the land. Calculating how clear was the coast. How deserted it might be below. Rufus clearly was wishing to consummate the confection that lay in my hand. He usually did. Intimacy occurred as promptly as was physically possible, after the passing over of presents. It had led in the past to hair-raising situations – a finger-width this side of scandal. Once on the tube-train I could barely believe it! Me in a button-through dress, jam-packed in the rush hour against his smooth front. Jostled to climax by the crowds, and the courtesy of London Underground. That was the time of the french knickers at Finchley Road. The fact of their wide-leggedness had at least aided Rufus' entry. Something he must have considered when suggesting I change into them in the Ladies.

'Free Traders,' he said now.

'Oh really, which three!' I looked round the restaurant with interest, wondering who had caused him to change the subject. Was there someone here I didn't know?

'That's what they're called, these little scanties. No gusset – for easy entry. Free Traders. Popular with prostitutes.' His knee now was starting to tremble.

'I see,' I said, looking down.

'Your legs go in here.' Rufus spread out his hands and slipped them beneath the fine cobwebs. 'This here, well, that's where your pussy—' He cleared his throat. 'What about it then – give it a try?'

I led the way down the banistered stairs to the dark recesses of the kitchen. Someone had left a gas ring on. It burned like a cool blue halo, lending an almost religious light, quite Catholic in its quality, to the romantic setting.

'What are you wearing? Which ones have you got on down there?' Rufus bent and felt under my skirts. He knew my underwear, eyes shut, just from touch. 'Oh those,' he said, stroking the crotch. I stood with my legs wide apart, towering high up

99

above him, whilst he groped around in the flowing folds of my Haute Couture. His hands ran around the bare flesh of my legs, sliding over my thighs to my buttocks, then easing up to the hip-bones on either side where the top of my pants smoothly ended. Hipsters from Holland. From Amsterdam, brought back from a flying visit when Rufus had been sent to submit a study on a particular point of pornography. His experienced finger-tips eased them down, brushing lightly over my labia. 'Lovely. Mm, lovely,' he murmured, lingering in there with one thumb. One of the first things about Rufus that had struck me with force was how beautifully he clipped his nails. Like the lawns of a well-kept country estate. Or a poodle, up for the Cup at Crufts. No cuticles, no rough skin to scratch where one might least expect it. I relaxed at the butterfly touch and stepped out of my pants as he asked me:

'Lift your dress, yes, go on. I want to see.'

It was easier said than done. The magnificence of my Zandra Rhodes lay in how much there was of it. I looped and gathered up as much as I possibly could, holding it high up above my waist, exposing the rest to his gaze.

'That's it. Leg up. And now the other. How do they feel – the Free Traders?'

'Tight,' I said briefly. They were cutting in. Cheap second-rate elastic. I'd be left with a dreadful, bright red indentation. Branded. By street-walker scanties. I looked down. The bright violet, dark puce in this light, stretched tautly over my stomach, beginning beneath my deep navel. It split, divided at the junction of pubic hair. I could feel it join up in the small of my back. Which meant my extremities were available to all the world, just as if down there I wore nothing.

Rufus was now, rather recklessly, removing the whole of his trousers. He often did that. He liked to rub legs – that's how he chose to explain it. But I wouldn't have thought this quite the time, or the place. Our tableau was occupying the direct route to the outside lav. We'd be probably better off there.

I patted his pecker, and held its head, and spoke as one might to a pet. 'Let's go in the lav—'

'In the lav! Oh good lord! Not that sordid God-forsaken sty!'

'Safer.' I led him away.

The two of us fitted in quite well. Just the right sort of squeeze. And I was able, by sitting on the lavatory seat, to lay back and loop my skirts on the chain. Rufus straddled over me, one hand for support on the lavatory roll, the other on top of the cistern.

We decided to leave the washing-up till the next day; the whole place was a scene of wild disorder. Ash and spilled drinks and fag ends stubbed out in pockets of pâté, and the atmosphere heavy with party fever. The normal end to that sort of evening. Soc and Ari seemed incapable of coping. When would they prove worth their hire?

'We'll see to this in the morning, Vince.' He'd obviously gone past the stage of caring. I took matters firmly in hand. My batteries after all had just been re-charged by Rufus. I could feel the brittle Free Traders biting my cheeks as a reminder. And I could feel as well his oozing spunk. I could have done at that point with a gusset. These open endings were all very well, but they didn't give much sense of security. I bade goodnight to departing guests, with both legs squeezed tightly together. That way at least his semen might swim in a direct route from my snatch straight into my shoes, instead of staining my Zandra Rhodes. It cost a hell of a lot to dry-clean.

Nutty was almost the last to leave. He lingered long after the others, looking imploring and wretched. 'What's the matter with you?' I snapped at him sharply. For once I felt quite as I spoke. It had been a long day, and would be again tomorrow. The realization was gradually beginning to dawn on me, to sink in, just what we had started. The daily grind of being in business, like starring in a long-running show. Except that this one hadn't yet got the necessary organization to run on efficient lines. But we'd get it right. In the end.

Soc and Ari sat slumped, half unconscious, Zoë had long since departed, muttering something about finding Stuffy. She must have been upset that he hadn't turned up. Vince swayed, frail and splendid in his finery – the evening had yielded nothing in the way of new relationships for him. But then it never did. His encounters were less straightforward than that. Would he go on the toot now or not? He seemed tense. We smiled at each other.

'Shall I drop you? Shall I see you home?'

But he shook his head. 'No thank you, darling. I don't know yet what I'll be up to—'

'How will those two get home do you think?' I pointed at Soc and Ari. I'd told them they ought to be going, what seemed now like hours ago. In order to catch their last tube or bus. It was obvious that Vince wouldn't share a taxi, although they lived in the same direction.

'May I be of help?' Nutty coughed and moved nervously forward. 'I'd be pleased to be used as a chauffeur, my dear—' Perfect. Demeaning. I yawned and turned to switch the lights off.

'O.K. Nutty. You can drive them.'

It wasn't until I was home and warm, stretched out in solitary splendour on my Slumberland mattress, that I realized my knickers were missing. The ones that I'd stepped out of for Rufus. I remembered I'd seen them clearly on the floor, by the light of the blue gas ring. But there was no doubt about it in my mind, they'd gone by the time we returned from the lav. Whoever'd taken them had certainly seen us.

Sydney Bummer, our predecessor in The Brick Bistro, had stayed open all day. Starting, in fact, by serving breakfasts. Neither Vince nor I were much good in the morning, though we might manage something midday. But in the actual effort of opening midday lunch had oddly not been discussed.

My telephone rang at half-past seven, before I'd even aroused the children. It was Vince, being bossy. He'd had a good night, fallen on his feet with an Irish chippy from Willesden.

'What about lunch? Will we do it?' he breezed. All action. The top of the morning.

I blinked several times to focus my sights. The room smelt

strongly of sleep. A not unpleasant mix of my bodily perfumes. The Old Man had always been keen on my smells. Like warm milk and cut grass and clean hair, he claimed. And so had Stephen, though I had liked his more than mine, his silky poreless body. So small beside my own. Perhaps that's what pleased me most about Vincent, he reminded me physically of Stephen.

'Lunch?' I'd actually forgotten the restaurant! 'Oh, the restaurant! You mean doing lunch today there.'

'I'm at Covent Garden. With the friend of my friend. A fruiterer and vegetable porter. He can get all the wholesale we'd possibly need. He knows everyone in the business. You should see him.' Vince dropped his voice. 'His shoulders—' His voice trailed off. 'And his friend supplies wet fish as well.'

'That's useful. Wet fish. What about smoked? Smoked trout, I mean. Or smoked mackerel?'

It was coming back to me now, slowly, all the things I'd ever eaten in other people's restaurants. The trouble was, should we make ours posh? Or rather more run of the mill, as in the days of Sydney Bummer.

'Yes, all of that. Smoked smokies, the lot. Shall I put in an order, do you think?' Vincent sounded over-excited. From one extreme to the other. 'Open up an account with these blokes?' I thought of Nutty's £500 cheque. Good for floating.

'Yes, why not.

Auntie accompanied me to the restaurant, when I'd dropped the three children at school. She'd slept the night in what she'd been wearing, her brushed nylon – minus all that went underneath. They lay, a neat pile, at the bottom of her bed. Covered decorously by her cardi.

I took her up a nice cup of tea, milky, four lumps as she liked it. With the tea-bag still at the bottom sending darkening swirls towards the surface. 'Nice cup of tea, there's nice.' She smiled, struggling to sit up in bed. A curler had somehow got caught in her pillowcase. It rose with her, attached to her scalp like a billowing growth. A goitre such as you sometimes see sitting on old ladies' lapels.

'Hold on, Auntie!' I bent to undo her.

'Thank you, love. There's a good girl you are.' I smiled; she said it with such feeling, such satisfied well-meaning warmth. As warm as toast, that's what she was. It made you feel good to be near it.

She thought that she'd wear her slippers again, though one had got splashed with champagne. 'A champagne slipper, like Cinderella! No Prince though, there's the pity.' But her eyes had remained as bright as ever, she'd never really expected one.

'All set, Auntie? I'd like to get off. Got your hat and your gloves? Got your handbag?' No need ever to ask that, of course. The Mock Croc, Marks and Spencer's bag had accompanied us last night, snagging the brave brushed nylon as badly as Soc and Ari. She was wearing outdated ski pants today with the elastic going under the instep, to keep them straight, un-wrinkled, looking as if they'd been ironed on. Her suspenders showed clearly beneath, and a bulge of spare flesh round the top of each leg where the edge of her panti-girdle ended.

'Do these look all right?' She felt sure they did.

'Do you really need the panti-girdle, Auntie? It might look better without—' I regretted it as soon as the words left my mouth.

'Go without!' It was as if I'd suggested she walk out naked. Go starkers all the way to Sloane Square. She shook her head, blinking hard, beside herself. 'No, I couldn't do that. Not go without.' It occurred to me what a comfort the corsets must be to all women who were like Auntie. Caught in the clasp, the continuing embrace of their own constricting confines. So that even if an approaching male were to want to, he couldn't not without considerable inconvenience to either party. And a lot of side-play with hooks and eyes, and zips and lacings and so on.

I calmed her down and at last we set off. 'We're doing lunches, Auntie. Dinner, I mean. We're doing dinners now, in the middle of the day.'

Auntie was still a little ruffled. 'When else would you do dinners then, tell me.' Despite her eagerness for progress and all things modern, she stayed stubbornly with the language she knew.

'We're trying them anyway, midday meals, but if it gets too much, we may well have to stop. We'll see how we get on today.'

We opened the door to a curious calm, the sort that precedes the storm. Soc and Ari, and Vincent, must all be in the kitchen. Upstairs there was no one at all.

It had all been cleared up though, beautifully – I had to say that. There was no sign of last night's festivities. And someone had dressed all the tables with flowers. Daffodils to go with the walls.

'There's nice.' Auntie blinked and bent down to sniff. 'Not much smell thought, never is with daffies. Fresias, they're what you want for a lovely smell. They fill the room, they do.' She burrowed her nose deep into the blossoms, then lifted it buttered with pollen.

'Stay still,' I said. 'Your nose needs dusting,' That close I could clearly see the face-powder on her skin, applied like flour on pastry. Puffed on too liberally and then just left to settle, like sand, in her finely etched wrinkles. Not that she had many of those, her cheeks were as smooth as a baby's. Smoother and pinker, plumper and altogether prettier than my own high-boned facial structure.

There was the unmistakable sound of singing down below, accompanied by a transistor. Two voices joining in to Pete Murray's signature tune. Two of them, Vince and another's.

Auntie looked startled. 'Who's that then?'

It wasn't difficult. I knew the timbre of Vince's voice quite well. He'd under-studied once in the Eastbourne production of *Oklahoma!* and had even auditioned, unsuccessfully, for *Hair*, wearing a borrowed wig.

'It's Vince, Auntie, obviously.'

'But I mean the other. There's someone with him I think.'

I felt a jolt of misgiving. Vince did do that sometimes, get carried away with enthusiasm. Who the hell had he found now? Though, whoever it was, he had a nice way with flowers, and clearing-up. I led the way down the spotless stairs; each one had been swept and swabbed. 'Hello,' I shouted. It was best to give warning, in case they might be making use of the architectural features as Rufus and I had done last night. Soaring in song together, in tune with the BBC. 'Hello!' I shouted again to make sure. 'It's us. It's Auntie, and me!'

There was a scuffle on the other side of the door. Were they re-arranging their clothing? 'Look, Auntie, this paint is completely dry.' I ran my hand round the banisters, lingering purposely. The door didn't open. There was silence now. The transistor had been turned right down. 'Why are we waiting then? Go on, go in there—' Auntie was getting excited.

I knocked just once, and was about to knock a second time when the door flew back in a flourish combined with a fresh burst of music. Quite apt as it happened. Shirley Bassey hammering out the opening of 'Hey Big Spender'. She shouted it straight at Auntie and me, the minute we walked in the door.

Vincent stood, wreathed in smiles, radiant as a bride with the band of gold fresh on her finger. His arms were flung out each side of his body indicating just where we should look. He was alone, that perhaps was the biggest surprise, though the room took a lot of beating. It was indeed a hive of activity. Hobs bubbling. Pans boiling. Things steaming. Stuff simmering. As if the engine room of an ocean liner had assumed a life of its own, pumping, gurgling, geared into animal action yet maintaining ferocious efficiency. Aware, like a row of prancing marionettes, that above was the hand of control and discipline. It couldn't be all Vincent's doing. And certainly not Soc's and Ari's. Whoever it was had that magical touch of coaxing life from the inanimate. Vincent this time might have stumbled on our salvation. The embodiment emerged from the lav at that split second, as my eye accustomed itself to the uplifting scene.

' 'Lo Missus!' The voice came from the North. Confident, curt and, though friendly, with a hard edge to it bordering on caution. Vincent turned theatrically, spinning on the balls of his feet and extending his fingers in introduction. 'Dick! I don't think you know him!'

I didn't know Dick. 'No, I don't think I do. Hello Dick.' I held out my hand. He ignored it, but nodded his head instead. 'This is Auntie,' I added.

' 'Lo Auntie!' He pronounced it Anty, like ants in your panty. She smiled back at him. 'Oh, hello Dick. My father's name was Dick, short for Richard. Though everyone called him Dai. I don't know why because that was his brother's name – and they used to call him, well, sometimes Billy. And other times Will or William, but we all knew who they meant—' Auntie's voice trailed away. Vince laid a kindly hand on her arm. 'Dick's our new cook. He's a wizard with food. What do you think of the kitchen?' He was looking at me when he said it, almost pleadingly, I thought. There was no need, no need at all for apologies. From what I could see of the activities of Dick, it was all I could have wished.

Dick turned his back and picked up a spoon, applying himself to a saucepan. 'I've got to get on. No time for this gassing. There's loads of things to be done. Who's peeling these sodding spuds for a start?'

Auntie stepped forward eagerly. 'I like to do peeling,' she offered.

'Right, roll up your sleeves then, Auntie, and get going on this lot.'

I admired his air of decisiveness, I could see why he'd impressed Vincent. It was quite hard to tell which way he was. My guess would have been he'd have either – man, woman, boy, girl, even the cat or canary if it happened to suit him and helped towards what he was after.

He was after a rather large share of the profits. Vincent thought he was worth it. 'But what about Soc and Ari?' I said. Vincent shrugged and consulted his wrist-watch. 'Where are they?'

True. Where were they indeed? Without Dick we wouldn't be open for lunch and probably not even for dinner.

Vincent and I went upstairs to the restaurant.

'Where did you meet him? Last night? But I thought you'd fallen on your feet with the chippy from Willesden—'

'One thing led to another. A whole lot of them lodge in this one rooming house. We had a bit of a ding-dong, that's how I met Dick. We're lucky, he's just between jobs.'

'Where was he before?' Not that we needed References. Soc and Ari had not had any. With good reason – they didn't deserve them.

'Joe Lyons, I think. Brixton Hill. But before that, the Gay Bistro in Barnet. And a fish and chip shop over at Shepherds Bush, and even at one point a stint at the Savoy.'

'Quite varied then,' I said with interest. He was young to have moved round so much. Mid-twenties, though possiby not even as old as that. People who worked in the catering trade, with long hours sweating in kitchens, seemed to age as fast as footballers. The strain of it showed in the face. It showed in Dick's. Deep lines ran down from his nose to his mouth, bordering concave cheeks. He was terribly thin, not like Vincent, not affected slimness like that. But stringy and muscled, quite small-boned. With an impression of restless energy, even, perversely, of strength. There was probably nothing he couldn't lift with ease. Even me. Though I was twice his height. The leanness was alley-cat as opposed to lounge-lizard. One more reason for Vincent to like him.

'What shall we do with Soc and Ari? Supposing they turn up of course, and there's no reason to think otherwise, Vince—'

He shrugged, an unlovely habit. 'Sack them I suppose.'

'Oh, no! I couldn't do that.'

'Why not? They're nothing to us. And we've never been that over-confident in them, have we.' Vincent had never held loyalty high on his list, though he felt it towards Auntie and me. But we, I suppose, were more like family. One he'd chosen himself to adopt. He leant forward and kissed my cheek. 'Don't be soft.'

But I wouldn't give in quite that easily. 'Soc's wife is expecting in no time at all – can't they take second place to Dick? We'll pay them the same as they're going to get now. It's just that he'll be in charge.'

Vincent looked doubtful. 'It's a very small kitchen. I don't know if Dick will agree.'

'It is a very small kitchen for the three of them. But they, all three, are very small people. And what you're suggesting, Vincent, is rather small too, if you don't mind my saying. I think that it's terribly mean.'

He stared at me, slightly taken aback. Then he sniffed. 'Well, we are partners. If you feel so strongly, all right they stay on. But they'll have to prove that they're worth it.'

'So will Dick though, Vince.'

'Well darling, at least he can cook.'

'I can see that he can — but the proof of the pudding is the eating!'

Zoë was not coming in today, but she would be in this evening. When I'd rung her up, she was still in bed.

'Stuffy's here,' she said.

'Oh! Is he really!' I could barely contain the surprise in my voice. 'Oh! Give him my love,' I said lamely. What on earth was Stuffy doing with her? Had he slept the night there? With Zoë?

'I don't know about that.'

'Don't know about what, Zoë?' I thought she sounded aggrieved.

'Giving your love—' She abruptly replaced the receiver. I sighed. It spelt trouble. We might well lose a waitress.

I saw Soc peering in through the window, then Ari, squeezed over his shoulder. The sight warmed my soul, they looked so familiar. They spotted me and started to shout. I hoped that Dick wouldn't be too hard on these two terrible little turds. I'd grown fond of them both despite their inadequacies, and I knew that the kids had. And Auntie.

We opened up at 12 o'clock sharp, and by half-past had done eleven lunches. All was chaos downstairs in the kitchen. The Dumb Waiter was refusing to work, which meant that every single dish was being passed up the stairs on a rota. Like a line of firemen passing buckets of water. Through from Dick, at the start of the chain in the kitchen, up to me who was serving the tables. Auntie was proving the weakest link, stationed half-way up the stairs. And Soc, it seemed, was barely better — screaming each time that Dick's plates were too hot, he'd dropped the first three on his feet. And so he stood now in a pool of stewed steak, with carrots stuck to his crêpe soles and creamed potatoes cooling on his socks – which made him completely immobile.

Vincent trembled at the top of the stairs in the grip of terrible stage fright, as if our disinterested clientele were distinguished drama critics. He was barely able to pass on each order, shouting it down the empty Dumb Waiter to Dick. No wonder he didn't get work. His diction was such that the back of the stalls could quite rightly demand reimbursement.

'What's wrong, Vince?'

'Don't know. Just jittery.' He ran his tongue over his teeth. A case of dry mouth.

'Have a drink. That might help.'

'Oh, I daren't, darling. Not in this state. How' – he looked round the restaurant fearfully like a criminal out on the run – 'how do you think they're liking it?'

I followed his eyes. 'They seem fine.' He was losing his cool for no reason, with this particular lot. They ate without appetite, almost mechanically, and would have done so whatever they'd been served. Which was just as well from what I could see of the quality of our cuisine. I studied a plate of Sausage and Mash, and another of Shepherd's Pie. Auntie was flustering up the stairs with Fish Fingers; I suspected she'd secretly stolen one from the state of her teeth when she smiled. 'Two Tinned Pears and Custard coming in a minute. And one Vanilla Ice with Jam,' she announced with an air of importance. Dick had decided on the menu. Auntie was all approval, as Tallulah and Zsa-Zsa and Bogey would be. All those under ten, or toothless.

But I'd held my counsel and kept all doubts to myself. It was hardly the time to start rocking the boat. Dick's approach to food was at least basic. And no one had so far sent anything back. Perhaps, with some subtle persuasion on my part, more sophisticated dishes might be introduced for the evenings. We hadn't discussed it together at all, Vince and I, me out of delicacy. Apart from his nerves, it was obvious that he'd defend Dick to the death. But I couldn't for the life of me see how our wines would wash down with this form of tuck. A vision of Rufus presented itself, delicately probing with his connoisseur's prong through a pile of Dick's overdone cabbage. Both Vince and I, though unable to cook ourselves, had done enough dining-out to distinguish the rough from the smooth. Perhaps on the other hand we might manage to make our notably mundane menu a positive mark of the place. Serve champagne with Dick's pork chipolatas. And port with our tinned pears and custard. It could be considered a kind of jape for the jaded palate – a return to childhood treats. I must make a note, a special request for trifle, and banana blancmange. And greengage jelly, that glorious bright green. And paper party serviettes with painted balloons on the borders.

'The bill, Miss!'

'Certainly, Madam.' I smiled at the woman before me. Her husband scowled sourly at Auntie's ski pants and then towards Vincent's half profile.

'You've spoilt this place. It used to be decent!' He said it with savage delivery.

'Oh, I'm sorry, Sir,' I answered him smoothly. 'Was the meal not quite to your liking?'

His wife chose to answer the question for him. 'Our peas were cold!'

'How were your Qs?' I asked lightly.

'Beg pardon?' They were openly hostile.

'Your bill.' I handed it to them. They left without leaving a tip.

Vincent had watched, standing well away.

'They won't be back,' he fretted.

'No, thank God. I don't think they will.'

'What was wrong?' He was biting his nails.

'What was wrong, Vince? Well, they just didn't like us. That's okay. You can't win them all.'

'Cheeky things! Cheeky things, that's what they were!' Auntie looked het-up and indignant. 'They didn't deserve Dick's lovely dinner. I had a good mind to say, I did, myself!'

'Oh Auntie, don't ever, please don't. If this goes on we shan't

111

have a business. No one will come anymore.' Vincent genuinely seemed to believe what he was saying. I looked at his worried face.

'Oh, don't be daft,' I said reassuringly. 'It's up to us how it all goes.' I lowered my voice and glanced around at the remainder of our grim patrons. What a gloomy contrast to the dazzling décor. 'Ghastly decorations!' 'Gives one quite a headache!' 'I agree, puts one right off one's food!' I'd been hearing all that since 12 o'clock. 'These aren't the sort we want in here in any case, Vincent. We're inheriting these from Sydney Bummer – this trade will pretty soon fall off.'

'That's what I'm afraid of.'

'And be replaced.'

'By what though?'

'By friends, Vince, of course, who else?'

He didn't reply. I knew why not. He was thinking the same thing as me. Dick's culinary range didn't match up to that. Just as we, and the Brick's gleaming face-lift, appeared not to suit its past patrons.

We ground to a halt at half-past two, by which time we'd served twenty-seven lunches. And survived the strains of the fierce fight which developed between Dick and Ari. Soc claimed to have had both hands badly burned, though close examination failed to show any signs. 'Him do it. Is Dick. Yes, Boss Lady, he a fiend. Dick the Devil. He vicious. He – he—!' The diatribe ended with violent spitting in the direction of Dick.

Dick coolly looked on, one eyebrow raised, 'Piss off, you Cypriot runt.'

An expression of pain and deep, injured pride on a national scale passed over Soc's twisted features. He turned to Ari and poured out an incomprehensible torrent in their native tongue. To which Ari reacted by grinding together his broken front teeth and kicking Dick hard on both shins.

'Christ almighty. You cunt.' Dick slammed a saucepan, fortunately empty, on the nearside of Ari's skull. The unexpected blow knocked him clean off his feet. Dick took the opportunity to further the fall with a few swift boots up the backside. Soc was shuddering, wild-eyed, against the knife and fork drawer hugging a clutch of wooden spoons against his heart like a crucifix. And moaning a continuous low-pitched growl like a zoo-reared lion in labour.

It was Auntie who managed to intervene and restore an uneasy order from chaos.

And it was only because of Auntie's continued presence in the troubled kitchen that we finally closed in dubious calm. Not one of us dared to enquire of Dick what he'd planned for this evening's dinner. With the way that things were between Ari and him, not to mention the still-smouldering Soc, who kept licking his hands like a beast with a wound – we'd be lucky if Dick deigned to show up.

My bright pink menus lay pure and pristine, still unwritten upon. Vincent had chosen to chalk up the midday choice on a piece of old board – Dick's suggestion. It might have done all right for lunch, despite disgusted reactions from already irritable regulars, but I didn't feel it would do for dinner.

'We ought to know well in advance what's on, for writing out all the menus. One on each table, don't you think, Vince?'

'Oh, I'd leave that all up to Dick,' Vince said fearfully.

'What, the actual writing?'

'Well, he's done all that. He must've done, with his experience.'

'Can he spell, do you suppose? Does he know there are two 'n's in dinner?' I knew perfectly well how Vince would answer: 'Don't be bitchy.' But I felt both that and frustrated. Something had got out of hand. The reins had been snatched from our fingers. The evening threatened ahead. I viewed it with a sense of foreboding, leaving Soc and Ari to clear up. Dick had got changed the minute he'd done the last orders.

'Where's he going?' I'd whispered to Vince.

Vince had winced and started perspiring again. 'Why do you keep asking me all these things? I don't know—'

I'd kept my silence. I could've been childish and replied: 'Well, he is your friend!' But instead I said, 'Perhaps that's what they do, chefs, go off in the afternoon. Shall I ask him?'

Vincent rolled his eyes to the ceiling. 'Oh God, no! For Christ's sake, no, don't do that. He's sure to be back. We haven't paid him yet. Just treat it as perfectly normal.'

Dick emerged from the lavatory, where he'd got changed – our only place for privacy – as Rufus and I well knew. He buckled the belt on his skin-tight jeans, almost as tight as Brad wore them, with a similar display of what was inside. I could hear Vincent's intake of breath. Despite myself and this lunch-time's troubles, due to Dick's aggression, I had to admit his attraction.

'This toilet here is a bit of a come-down. Full of crap!' He frowned in disgust, tucking his tee-shirt into his jeans, a black one with very short sleeves which barely covered his pectoral muscles. Like the ones Marlon Brando once wore. We stood like an audience looking at him, ashamed at our faulty facilities. Full of crap! Who'd done that? Who'd sullied our sanitary arrangements?

I stepped forward. 'I'll clean it,' I said. 'But who's been? Was it one of the customers?' I didn't think so, no one had asked me the way. But then they'd all been here before and must've known what to expect. Not many, not those forearmed with knowledge, would brave coursing through our kitchen.

Dick slicked a comb through his long side-burns and over his smooth straight hair. I knew the style, from way back in the fifties.

'It's not a clean-up that's called for, it isn't that, Missus! It requires some re-decoration. A more modern toilet and hand-sink put in. I've got a mate who could do it for nothing.'

'Nothing?' Vince echoed before he could stop.

Dick spun round. 'Well, not nothing! You geezers expect sodding blood from a stone! A fair rate for the job's what I mean—'

Vincent quivered, beginning to blush. His reaction reminded me of Nutty, when I gave him the hard word. Did we appear, with our exchanges, as unpleasant as this to onlookers? But even so, I stood saying nothing. I could hear Auntie's stomach behind me, gurgling with emptiness – we'd none of us eaten. Not that I felt like it now.

'Right. I'm off then. I'll see you—' Dick flung over one shoulder, stopping briefly to light the cigarette that he'd already rolled. I watched him cup his bony fingers round the flame, as taut and tense as an animal trap. Like a cage. He slid a sly shiny eye in our direction, winked swiftly, 'S'long!' And was gone.

'Auntie's flagging, I'm taking her home.' Auntie sat at the top of the stairs. Things seemed better since Dick's departure. Vince had become more himself. Even Soc and Ari, scuttling between pot-scouring and swilling out cloths and swabbing down the kitchen floor, seemed to be humming in some sort of harmony. It was as if the troops were now on time-off. But it was as well to remember the necessity for a commander-in-chief. We'd probably learn to work as a team, with our leader, before very long. And it was in that mood that I'd taken Auntie away, dropping Vince at Sloane Square Tube Station. We were meeting later, it was all arranged. In the meantime, Vincent was off home for a rest. 'Sleep at our place, if you want a lie-down,' I'd invited. 'Rather not, darling. I feel I need absolute peace, your place is like Paddington Station – the children and all that. you know what I mean. And the off-chance of Gentlemen Callers—' He waved his limp wrists wanly in the air. Looking drained out and defeated. I squeezed his arm, and kissed his cheek. 'You know best, Vince. I'll see you. About six.'

The telephone was ringing as I opened the door. 'Just a sec, Auntie. Stay there while I answer it.' She'd fallen asleep, chin slumped on her chest, half-way along the Kings Road. I'd taken a short-cut off to the right through the quieter side streets so that the noise of the traffic wouldn't waken her. She swayed where she was, just inside the front door, still sleepy and dazed from the drive. I would put her straight to bed of course and see that she didn't come to the restaurant tonight. We sometimes overlooked her age and the effects of that limiting factor.

It was Brad on the phone. 'Can you hold on?' I said.

'No, I can't. It's a call-box. No change.'

By the time I'd got back out to see to Auntie, she'd already gone up to her bed. 'Auntie?' I knocked softly in case she was sleeping, and peeped round the door to make sure. She was. She lay spread-eagled on her coverlet, a quilted relic of her girlhood, now frayed and thinning at the edges, but still sweetly beckoning with blushing carnations. I covered her lightly with one of her coats, she usually complained of the cold when she woke. She'd undone the side-fastening of the fitted ski-pants, it revealed her elasticized stomach. I stared for a second at the fascination of stretch and shrinkage as each breath was released from her body. At the end of each of her legs her slippers hung down, a snug fit. They'd been a good buy, if not exactly suitable for wear in our restaurant kitchen. I could see a slight film of grease on each sole, and discoloration on one upper. Bedroom slippers were intended for boudoirs. I took them off, easing each in turn, and placed them next to her handbag. Then I left the room and went down the stairs to await the arrival of Brad.

'Sweetheart, you stink! Jesus, open the window!' Brad was recoiling in horror and I'd barely got in the car.

'Care for a run, kid?' he'd said on the phone. 'I'm off out to Roehampton, delivering documents from the British Museum to some barmy old trout, Professor something. I don't have to be back on the dot, I thought we could doddle, you know—'

'Doddle? I see, Brad!' I'd laughed at the word. It was one we recoursed to quite often, dating from our very early days when getting together had been difficult. 'I'd love a doddle, a real one. Best bring a blanket I suppose. Where are you thinking of, down by the river?'

'Same spot, kid. In view of the lock. Deserted at this time. It's not that good weather.'

I'd noticed a certain amount of oiliness as I'd pulled the comb through my hair. An unfamiliar sensation these days since the drying effects of my perm. But I wasn't concerned as the curls slid about, the end result was quite flattering. The whole head of hair resembled a ragged chrysanthemum, glossy and bronzed, certainly striking. It didn't occur to me that I might smell.

Brad hissed a long breath between his straight even teeth, a Hollywood set, all his own. 'Pooh, what a pong! Where've you been, in the frying pan?'

'Is it that bad?'

'It bloody well is!'

I bent my head down and opened my jacket, then plunged my nose into my blouse. I sniffed. Was there an odour? It was so hard to tell, oneself. But I certainly knew what Brad meant. On mornings after I'd eaten out in certain restaurants you could smell right away which they'd been, from the lingering whiff on whatever I'd worn. And even sometimes on my hair. Insufficient air-conditining. Faulty ventilation. A coagulation of the atmospheric conditions collecting in people's clothing. If this continued I could clog all my pores and slide from my sheets on the sheen on my scalp.

'Just as well then,' I said.

Brad was getting up speed, pressing his spruce, plimsolled foot on the pedal. Thick rubber-soled 'Red Flash', he wore, the same as Wimbledon champions. It used to be Running Track, blue and white, shoes. But not any more. They were out.

I looked with interest at the footwear of all my admirers. The contrast pinpointed their characters. Rufus for instance had always worn suede, punched with holes and tied up with neat laces. A Bourneville brown, except in Court when they were leather, in black, and lacking the punch holes. Even in summer there was no deviation, no concession was made to the weather. Whereas Nutty for instance made a big thing of peering at the barometer each morning and would attire his extremities accordingly. The fact that he invariably chose to wear wellingtons whatever the state of the sky said more about his sexual leanings than his degree of sartorial interest. Lionel Striving wore boots, with elasticized sides, in the same range of shades. From a khaki-kind of an olive-green right through to a subtle toad. But in the summer, he favoured shoes. Sharp, plaited-leather, Italian style. The sort worn by successful gigolos. With his head for business and his esteem for high finance he might have done well with the Mafia. Ulysses, Stuffy, like Stanley Spencer wore sandals all the year round. Open-tied like Christ, Our Lord. But with warm socks when winter came round. Auntie was knitting old Stuffy some socks, navy blue but with Fair Isle toes. She'd reasoned, quite rightly, that unless they were there no one would notice the work.

'Yes, it's just as well,' I repeated to Brad, 'that we're going to be out in the open!'

He kept his eyes firmly fixed on the road, skilfully overtaking, then reverting to the left-hand lane which would take us through to Kew and eventually to Roehampton. 'I'm not sure I'll fancy it even then!'

I laughed. 'Well, I will have enjoyed the ride.'

He turned his head to look at me. 'I shall have to spray this interior. Shout when you see a shop, sweetheart, for some Fresh Aire or something like that. I'm planning to pick up more fares later on — I wouldn't survive the shame. What sort of stuff are you cooking in there? It could finish us, this sort of stench!'

I didn't laugh now. I knew he meant it. How fastidious he was, and how clean. Like a cat. He'd been shocked by the state of my place and my personal hygiene come to that. I hadn't given my personal hygiene much thought until I'd met Brad. Stephen had been as obsessive, it's true, about bathing and constantly changing. But not The Old Man, his mind had been occupied with higher things — 'The Philosophical Significance of Paradox' — and other associated themes. Mundane matters such as bodily fragrance were dismissed and tolerated along with animal functions. In his final four months we'd had a hell of a fight, the daily nurse and myself, to even achieve the necessary bed-baths now and again. He preferred his sores, so he said.

'I could dip in the river, Brad. How about that? When we stop off I'll buy some shampoo!' It was April, cold enough, in the water anyway, to freeze the brass balls of a monkey. Madness. I hadn't meant it.

'Yes, that might do it!' He didn't smile and, spotting a shop, drew into the side of the road. My fault of course. I should have known better. Bradley was slightly short on humour, especially the sort laced with heavy irony. It quite often sailed over his head.

But when I was in, it wasn't all that bad. Not a soul to be seen for miles. I undressed by myself behind a bush whilst Brad kept cave round the front.

'There's no need, Brad,' I said. 'There's no one around. And if there is I've got my bra and pants on—'

'Take them off I want to see you naked.' I crouched, goose-pimpling, in the breeze despite the weak shaft of sunshine. It could as easily start to shower at any minute. 'April Showers Bring Forth May Flowers.' I'd recited that in one school concert and spoilt the whole of our class's show by not being able to produce my spring posy. It had somehow got stuck up the sleeve of my cardi. Which meant that I mucked up the punch-line.

I debated whether or not to relieve myself, hidden on all fours in the bracken. Probably best to save up the warmth, I should need it much more in the water. Passing my own, as we called it. Supplying the hot tap – Tallulah and Zsa-Zsa showed particular affection for the process in our local swimming pool, but more often in icy seas.

'Are you ready?' Brad was sounding impatient. I'd forgotten that after all this sluicing he was expecting a poke of sorts. When I smelt that much sweeter of course. I picked up my shampoo and ran to the bank. 'Here I go!' – and splashed in like a dog, starting to swim right way. He stood there staring after me, now grinning in open approval.

'How is it?' he shouted.

'It's lovely,' I lied. 'Really warm! Why don't you come in and see for yourself.'

I looked down, whilst keeping on the move. The first shock of the icy contact had subsided to a general numbness, but by swimming as vigorously as possible I felt the return of my limbs. The water just here was surprisingly clear and appeared to be teeming with fish, almost as if I'd stumbled straight into a shoal. I switched from breast-stroke to crawl to keep my legs closer together. What if one of these piscine particles chose to swim into my person? Silently easing its scales inside, flapping its fins up my uterus and trailing its tail on the lips of my labia. I suddenly felt very alien and vulnerable, swimming alone.

'Come in,' I pleaded. 'And keep me company—' I needn't have, Brad was already half-stripped. I trod water, watching the rest of his torso emerge. He must've been, physically, the most perfect specimen a woman could find. A tanned, muscled triangular mould, with a long neck and member to match. Even off-duty, limp as it was now, it swung seemingly half-way to his knees. Christ Almighty, could I take all that? Full marks for Accommodation. Perhaps I should think of putting the sign up in my bedroom window, and when my Gentlemen called switch to Full. The thought of the bedroom reminded me of Auntie, which in turn brought the children to mind. I should have to be getting back quite soon to feed them, at least to see them before getting off to the restaurant.

'Buck-up, Brad! I'm getting lonely—' He was carefully folding his clothes!

I turned and swam in the other direction. 'Race you!' I shouted over one shoulder. 'To the other side, right?' The splash as he dived in was answer enough. I concentrated hard on each stroke.

There were cows in the field opposite, strange that, somehow being so close to London. They stood rooted solidly to one spot, like lumps of chocolate mousse splattered with whorls of white cream. Several were lying on the grass – supposed to be a sign of rain, that parking of arses, making sure of a dry spot to sit. They weren't that daft then, cows. I harboured a fondness for the gentle beasts, myself. They put me in mind of Auntie, that same bovine quality she had.

The other side still seemed far away; I glanced over my shoulder to see how far Brad had progressed. It was quite an even race between us, I wasn't often beaten by men at swimming. The powerful width of my shoulders, and the length of my arms and legs coupled with my natural ease at athletics made me a formidable competitor.

He was nowhere to be seen! I turned, and stopped swimming altogether, treading water again on the spot. 'Hey, Brad!' I broke off as his hands brushed my feet – 'You bastard – let go.' My 'go' ended in a gurgle as the river entered my mouth. He was pulling me down under to join him and I only just managed to snatch breath.

He looked like a blurred impressionist painting. One of a God under water, or of an angel flying through space – streamlined, with a shimmering edge. And amazingly pale and amorphous, his usual symmetry destroyed by the weight of the water above. Did I look like that too? A slow stream of bubbles escaped from his mouth. For a smoker his lungs were remarkably sound. So were mine, but I wouldn't have liked to stay down much longer. His arms encircled my waist, he slid, wrist crossed, both hands on my buttocks so that one little finger was snugly fitted between them. And then he tightened his hold. We had, from necessity, to keep moving our legs in order to remain where we were. But somehow with a skill born from mutual needs and an intimate knowledge of each other's bodies, we met at our pubic zones. His erection took longer than usual to rise. He must have been running short of breath, like balloons before they blow up. I very much hoped that he wasn't planning an under-water eruption. We both could explode if he chose to shoot-off down there with the shoals and the slime. A tiny team of teenage tadpoles wriggled their tails past my toes and beyond, a gossiping group of minnows made gestures over Brad's shoulder. I'd somehow managed to sit on his lap, each leg either side of his hips. His cock was inside me, like a cork in a bottle. Had he trapped half the river up there? I had a brief vision of Roehampton Water flooding the width of my womb, crammed with the vast minutiae of sub-aqueous life. 'This woman is giving birth to two carp – twins by the look of them, Doctor!'

I waved my legs in a regular rhythm, as if I was on a bicycle, my hands tightly crossed round Brad's neck, employing my elbows as paddles as well in case we should drift to the surface. Behind me and underneath my upper thighs I could feel his knees doing the same. They rose and banged my slippery bum with monotonous regularity.

But now, at last, my lungs were giving out, I couldn't remain any longer. I brought my face around closely to Brad's and rolled my eyes to indicate desperation. He was pretty near the end, I could tell by the veins distending along each temple and the stretched-tight look of his neck. I removed one hand and pointed above. Would he come out – of me, not the river? Apparently not, his plan was to stay. We rose to the surface as one: Like two stuck dogs before water's been flung.

'Whew, whe-e-e-e!' We said it together, heads back, both gulping in air. Was it free, this stuff? One of life's necessities, the only one – under water. Delicious relief eased through my body, my head had begun to thump and inside my ears a pounding had started, like an amateur on his first drum.

'I love you!' Brad said. He meant he loved Life. We both understood what we meant. I hugged him.

'I know. Isn't it glorious?' I said. 'Let's get out and go under a tree.'

'You make it sound like the toilet,' he said.

'You've reminded me. I wonder if I can.'

'Can what? Eh, sweetheart? What?'

We struggled to stay joined together, united by his strip of gristle and the plaiting of our pubic hairs. It wasn't easy, not as simple in fact as down under. We appeared to be caught in a criss-crossing current, maybe matching the mood of the moment.

'Pass water. In the water I mean. I wonder if I can with you in me. I doubt it, but let's see now, I'm trying.' I shut my eyes in an effort to concentrate, and willed my bladder to burst its boundaries. Nothing happened. Nothing at all. I tried to relax. 'Will you talk to me, Brad – tell me something, any old thing. To take my mind off, perhaps that'll work and release the tension—'

'Aren't you attempting the impossible? I think we've got too much going here.' His words petered off in a gasp.

It was pretty gruelling, we'd be better standing. The thing was becoming a farce. I kissed his neck. 'Let's go to the side.'

'I shall lose my hard-on.'

'Don't look so tragic. I'll hold it, and swim back one-handed.'

It didn't take long, and when we could stand I guided my handful inside, barely softer than when we had stopped. He wrapped himself completely around my body. One leg over mine, his hand in the small of my back, the other playing with one nipple. We kissed and kissed. It started to rain, very gently at first then more freely. Like in a film, symbolical. Except if it had been a film the camera would be trained in another direction by now and not on our ecstatic bodies.

'I'm coming.'

'So am I.'

'No, I'm not. But I'm something.' I was. It was hard to know which though, or what. I was gripped in my entrails with an agonized sweetness, dissolving deliciously now. 'Oh, ooh, I'm doing it!' I gasped and let myself go.

'Doing what?' Brad managed to ask between moans.

'Can't you feel it?' We were waist high in water.

'I'm coming—' Brad's voice dropped to a whisper, full of vibrating intensity.

'I'm pissing—' I struggled to finish. 'But now I'm coming as well, just like you—'

Auntie was in tears by the time I got back. She was standing, crying silently at the kitchen sink, chopping a sprig of spring onions.

'It's best, Auntie, when you're doing onions to run them under the tap, then the juice doesn't get in your eyes. I read that tip in a *News of the World* that someone had left on the train,' I said, trying to be helpful. But she barely acknowledged my presence.

'Auntie?' I said anxiously, it wasn't like her at all. 'Are you all right?' The children were due back home any minute, all being dropped by the new rota that I'd managed to join. In a fortnight's time it would be my turn. For the moment I could relax.

Auntie's shoulders drooped even lower, she gave a shuddering sob. Two transparent tears welled over her lashless lower lids and came tumbling down each of her cheeks. The sight was somehow immensely moving. Something was badly wrong.

'Auntie, what is it?' I walked towards her and put both arms around her neck. Her head fell on my chest like a broken flower. We stood there together just hugging each other, me strong, and she weak as a child. I picked up a tea-cloth and wiped her tears. 'Now then, Auntie, you tell me. What's the matter?'

Her handbag stood on top of the stove, covering the two front rings. It was wide open. Inside, I could see, from where we were, the confusion of Auntie's conglomerated possessions. Her keys, a clean hanky, several carefully folded serviettes for servicing Bogey's nose, a whole range of assorted cosmetics and creams, from Savlon to an old pot of Snowfire.

She gestured towards the bag with one hand, clinging numbly to me with the other. 'My money,' she whispered brokenly, 'It's all gone. All gone, but for fourpence ha'penny.'

'All gone, but for fourpence ha'penny!' I heard myself echoing foolishly. Her words were quite difficult to grasp, their significance failed to sink in. What did it mean, the missing money? I felt myself growing cold.

'Now, Auntie.' I shook her very gently. 'Did you drop it, do you think, somewhere?' It didn't seem likely, I knew perfectly well. She kept it sealed up in an envelope, the bulk of the notes, with loose change floating haphazardly amongst all the other things. In this case the loose change was the fourpence ha'-penny, hardly worth anyone's time.

Auntie started to sob again, this time not quite so quietly.

'Now, now,' I soothed. 'It's not that bad. How much was there anyway?' She didn't answer. I repeated the question. Auntie still worked in old currency. Her reply would include things like shilings. It did. She cleared her throat, then managed to mumble, 'Four hundred and ninety-eight pounds. And ten shillings. A brand new old ten-shilling note—'

The 'brand new old ten shilling note' snagged my attention, distracting me momentarily from the shock of how much there was missing. Was it illegal to harbour the note? Would it increase its original worth in future years to come, for novelty value or as an antique?

'Good God!' Now it hit me. 'Almost five hundred!' It was madness to carry so much, but pointing that out would do no good. Recriminations wouldn't vouchsafe its return.

'Let's sit down,' I suggested. 'And think where you've been, and when you last opened the envelope. You've looked in your room?' It wouldn't be there. It was never separated from the handbag. And the handbag was rarely, if ever, separated from Auntie. Except, of course, except – I tried to divert my train of thought. It was useless. Except at the restaurant.

'Do you think it's been stolen, Auntie sweet?'

She nodded like someone struck dumb. I could judge her reaction. I knew how she was feeling. Betrayed. Not just the money, but the fact that someone could quite cold-bloodedly have plundered her precious handbag. The act itself was deeply shocking, quite apart from the actual loss.

We sat side by side on the black leather sofa, not speaking, trying to think back. 'I last saw it, I think, no I didn't, not then – or did I—' She couldn't remember.

'Just go easy,' I said, exercising my patience. It was hopeless to know where to begin. 'Right, then, what about yesterday? You had it then, you remember, because it was a toss-up wasn't it, over who should pay for your primrose slippers at Peter Jones.'

'That's right, love, I had it. Right here in my hand.' She looked sadly down at her fingers. They trembled badly like someone in shock, which she was of course. So was I really. I tried to remember all the people who'd been present at our opening last night. It could quite easily have gone in that crowd. After all, who had taken my knickers? But the two, I knew really, were unconnected. The motives were hardly the same.

'Did you put down your handbag, Auntie, at all – at the party last night?' She didn't. Not once, not to eat or to drink. It had hung on her arm all the time.

'That means then,' I chose my words carefully, 'I suppose, that it must have been taken this morning.'

Vincent was walking down Holbein Place going towards the restaurant. I spotted him as soon as I turned the car around the bend leading from Sloane Square. His walk had a certain jauntiness in contrast to how I'd last seen him. You could tell, it was strange, even from this distance, that he was a homosexual. He waved his spine like a wand. Bringing a fairy to mind. The association of ideas. Should we bring in the law? Consult the police? We ought to, about Auntie's theft.

I drove slowly along. A passing car hooted me from behind. I waved it on, the woman driver frowned as she overtook me. For some reason, barely known to myself, I dreaded breaking the news to Vincent. His psyche was fairly frail at the best, how well would he take this fresh shock?

'You think it was Dick.' Vince sat in the car. I'd parked it not far from the restaurant.

'I don't think at all.'

'You bloody well do!' His voice quivered with accusation.

'It might have been me. Only I know it wasn't. It might have been you, come to that.' I spoke with exaggerated reason. It was the only way to keep the situation calm.

'Oh sure!' Vince said sarcastically. Our friendship seemed suddenly sour. Business partners were probably best chosen from people one barely knew, to keep a degree of distance.

'Or Soc and Ari. Or just Soc.'

'Or Ari—'

'Exactly,' I said. 'Oh dear. How very depressing. What should we do, do you think? Call in the Yard, or confront them ourselves?'

No one was likely to voluntarily own-up, and a search was out of the question. I couldn't see Dick accepting a frisk. Though Soc and Ari would undoubtedly enjoy my fingers searching their persons. In any case, it would be to no avail.

Dick had vacated the premises, and Soc and Ari had had all afternoon to do whatever they wished with anything they'd taken. If indeed they had taken anything. Would they do that to Auntie, of whom they seemed fond? With money as motive, who knows.

Vincent was silent. He sat looking troubled. The light glinted on one silver hair that I was sure I hadn't seen before. Were our worries turning him grey? I decided I'd better not mention that fact, for fear of a full-scale breakdown.

'What do you think then, Vincent?'

'Do nothing.' He spoke as if to himself. 'Don't tell them. Pretend you don't know.' He turned to me. He was clearly as upset as he looked. 'Just to get through this evening.'

'I see your point, Vince. It'll be a strain, but it's probably best. We can go into it all in the morning, then if for some reason anyone walks out, there's a chance of getting new staff. Tonight is too much the eleventh hour—'

Would it show, I wondered, the shadow of guilt? Would the evening reveal any remorse?

I'd put Auntie to bed with hot milk and two aspirin, with Tallulah in charge of the others. Even Bogey seemed stung by her air of grief. He'd sat on her lap sadly patting her cheek, trying to lift up her lips in a smile. She'd gazed unseeingly at his round little face, not even tending his nose. The girls had reacted quite characteristically with over-dramatic blood curdling cries of what they'd do to whoever had done it.

'Let's go in then, revisit the scene of the crime. Oh, Vince – not with that expression!'

'Which one?' He turned his face towards me.

'That one. Tragic as Hamlet.'

'I've never played Hamlet, that's one thing I haven't—'

'Well, don't start rehearsing it now.'

Soc was wearing new shoes, I noticed them straight away. And Ari was sporting a brand new tee-shirt with a picture of Popeye printed all down the front, the outline deformed by the shape of Ari's low-slung stomach – so that Popeye appeared knock-kneed.

'You like, Boss Lady? Is Popeye, see!'

'Popeye! Popeye!' Soc started scoffing. 'Pooh, pooh to Popeye. Is silly person. He go stuffing the spinach – is not true. It no make nice big muscles, the spinach. That Popeye, he got a loose screw!'

Soc raised his finger in a corkscrew action against Ari's nearest temple. And playfully punched Popeye's raised clenched fist. Ari howled his displeasure, Soc's hands were both wringing wet. The sound must have been much the same as those twins, fabled to have been reared by wolves – Romulus and Remus, if I remembered right. The one voice now joined by another, Soc's own, as Ari stamped viciously on his new shoes. They were canvas, a pale baby blue. The sort of shade that show every mark.

'Boys. Boys. Keep calm.' Could we last without Auntie sleepily keeping the peace? 'Where's Dick?' I looked round.

'He no here.' Soc looked sullen. 'But is fine by me. Dick big prick! I no like.'

Ari nodded vigorously in perfect agreement, their own tiff forgotten already.

'Is not nice person, is nasty man, this Dick no good for the restaurant—'

They stood hunched together looking solemn, and shaking their heads to and fro. Like those little dogs, a cross between toy and ornament, that car owners put in their rear windows. The ones with heads on a separate spring so the thing is on the move all the time, mile after mile of canine activity.

'What time are we opening, Vince?'

'Around half-past seven, I think Dick said—' Vince trailed off looking disconsolate.

I looked at my watch, it was ten past six. 'Plenty to do then—'

'Oh, really. Like what?' We were totally lost without Dick, which was plainly ridiculous.

'Well, Vince. Dick only does cooking – what about all the

drinks? It's different in the evening to the middle of the day. For a start, have we got any ice?' My mind was beginning to chug into action, it was simply another party. Dispensing, just like a chemist. All that had to be planned were prescriptions. The phone should start ringing with bookings soon. It was strange that it hadn't done so already.

'Has the telephone gone? Have people been ringing?' I turned to Soc who was nearest. He lifted both hands like a Jewish Momma. Oyvé, in a Cypriot accent. 'Is ringing, and ringing and ringing! I no touch. I no like the telephone. No!'

Ari pointed. 'Is dangerous electrics to touch telephone with wet hands! I say to Soc no do it!'

'Couldn't you have answered then, Ari?' Vince's voice held a certain strain, but he was trying very hard to overcome it.

Ari rolled his eyes in alarm. 'No, no, no, not me. I no speak the English. I no understand. I make bad mistakes in the message!' He clearly spoke from experience.

'That's all right – they'll ring again—' As I spoke, as if to prove my point, the telephone started trilling. I curtsied to Vincent and gestured him on. 'Patron, the first of your bookings!'

There was no ice. There was some, but it wasn't enough. Dick arrived as I made the discovery. 'So what, there's no ice! Makes no odds!'

He'd bought a very big bunch of freesias. 'For Auntie, where is the old girl?' The question was posed so innocently it reversed my rising suspicion. Were the flowers some sort of suppliant, or did they stem from genuine fondness? How significant were Soc's and Ari's new purchases – had they suddenly come into money? I decided I'd have to do as Vince said, put the matter right out of my mind. In any case, there were at this point, more immediately pressing problems. The question of ice for a start.

'I know where I can get some. From that ice-cube machine in Sloane Avenue. They've got one there, in front of Moon's Garage. Zoë was saying about it.'

'What's the point? The previous bloke who ran this—'

'Sydney Bummer,' Vincent supplied.

Dick didn't acknowledge the information, and pointedly ignored its source. 'The previous bloke who ran this joint didn't have fancy ice, I'm sure. Nor much in the way of wines.' He nodded dismissively towards Soc and Ari. 'Cypriot shit, I don't doubt. El Bull-Ox, something like that.' The temperature had escalated since his arrival, you could almost touch the tension. The telephone was ringing now non-stop as if we were the only restaurant around.

'How many friends, would you say?' I asked Vincent. He had chosen to sit in the hot seat, with the responsible role of juggling the bookings. Not one I would have undertaken lightly. How could you tell when people would leave? What if they lingered on?

'An hour and a half, I'm allowing them. Is that right?' Vincent had drawn up a plan of the restaurant, with each table numbered from one to ten.

'I don't know, Vince. It seems to be cutting it fine.' I couldn't recall for the life of me how long I spent at a meal. Wherever I'd been to, we'd sat there all night. Start to finish, until it closed.

'Make it longer for friends, Vince! And anyone we vaguely know!'

'There aren't that many, actually, darling. Mostly strangers. The friends don't seem to be bothering, the buggers had it all free last night. I knew that was foolish, I said so—'

I left him juggling with his lists, and went in search of ice. Soc and Ari were working with Dick, maintaining a tight-lipped silence, and nudging each other at his every order. It seemed the right moment to go. As I got in my car, Zoë arrived in a taxi. Our quota of staff was complete.

I got back with my bagful of ice-cubes, two hundred and fifty I'd bought – a waste, Dick would say. But it wasn't in me to serve drinks like Scotch, and gin and tonic without the clinking of ice. It seemed so uncivilized, so second-rate. Someone had to maintain some standard.

It wasn't Dick, as Zoë had noticed. 'I don't think much of our menu, dear! Or of the chef, come to that—'

'Oh, don't you? Dick? He's very nice – he's – efficient.'

'He's damnably rude. "Short Snout", he called me. "Hey, Short Snout, come here!" Can you beat it! ' She smoothed her hands over her waist-line. 'An extremely coarse little morsel.'

'You look nice, Zoë. Is that a new dress?' I put off picking up a pink menu. They lay in a pile, next to the till, badly crossed-out, with lots of corrections.

'No, not quite new. Second hand, pure silk. Do you like it?'

She looked quite different to how she'd looked last night. Today she was favouring the twenties. Her dress, cut on the cross, was ultra-defining and designed for someone much smaller. Her curves pouted out before and behind, with an arousing display of cleavage.

'This neck wasn't like this originally – I've spent all afternoon on alterations.' She stroked the firm line from her chin to the start of the swelling division. 'Is it too much? Have I gone too far?'

'Not at all. It's very provocative,' I said, and added, making sure no one heard: 'It'll take their minds off the food.' She seemed now quite different to how she had been on the telephone earlier today. I wondered whether or not I should tell her all about Auntie's trouble, but decided it wouldn't help matters. I picked up a menu instead.

'Cauliflour Cheese', I started to read at the top, followed by 'Livar and Bacon'. My eyes slid down, I was suddenly sweating. 'Pork Pie' was underneath 'Cold'.

'Lovely puddings, dear! ' Zoë perched her chin on my shoulder, pretending to talk like a parrot. 'Oh my goodness, I say – "Mince Pies and Hot Custard", I haven't had custard for years. With luck he might whip up a blancmange.'

'That's what I thought of this morning. And jelly – as a sort of snob joke.' I turned a tragic face to Zoë.

'It's not funny,' she answered.

'No, I know.'

*   *   *

'I like your menu. I like it, Dick. Some spelling mistakes that's all.' The heat was immense in the kitchen. Dick turned.

'That's all right then, some spelling mistakes. The bastards can read it, they know what it means. They've come for the grub, that's the main thing, not for a lesson in grammar.'

Vince popped his head round the door. 'We're open! Someone's just come in. Jump to it – we're almost completely booked out! I can hardly believe that it's true.'

They had managed, in the short while that I'd been for ice, to mend the ailing Dumb Waiter. Dick had done it, he'd brought his tools. The whole thing now swung up quite smoothly. It wasn't everyone who could've achieved such a miracle. Certainly not Soc and Ari, or Vince – he had certain virtues then, Dick.

'Are you coming up, to see to the drinks?' Vince was overexcited. I'd been made Barmaid to his Major Domo. Zoë was Resident Waitress.

'I'm coming, just getting my ice.'

My very first order was for two Gins and Tonic, and one Straight Scotch–on–the–Rocks. 'There you are, you see!' I hissed at Vince. 'I couldn't have done that with no ice!' His answer surprised me, even rankled a little. 'Don't start making trouble, with Dick.' But I had no time to dwell on anything. Dick. Vince. Me. Even Auntie was swept from my mind. Twenty minutes, I reckoned later, it had taken to transform our restaurant from rather a restful room of tables to a tower of blathering Babel.

'Two Sausage and Chips for Table Two! And where are the Coffees for Number One! And I still await Three Sardine Salads, half portions to do as Hors d'Oeuvres – you've sent me up Stuffed Tomatoes instead, shall I suggest where you shove them!' Zoë bawled cheerfully down the stairs. Dick's answer could clearly be heard. I turned up the music slightly louder, which made it near maximum volume. I thought my eardrums would burst, explode like two fireworks each side of my head, a mix of fine bone and warm wax.

Vincent was clearly hysterical. He ran like a rat with a bad case of rabies from table to table taking orders that Zoë'd just taken, and delivering all the wrong dishes. 'The bottle of White, the Dry, where is it?' he shouted wildly at me. We were selling a surprisingly great deal of wine, despite the food's unsuitability. And what was more, our Menu was being received quite favourably. Dick had priced it astoundingly low. But we were making it up on the wines. 'The bottle of White, the Dry?' I repeated. 'You've had it Vince, ages ago!'

'I haven't!'

'You have!'

'You liar!'

'Vince,' I protested. 'Look, I'm checking it here. See this chit? That's Dry White, Table Ten.'

His eyes swivelled ceilingward. 'Well, what's for Four?'

'The cheap stuff, the Red. You remember. Here, look – Three for Four—'

'They don't like it. They say they want White, just the one – there are only two at that table—' I looked over there were.

'Well, why did you order "Three cheap Red for Four"?'

'I meant to say Five—'

'Vince! How am I to know! I'm not a mind reader – you're mixing me up now. I'll have to re-do all these records! Otherwise it's all to cock when it comes to paying the bill—'

'Bill please, barmaid, for Number One! They say they can't wait for Coffee!' Zoë made sure to scream as loud as she could in the direction of the Dumb Waiter. 'They've timed it, they claim it's taking longer to come than the rest of the meal put together!'

At her words, the Dumb Waiter delivered Four Coffees. 'Too late,' she yelled gloatingly back. 'Returning Four Coffees, a spot more expresso next time!' Tempers were tingling. I glanced around. Everyone seemed to be drunk. Or was it just my imagination? Zoë tottered past with a tray of greasy plates. 'Dirty dishes coming down, Dick, on the Dumb Waiter – would it be asking too much to wash them before serving up?' Theirs was a running verbal battle. 'Come and wash them yourself, you big cunt!' I didn't dare to dwell on how things were down there with poor Soc and Ari. Soc had appeared sweating profusely at the top of the stairs, wiping his face with his apron. 'What are you doing?' Vince had demanded. Soc had puffed out his cheeks. 'I come up for air. Plenty hot! And that Dick – he just hit me. I—'

'Go away! Get down, go – go—' Vince shooed him away like a hen. 'He can't stand here in front of the customers surely—' Vince appealed to me. Soc stood there streaming like a fountain statue. I could see he might well put people off their food; it was as if he was actually steaming, like a horse at the end of a race. Though some restaurants I'd seen did allow their kitchen staff out, if not exactly to mingle amongst the diners, at least out on the street for a smoke.

'You do have the door open down there, don't you Soc?' I said kindly. He looked at me as if bewildered; the question seemed simple enough, had Dick been poaching his brains?

'It's perfectly true, though, you must admit, Vince – our air-conditioning needs some attention.' My own eyes were smarting badly already from the smoke and the sweat and the steam.

'Oh, never mind that, darling, not now – one thing, for Christ's sake, at a time! Now go away Soc, I shan't tell you again.' Vince waved his fine wrists towards the kitchen. Soc shambled away like a dog.

'Poor Soc,' I said.

'Poor Soc! Poor me, my God, what's up now with Seven?'

Someone on Seven required the Ladies; it meant half the table standing up to let her get by. Which in turn required a great deal of scraping and drawing-in of chairs around Table Six.

'Bloody hell!'

'Beg pardon?'

'You've snagged my tights!'

'Old fellow, you've spilt half my drink!'

The interchange was taking place between two very different groups. Table Six, upon which the drink had been spilt, consisted of four Hooray Henrys, young ones, aged around seventeen or so. With spots on their spots, and high voices still amazingly unbroken. What age were we allowed to serve alcohol, was it sixteen? Or more, perhaps eighteen? We might be breaking the law with this lot, though if we were, we weren't the only ones. They were pretty drunk on arrival. One had had the audacity before they were seated to slip his index finger down Zoë's flamboyant cleavage. Whilst another, I'd seen behind Vincent's back, was attempting a camp imitation. They'd ordered a bottle of Moët Chandon, Non-Vintage. I planned to charge them a fiver for it. They were now already into their third.

The five-some on Table Seven were mixed sexes with a very wide range of ages, and backgrounds, as well, on the surface of things. Three middle-aged balding, stock-size business men who'd exclaimed with delight at our prices. And two very tarty girls in their twenties, disgruntled at not being taken out on the toot to somewhere much smarter than this. One had decided to stick with her Whisky, all the way through the meal. It was she whose unfortunate tights had been snagged. The Scotch had released her aggression. 'New on today, weren't they, Dawn!' She turned to her friend, lip quivering.

'Yeah, new on this evening!' the friend, Dawn, shrilled. 'It's the fault of these fucking tables! They're too close together – there's no bloody room to swing a cat – in't that right, fellas?' she challenged her companions. They didn't want trouble.

'Girls. Girls. All is well. Plenty more hosiery where they came from.' Then to the truculent Table Six. 'So sorry, young chap, about the spilt drink – might one be allowed to replace it?'

The girl accosted me on her return from the Ladies. 'It's fucking ropey, your toilet arrangements! It could ruin your hairdo, a trip through that kitchen – look, mine's falling already. Not to mention the grease on your clothes—' I could hear her exclaiming, expounding the theme later as they were leaving.

'No, Dawn, I definitely don't advise it. Can't you hang on until you get to Harry's hotel? It won't take long in a taxi. Cross your legs and think of the Crucifixion.' I wondered if they were Catholics.

We were glad of their table, of any table, in fact. A small queue had formed just inside the front door, and was severely hampering service. Zoë had already dropped half a Lager and Lime in an old lady's open handbag. I'd seen her do it, the old lady hadn't. She might not discover it until she'd left and gone home. 'But my goodness, my contents are floating. A large bubble appears lodged in my wireless licence, now how did that ever get there!'

Vincent darted hither and thither, a desperate smile on his lips. 'Would you care for your bill, Sir? No? Yes, of course it's no trouble, your tenth cup of Coffee. Just coming—' Each time he passed me, he made a terrible grimace. I made one back out of sympathy. 'The buggers won't go,' he muttered through clenched teeth. I could see that they wouldn't. But why? Were we making the welcome too warm? Was I making my measures too large? Zoë came for a tray of Zambucca. 'Seven Crême de Menthe Frappé for Table Ten,' she sang out. 'And two more Brandies for Five.' Vincent was passing. 'I think she means Four—' I breathed hard. 'Four for Five, Vince?' My voice sounded strained.

'Two for Four.'

Zoë, thankfully, heard. 'Two for Five, as I've said. Fuck off Vincent, old bean. If you don't mind.'

The small queue at the door had suddenly grown. Vincent tried hard not to notice. 'There's a lot of them there, Vince,' I felt bound to say. 'Never mind, we'll know another time not to over-book.'

'Bitch.'

'Not meaning to be, but let's face it – each small mistake. It has to be out in the open, don't brood. I'm not doing all that much better with the bills!'

His face cheered up ever so slightly, to hear of my own inefficiency. If I'd been in charge, instead of him, or instead of Dick – everyone seemed in charge but me – I wouldn't have put me on the till. Money, the adding up, etcetera, had never been my forte. But thankfully most of these paying customers were considerably less in control than me. And as I was erring on the side of our profit, the Brick Bistro couldn't complain.

They went in a rush, just as they'd arrived. Six tables emptied at the same time. So that now the entire central corridor was blocked with a queue at each end. One waiting impatiently to get to their tables and the other fighting to leave. The word must have spread about our sanitary arrangements. Since Dawn's friend went, no other woman had been. Six or seven men had disappeared down the stairs at different times and come back with a look of disgust. Now and then I could hear from the kitchen the sound of a bellow from Soc, and various high screams which sounded like Ari. And ominous scrapings and thuds interspersed with Dick's demonic swearing. But other than that there was not much to choose between the tension above or below stairs.

'You've got those receipts, Miss? I've worked it out – you've overcharged by two pounds. Two pounds and twelve pence, no I tell a lie, two pounds and thirteen! Look here!'

I studied the man instead of his bill. He was sandy all over like a spadeful of beach, with a bristling moustache in each earhole. His process of hair growth was somehow reversed. The centre of his head must be full of strayed filament from the inside-out setting of his follicles. His ears represented small exits. What discomfort the poor man must suffer. How could a person begin to think clearly, with a brain box of tendrils and curls?

'It's all correct.' I spoke precisely. Quite confident that I could cope. This wasn't the first query of the evening. I was becoming practised at pulling the wool where totalling was concerned. 'Look, Sir – Three Prunes and Custard, you had with your Port. And the lady had Peppermint Creams. That's the discrepancy I think you'll find. You hadn't allowed for those four.'

'What four?' His voice was getting louder.

'The Three Prunes and One Peppermint, Sir.'

An ugly flush was suffusing his sandiness, each moustache stood on end in his ears. 'Are you trying to stand there and actually say that you're charging that much for those sweets?'

I smiled at him tolerantly, he was shouting so much he was drowning my latest Stylistics' 'You, You Make Me Feel Brand New!'

'Now then, Sir, by sweets I take it you mean the Peppermint Creams? Rather than what we loosely term in this country to be the "Afters" or the "Second Course", or more accurately, the "Pudding"?'

'You're trying to fox me!' He was losing control; people at the nearby tables were nudging each other. 'What I'm asking is how in hell this bill has become so exorbitantly high! Seventy-five pence for a plateful of Peppermint Creams! I ask you – not even After Eights!' He was looking around, attempting to recruit support from adjacent onlookers. Several people were waiting impatiently now behind him to settle their bills.

'I couldn't get After Eights,' I said. 'The shop had sold out. I'm sorry. Tomorrow perhaps.' He stared at me disbelievingly, as if I were not quite all there.

'I can't believe,' he said eventually, 'that you'd charge, for what most restaurants give away as a matter of course—'

'They're more established than we are, Sir. We can't afford charity yet. The lady ate every single one. They're quite a superior brand – let me see – the full dozen, twelve I believe we gave? That's only sixpence a peppermint. Served on the premises, you see. You're actually getting our seat, our lighting, electricity, decor, ambience – in short you're paying for overheads. Now, do we agree that's quite fair? Quite. Thank you, Sir. Next bill please.'

'That seemed to go smoothly enough, you see, Vince.' I turned to him after I'd skilfully cleared the small queue. Vince looked dazed. He moved now like one in a trance. No mad table hopping. No manic hysteria. He'd played his crescendo already. It was my turn now. More mine and Zoë's. His Head Waiter role had dissolved. He'd ushered the public into our emporium. Zoë and I had to ease them out, making certain they all paid first.

*   *   *

My additions were becoming more wildly erratic hour by hour, as the evening wore on, as in a sense was the general service. But amazingly, most people seemed to accept it all as part of the normal procedure. If asked, we could quite truthfully have stated that our first night was proving successful. 'I've made two pounds in tips, just from Table Ten,' Zoë confided exultantly. 'And I expect to make even more from Four. They're Red Indians, they don't know what day it is—'

Vincent was standing within earshot as she said it. 'Your tips should go straight in a Service Box and be shared amongst everyone, Zoë.'

'Bollocks to that, Vince!' She turned on her heel and narrowly missed colliding with a courteous American couple who were just on the point of departing. The man came towards me first to pay his bill. His blue-rinsed, plump wife hung behind. He smiled behind his rimless specs. 'My, what a cute little place it is you have here! I can't tell you how we have enjoyed it!'

His pleasant wife approached and nodded. 'Your food is so typically English – we're from the Mid-West, it's my first trip, you know. But my husband was stationed in Britain during the War. He said our little meal here tonight took him right back to those wartime years—'

'I can believe it.' I smiled back winningly. 'Whereabouts were you stationed?' I looked at her husband.

He beamed. 'Ilkley Moor—'

'Oh, Ba Tat!'

He looked thrilled and astonished, and so did his wife. 'Ilkly Moor Ba Tat – why we sing that back home!' She turned to her husband. 'Don't we, dear – I know all of the words, don't I!'

'How amazing,' I said. 'As a matter of fact, I'm not sure, but I think our cook Dick comes from Ilkley.'

'No, really!' they chorused together.

'Yes, Dick, he's downstairs.'

'Why, you'd sure like to meet him – wouldn't you, dear?' the woman said to her husband.

'Surely!' he agreed. 'Just to hear the great accent again—'

Vince stood guard in my place at the till, whilst I led the

Americans downstairs. 'Whoo, whoo!' I went, to give prior warning. I couldn't be sure what to expect in our kitchen.

They couldn't have heard. Soc was picking his nose over a plate of stewed prunes. And Ari had his flies half undone. Dick was in the middle of scraping someone's left-over custard back into the saucepan on the stove. Was this what our patrons were privileged to glimpse whilst tripping out through to their toiletries? I could see by the light shining under the door that someone was out there this minute. From the sounds there seemed to be trouble with the flush. Introductions were effected against a background of persistent chain-pulling.

Dick scowled as the American offered his hand. 'Pleased to meet yer! My mother got knocked up by a Yank in the war. The bastard scarpered before she had the chance to pin it on him. She tried to abort, but it didn't work – I came along instead!'

Soc and Ari were listening with fearful fascination. Dick's reaction was so unexpected in face of the American urbanity that it took seconds for me to realize exactly what he'd said. The man blinked. His wife smiled. Both were taken aback, but sheer good manners and years of social training saw them through. He showed his teeth, top and bottom, in a good-natured grin.

'Why now, what the heck – I know our boys weren't as well-behaved as they might have been – but those Yorkshire lasses were so darned cute, I suppose one could barely blame them. May I offer my own apologies on behalf of the American Army, son.'

The 'son' was unfortunate, I afterwards thought. It heightened Dick's obvious hostility. It certainly could have been quite on the cards that this dignified man was Dick's father! I made matters worse by unthinkingly enquiring as to whether or not they had children. The woman's sanguine expression had slipped. 'Our Lord saw fit not to bless us with offspring, and my gynaecologist later concurred.' She'd leaned confidingly towards me, as she said it. Soc and Ari strained forward to catch what she was saying, not wishing to be excluded from any of these exchanges. Soc obviously got the wrong end of the stick as he watched the woman pat her stomach. He took the action and her overall plumpness as a sign of a late-stage pregnancy. He patted his own and broke into a grin. 'Yes, lady, I coming a baby too! Soon, my wife she have it. I hope very much for a little girl baby. I have plenty plenty boys!' He raised his eyebrows high in his oily hair and, putting on a look of concern asked with commendable interest: 'You, lady, want little girl? Or want boy?' And he picked up a nearby loaf of bread and began humming 'Rock-a-Bye-Baby' with it cradled along his arm.

This affecting tableau was interrupted by a tearful young girl at the end of her tether. The unfortunate phantom flusher. 'I can't just seem to—' Her high voice broke unsteadily. She completed her sentence by pointing. No one spoke. The American moved forward. 'May I be of assistance?'

'He understands closets,' his wife whispered proudly to me.

The girl gave a whimper as a sign of distress. I walked forward in front of the American; the girl greeted me with relief. 'It's my—' she lowered her voice, and continued, 'my Tampax, you know, the cardboard container – it keeps bobbing about on the surface. It's frightfully embarrassing if a man—'

She was aged about eighteen and had been well brought up. Home Counties, by the cut of her hair. It hung each side of a centre parting, burnished brown, like a conker. She spoke with bit of a lisp.

'Run along,' I said. 'I shouldn't worry. That sort of thing often happens. It'll soon go away as it gradually gets soggy. No reason to get upset.'

She gave a trembling smile of heartfelt gratitude. 'Are you sure?'

'Quite sure.'

'Thanks awfully, you're terribly kind.'

Dick was throwing a rasher of bacon, recently fried, on a thick slice of bread, upon which sat a lightly poached egg. He reached to a shelf and unscrewed a large bottle of Crosse and Blackwell Tomato Ketchup and shook it on top of the bacon.

Then, ignoring us all, he opened his mouth and crammed in as much as he could. 'My, my boy – that looks good!' the American said, all geniality.

Dick looked at him with open dislike. 'Would you two Yanks sod off outa this kitchen?'

'Well, darling, I suppose you can understand it. His reaction – in defence of his mother – upholding her honour for past humiliations. Unwed and seduced by our Allies. After all—'

'He's a bastard!' Zoë stated, quite accurately. 'And added to which he's a bully. A bloody sadist with a very peculiar sense of humour. He's stopped "Short Snout" for me, now it's "Dung Drawers"! There's no depth to which I'm sure he wouldn't stoop.'

Zoë was dearly drawn to the double negative. 'These poor patrons of ours, I pity them really. He could be peppering them all with powdered glass!' She shuddered. 'You'd never catch me eating here. The food's frankly rubbish. I'm amazed that they've eaten it – aren't you?'

I was amazed, but I'd gone past caring. We could've served Fried Lice and Camel, people would probably have been just as pleased. But the evening quite suddenly was taking its toll. 'Aren't you tired?' I sat down. 'Zoë?'

She shrugged. 'I should be, but strangely enough, no, I'm not. I'm conserving my strength for much later. I'm crossing fingers that Stuffy'll come round. He did last night, but—' she pulled a doleful face. 'He didn't do much. I have to say that.' I didn't answer; she continued without noticing. 'He was here, you know. He was here at the party last night. But it must have been seconds only, because I didn't see him. Nor did you, by what he said to me afterwards.'

An uproar had surfaced now unexpectedly between a couple who sat near the door. 'My God!' Zoë gasped. 'What the hell is she doing? Quick, go and get one of the boys.' Vince was downstairs smoking with Dick. Poor Pot, from what I could smell. Cooking had ceased, we were trying to clear up, but six tables of people remained. All couples, cooing and doveing, except this one now, Table Two. They struggled together in a fight to the death and could well go straight through our window. The woman was hitting her companion with his briefcase, whilst he retaliated fiercely with her handbag.

It was strange, but I hadn't seemed to notice them before, they'd appeared to be so featureless and grey. But now I remembered another fight of this same nature taking place between a similarly undistinguished pair, half way along Park Lane. And the ages, too, had been about the same, mid-fifties or thereabouts.

Neither spoke, neither uttered a sound, not of pain or surprise or outrage. They just lunged, grim and silent, scuffling together as the chairs all around them started falling.

The other tables stared over, appalled. 'Shouldn't we stop them?' I heard someone say. 'Best not, darling. They know what they're doing,' came the guarded reply.

'Have they paid their bill yet?' Vince wanted to know, standing well back in the shadows.

'Oh, for God's sake, Vince!' Zoë exploded. The couple in combat looked like Kung Fu fighters in a momentary pause, preparing to pounce. The woman's grey hair had been piled in a bun, low at the nape of her neck. It now hung like a heavy London fog, drifting in wisps round her shoulders. Her companion's locks had been carefully combed from a very low, left-hand parting over the hill of his balding scalp. The arrangement was sadly disturbed, so that now the top of his head was revealed, as bare as a baby's bottom, whilst on the left, a long strand of hair curved to his cheek in a ringlet.

Vincent's question was more sensible than Zoë'd supposed, but they had paid their bill as it happened.

'Chuck a glass full of water – aim it straight at their gobs. Or better still, a bloody great bucketful. That should see the buggers out!' Dick had suddenly joined us. He stood at the stairs staring over. 'I'll do it. I'd love to.' He shot down for his bucket.

'I bet he would too,' Zoë muttered.

Vince slipped past the pair to open the front door and prepare the pathway for Dick, who planned to flush them out like fleas and had brought up not one, but two buckets.

'Ouch!' I shivered as his torrent of cold water made first contact with the two forms. Their bodies buckled and fell apart.

'What a bastard – he's really enjoying it. Quick, look at his face. Just catch that expression. I wouldn't like him at the end of a whip!' Zoë caught hold of my arm. The combatants, in shock, seemed stuck to the spot. Dick continued; he planned to get rid of them. The remainder of the restaurant patrons were making small movements to prepare for their own departure, as if feeling that unless they went out under their own steam this demon usurper might start on them with the watery whip from his buckets. Three slurps saw the pair to the door and the rest of both pails pushed them on to the pavement. We clustered, Zoë, Vince and I, watching Dick chasing them up the street. They ran like defeated rats – he, ludicrously, still holding tight to her handbag, whilst she wielded his masculine briefcase. As they rounded the corner of Pimlico Road I watched her raise it once more. Soon the frontage of Casa Pupa might be imperilled, but for the moment our windows were safe.

The restaurant was empty. Our patrons had fled. It was quarter past twelve by my watch. 'Clear up tonight? Or finish tomorrow? Lunchtime – are we doing it or not?' It seemed we were. Dick said so. 'A chance to get some coins in the kitty!'

I couldn't help noticing how confidently he hailed his cab, as if to the manner born. Vincent was rushing to catch the last tube, closely pursued by Soc and Ari. They bounced bowlegged, badly, like worn tennis balls, never higher off the ground than the width of their shoes. Soc, of the two, moved more painfully. His new shoes were pinching his feet. The thought of his shoes, Ari's tee-shirt and the cool insouciance of Dick's cab-hailing reminded me of poor Auntie's loss. Which was the culprit amongst our kitchen staff? And would tomorrow bring confrontation?

Stuffy and Nutty were sitting together, singing, in the back of the yellow Rolls-Royce. It spoke much for the vehicle's soundproofing properties that from the pavement you couldn't hear a squeak. In fact, driving towards it in my Morgan, I wouldn't have known until I was parking behind it, in front of the house – I wouldn't have known that anyone was in it at all. A flaring match had caught my attention. My first thought had been that a wino, or one of those roaming old women with their worldly possessions in one carrier bag, had decided to squat for the night. I couldn't blame them, in their position I probably would've done the same. Why should all these empty cars, clean and warm and dry, occupy so many miles of street when gipsy souls were simply seeking a temporary roof? A whoosh of Fresh-Aire, that's all that was needed the following morning. Fumigation for critical cases.

I walked past, not looking, up to my front door. Nutty wound down one window and stuttered, 'G-good morning, Madam.' I turned round. Stuffy still held the lighted match, it must almost be burning his fingers. 'Good morning,' he echoed, smiling foolishly. 'We've been waiting for you to return.'

They were drinking Champagne straight from the bottle, it bubbled down over their chins. Stuffy had perched it between his corduroyed knees, the green shone in front of his match like stained glass. I was tired. They were drunk and behaving like children.

'I didn't know you knew each other?' I wished they'd both go away. What would happen if I, like Dick, resorted now to two full buckets? I held my watch to the light – well past one o'clock. Further up was a cop on point duty, permanently positioned outside the house of some Judge, Lord Chief Justice Something, noted for the severity of his sentences. A likely victim, a certain target for retribution and revenge. The cop, I could see, was looking this way. I recognized him at once; Tom Twiddle, deceased – his nephew no less. The young policeman who'd called round at our restaurant on the morning his uncle had died. How remarkably small the world was really. 'Don't talk rubbish!' The Old Man would've retorted. 'Don't talk rubbish!' were the very first words I'd heard him say – not to me, but to someone behind me. In the Turner Room at the National

Gallery. For years after he told people that he'd picked me up, just like that, in Trafalgar Square. The startled recipient of his scorn, a total stranger to each of us, was extolling the virtues of Turner's Venetian Period. He'd quickly moved on at The Old Man's outburst. I'd remained rooted with shyness. We'd looked at each other, he was hard to ignore – especially since now he was winking. He was wearing a hat, a Homburg, I think. Beneath it his hair was quite white. It rested on the black velvet collar of his thick black cape, under which emerged bright yellow trousers. He made an arresting figure, a cross in his stance between Robert Graves and Augustus John with the long upper lip of a horse.

My shyness increased. I was used to oddness, with Stephen – but his had been secret. And anyway, we two had been so young together, more equal from all points of view. Education; we both had left school at fourteen. Both orphans, though he was from an orphanage. And sexually, we were like brother and sister. At his death I was technically virgin.

The Old Man spoke. 'How lost you look, child. I might care to make you my mistress. Come and have tea, we'll talk about it. I shall take you this evening to the Last Night of the Proms. Malcolm Sargent has a waist-line very much like yours. But I'd like you with a little more meat.'

After the Proms we'd walked in Hyde Park and then through to Kensington Gardens. We'd sat on a bench watching strange men walk past. 'They're all Homos,' he said. 'Homosexuals.' I knew what they were, they were what Stephen had hated, vehemently so. But I looked back at The Old Man innocently.

'Are they? Oh, really?' I'd said.

He'd continued explaining the subject to me, fifteen years ago few would have done so. But I knew all about it already from Stephen. I was more interested in straight-forward sex, that's where my ignorance lay.

'Do you know—' he'd said suddenly, taking my hand, 'why the breath smells after people make love?' I didn't. 'It's because,' he continued, squeezing my fingers and now lifting them to his tongue, 'it's because the seeds of life are dying, even before they've lived.'

I couldn't begin to understand what it was he was saying. But by then he was running his lips very gently all over the palm of my hand, and pressing his tongue to the centre and breathing soft breath on my wrist. My elbow ached from the awkward angle, but I wouldn't have cared if it cracked. Because his other hand was inside my blouse, drawing blood from a sleeping stone.

That night he forcefully de-flowered me in the large front bedroom of Old Church Street, the same one that the girls now slept in. The bloodstain is still on the carpet, he'd encircled it with Quink Blue-Black Fountain Pen Ink. It lies approximately beneath Zsa-Zsa's feet.

'Where are you off to, little one?' He'd fallen asleep as soon as his body had rolled off me. I didn't mind, it had given me a chance to study the room I was in. Auntie's bedroom, back home, the one that we'd shared, had aways been terribly cold. We used to rub each other's chilblains since as far back as I could remember. Getting up in the mornings was agony. I dreaded the icy embrace of the lino, and the chill china rim of the Wo-wo.

'Wo-wo? What's a Wo-wo?' Stephen had asked. 'It's a—' I'd found it difficult to find the right word. We'd always called it Wo-wo in our house. Was it perhaps Auntie's invention? 'Well, you probably know it best as – potty.'

'Oh, po! Or a "Gozunda"? Have you ever heard that one? I haven't, I just read it in a comic.' Much of our culture had come from comics, Stephen's and mine – Desperate Dan, and Keyhole Kate and Lord Snooty – all that team. The Old Man had been quite genuinely amazed, for all his voracious appetite for reading; he'd never heard of one of these people. But in his later years his sight so frail that he could barely see the pictures, let alone the words, it had been one of his greatest joys to go through old copies of *Beano* and *Dandy* with Tallulah, when she'd been tiny.

I'd lain that first night, simply looking around. The Old Man always slept with the lights on throughout his life. It sprang from a dread of the dark. But I didn't know that – I just thought how wasteful to be going to bed with them on. Though in a sense it wasn't like light at all. Light, at home, had consisted of candles, until much later on when electricity had come. Though even then, for going to bed we rarely switched on the lights upstairs. Simply to economize. It hung in each room from the centre of the ceiling, on a wire the length of the rulers at school, ending in a clear, low-watt bulb caged in a hideous shade of mock vellum. Pale beige with loops of brown cord. I'd spent years of my life studying its ugliness, whilst Auntie lay snoring beside me.

The Old Man's bedroom was entirely different, not like a bedroom at all. Ours had been empty of all save the bed, a brown wardrobe, and the wash-stand, of course. On top of the wash-stand stood a wide off-white bowl with a jug of cold water to wash with. And a matching container for holding the soap. All displaying the same dying rose.

Stephen and I hadn't had a bedroom, simply a room with a bed. And a small metered gas ring and fire and two chairs of the hue of stale cocoa. Not even a table to eat our food from, or a surface for Stephen to write his songs. But it didn't matter, we ate off the floor. The whole of our life was a picnic.

The Old Man's bedroom was wallpapered with volumes and volumes of words, in the form of books, folios, periodicals, pamphlets, theses, essays and exercise-books full of jottings. There must have been, I lay there counting, at least eleven or twelve lights in the room. None hanging from the ceiling. All Art Nouveau original lamps, The Old Man had carefully explained. And he'd drawn my attention to the succulent colours, to the turquoise, sea-greens and serpent yellows. And to the loving, looping lines and the curves. I'd listened, and looked, enthralled and aroused. I'd never seen light presented like this. Stephen and I had had in the corner of our Kilburn bedsitter a very old standard lamp, as brown as the cocoa-coloured chairs. A print of a billowing ship in full sail glowed dully over its shade. It was the first piece of furniture Stephen had damaged as his drinking grew gradually worse.

And from stroking the sensual lines of his lamps, we stood before each one in turn, The Old Man turned his attention to me. 'Will you take off your clothes.' It wasn't a question. I couldn't say no. He'd laid back, fully dressed with his hat on his head, smoking a pipe – simply watching.

'How incredibly elegant you are for a child. What style to that long, pale young body. But it needs to expand, to mature and to realize what power it will hold over men.' The Old Man had spoken as if to himself. But now he spoke gently to me. 'Come here, my gauche and blushing girl. I'm going to teach you to love.'

And he had. I turned my gaze away from the room, slowly towards his face. His head, mouth half open, lay back on his pillow. The closed lids of his eyes lay like eggs in the shadowy depths of his sockets. The profile resembled that of a Roman Emperor, the sort you see on old coins. And it also looked, for some reason, religious. I felt I was in bed with God. Had he entered, the Spirit of the Holy Ghost? I certainly felt quite spiritual, quite other-worldly and extra-special. My Inner Being had been softly brushed, it was still sightly trembling at the touch. We'd lain side by side at the very beginning, and he'd kissed me from my mouth to my neck. And from my neck he'd gone down further still, till his head was in line with my titties. And then he'd done what I'd thought wasn't possible. He'd put the two of them into his mouth, pressing them so close together each side – cupping them tight with his hands.

I'd shuddered, it was such a thrilling sensation to have him actually – suckling! I wonderingly touched The Old Man's large head. I fondled the nape of his neck where I'd liked him touching me, as he'd done just before. His sucking stopped quite abruptly and his body moved further down, now past my navel. I could feel myself sweating with shame. What was he hoping to look at down there? Except a large landscape of hair! I stared straight ahead. Oh dear, wasn't this rude? Stephen and I had both slept in my nighties, entwined and slithering as our shiny mock satins had slipped and slid against each other. Our actual flesh never met. But The Old Man was going much further than that, entering another area. The introduction of our, not merely outer, but inner flesh was about to take place.

I shut my eyes. He was certainly making a wonderful meal of my – thingy.

He was speaking to me! But I hadn't heard. He repeated what he had said. 'You're intact, little one. Your precious jewel is here for me to possess. See, I introduce my evil snake into your innocent Garden of Eden!'

I watched with astonishment as he fell back on his haunches, like a drawing I'd once seen of Pan, and proceeded to hoist with one hand something I'd not noticed before. Was he wearing that there when he'd got into bed? He'd thrown back the sheets in a flourish when he'd moved from my neck at the start. The bedclothes lay crumpled, hanging half off the bed. Now he pushed them down even further and started nuzzling with his banana – that's what it looked like to me. He was running the tip of it from the top of my slit nearly right the way back to my botty. And each time he did, he spat on his fingers and transferred that same spit to his tip.

I liked it a lot, I had to admit. It was silly, but also exciting. It was naughty, all right. But it wasn't enough. I began slowly moving my body. He was pleased, I could tell by the soft deep sly chuckle. And he'd chosen that exact point to enter.

He'd started to talk to me as soon as his thing eased inside, probably on purpose to take my mind off the pain. And it was very painful too, what he was doing down there. I tried my best to widen myself. It was as if I'd had to open my mouth, stretch it in order that someone might fit in a Thermos flask, those were the relative proportions. I gazed at him, my head on my pillow, as if from another planet. He'd taken his own pillow from the top of the bed and placed it beneath my pelvis, explaining how if he hadn't done this, my 'cunt' would be at the wrong angle. He kept saying 'cunt', the word seemed to please him. But my mind was more on the pillow. I was worrying now about whether I'd stain it with the juices that seemed to be

150

flowing. Would he change it, put a clean pillowcase on after all this was over? Or go to sleep with my feminine odours nestling around his nose?

'Your cunt is perfection,' he murmured. 'My angel—'

'Is it?' I'd bitten my tongue to transfer my attention away from the source of the pain. He was penetrating now so deep inside I feared he might fracture my womb. Or worse, rip right through my internal workings and emerge at the top of my head.

'Perfection.' The Old Man murmured again. 'A pulsating pathway of petal-soft skin teasing me slowly to Paradise—'

Me? Who, me? Apparently so, there was no one else in the bed. He was going round in a corkscrew fashion, holding tight to the base of his stem. And from that he quite suddenly changed direction and went in the other way. The switch took a few seconds, though it must have seemed more, to set up a new set of sensations. It was as if my insides were made of suede, and from stroking the surface in a certain way someone had now gone against the grain and created a quite different texture. I could only just about stand it.

'I'm not hurting you, am I, little one?' The Old Man whispered solicitously. I unclamped my jaws and whispered back, 'Not all that much. A bit. But it's nice.'

He'd positioned himself in such a way that his head was framed by one lamp. The light surrounded his head like a halo, suffused by the mane of white hair. I wanted to lie there for ever.

'This is the first and the last time I shall allow you to lie there.' My heart leapt to my throat at his words and then as quickly dropped from the sheer disappointment. What was I doing wrong? Where had Paradise suddenly gone to, and the tease of my petal-soft skin? But the tone of his voice became tender. 'I tell you this as I pillage your innocence and remove you from youth's pedestal. But after tonight we prepare to be partners, each equal in love to the other. You'll be mine for as long as I live—'

*   *   *

Stuffy and Nutty continued singing, both so slurred that the tune was unrecognizable, but it might well have been the Eton Boating Song. The Old School of both of them, I suddenly realized. It was strange to think that Stuffy had been there. He so hated everything it stood for and made such efforts to conceal that fact of his education. And indeed had made such remarkable progress in declassing his accent, it would have taken an expert to know.

I'd joined them temporarily in the back of the car. 'You can't sit in here all night, you two—'

Stuffy put his hand on my knee. 'Can't we come inside? Can't we share your couch, my comrade and I, can't we please?'

'Don't be so silly, Ulysses. Why don't you just go home? Where have you been,' I turned to Nutty, 'to have got into such a state?' I frowned and spoke with extreme severity. Nutty's eye started nervously swivelling. 'I, we – well, you see, w-w, we—.'

Stuffy came to the rescue. I'd never seen him more confident. Nor for that matter, more drunk. 'We collided up in Camden Town, I was coming out of Compendium – I'd just bought a book which you will enjoy, but be that as it may, my dear – and from there we've pub-crawled our way across town. Several stiff ones in the French, a swift visit of course to the Colony to pay my respects to Muriel, and a taxi to dear old Sean Treacy, here at the top of the road.'

'The Queen's Elm. That's where you've been. Have you eaten?' They both shook their heads, silent, like two bad boys being told off by their mother. I could see the whole scenario, I could tell what the saga had been. United by joint adoration of me, drowning in mutual sorrow. 'Well,' I said sternly. 'You should have thought earlier, and come to the restaurant to eat, instead of drinking like that on empty stomachs.' Stuffy groaned as I mentioned restaurant and Nutty immediately joined in.

'What's the matter with you two?' I was losing patience, tomorrow had turned into today. 'I'm going to bed.'

'Do you have to, really?' Stuffy suddenly said.

'Yes, I do, I'm afraid, I'm terribly tired—'

'Run this ridiculous restaurant? Do you have to?' Stuffy's expression was terribly serious, making him even more Stanley Spencer-ish. I thought of the hours we'd lain together, his scholar's body so enveloped by mine like a small boat alongside a ship. They sat facing me in the luxurious interior of the faded, old-fashioned Rolls. I'd perched myself on the pull-down seat, the one to the left of the door. It struck me how very similar they seemed, Stuffy and Nutty together. Even down to their ridiculous names – Ulysses and Hannibal – Stuffy and Nutty. A music-hall touring team, clog-dancing and tapping the spoons. They both gazed at me as if I was their life-blood and about to cut off their supply. Nutty's left elbow had started to jerk, it echoed the rhythm of the eye. Up and down, and left and back. The puppeteer must have gone for his tea and left the poor marionette in first gear.

'Actually,' I said, making movements to leave, 'it was really rather nice in our restaurant tonight, though in one respect I must say, remarkable. The occasion was noteworthy for one reason – not a single friend turned up. Not even to give moral support.' I opened the heavy door of the car; they sat there in joint dejection. 'But never mind, there'll be other nights – now I bid you good-morning, gentlemen.'

At just about dawn the telephone rang. I'd been dreaming that the telephone was ringing, so at first I didn't bother to answer it, believing it to be a dream. 'Were you sleeping?' The voice sounded almost next door.

'No, just dreaming.'

'It's been ringing and ringing for ages—'

'That's what I was dreaming. I'm sorry, who's that?'

'It's me.'

It was Lionel Striving, all the way from New York. 'How near you sound.' I was surprised.

'That's the third time you've said that!' How impatient he sounded – as well as sounding so near. I must have been very deeply asleep, my brain felt exceptionally sluggish. I coughed in an effort to clear my head, at the same time clearing my throat.

'Have you got a cold?'

'A cold? No, I haven't, Lionel. Have you?'

'No, not a cold – but I tell you what—'

'What?'

'I've got a bloody big erection. I can see it now. It's sticking right out of my pyjamas, that's why I'm ringing – to tell you!'

I looked at my watch, it was ten past five. Was it worth being woken up at this hour to learn that Lionel was erotically aroused? Which part of his pyjamas might the prick be poking through? I'd place bets on the bottom button-hole.

'Yes, I'm sipping this brandy and reading in bed. These Reports are confoundedly confusing – then out of nowhere, your face appears – and you're bending to pick up a sweater, or something that's dropped to the floor. Do you remember, when you did that – when? A week last Tuesday? And you'd taken your tights off already? Do you remember?'

'I do remember.' I was growing sleepy. His voice was becoming excited. 'I'm holding it now, this erection. Because I remember exactly. You were wearing that beautiful dress, bright green. And you were wearing lots of rings, little tiny turquoise ones, and you'd painted all your fingernails to match. And as you bent over—' I stifled a yawn. 'As you bent over. Christ, my bloody prick might burst – I could see the bare backs of those beautiful thighs and all the dark hair of your bush. It really turned me on, do you remember? And I had to have you, I couldn't wait even to take off your dress – uh, uh—' His voice slowed down. 'Uh, uh! I think this is doing it! It is – by Jesus – I'm bloody coming – I'm coming, my darling, can you hear it?' I heard his gasp and strained for more, for the sound of a fountain, an oil-well erupting, a saucepan of milk boiling over. But all I could hear was the wash of the waves and the fish as they snoozed in whatever ocean lay between Lionel and me.

The next day was Saturday. Rather, that day was Saturday, this one – the one I was in. I lay in bed reflecting on that fact. Lionel's call had disturbed me, I couldn't drop off again, not completely. I hung instead on the numbing ledge that exists between sleep and half consciousness. My thoughts droned in depressing circles over what to do about Auntie. Would it perhaps not be better all round if we chose to ignore the theft? I could forage from my various accounts for five hundred pounds and just reimburse her. After all, why not for once let the guilty party off, the thief get away, the culprit escape? The poor bastard was, in a sense, just as much of a victim. It all evened out one way or another. I had plenty, and because I had, so had Auntie. A confrontation would serve no purpose except to create an atmosphere. The more I pondered, the more certain I became that this was the wisest course. In time, whoever it was who'd taken Auntie's money, might carelessly leave some clue. Inadvertently give themselves away. By then, though, we might not even be interested. Zen and the wisdom of Solomon. The Old Man, I felt, would have approved.

Around seven o'clock I could lie there no longer and got up to make myself coffee. Now might be the right time to test Bogey's bed, to see if he'd managed to stay dry.

He had. Good boy. His lashes fluttered, a small smile flickered over his face. As if even before he'd opened his eyes he could sense I was standing close. I studied his mouth, the bland curve of his lip. Did it resemble Brad's? Or could the chin be said to be nearer to the confident jut, say, of Rufus? And what about the soft grey eyes; when solemn didn't they look most like Stuffy's? But the hair, the mop of tight dark curls – the same as Lionel Striving's, only longer? Poor Nutty, the only one not on the list. And the only one of all my Gentlemen who genuinely did like children, who would have been overjoyed to have assumed the mantle of fatherhood. If I'd granted the honour to anyone.

Bogey woke up and from simple pleasure proceeded to wet the bed. Who of my lovers had the weakest bladder? Perhaps the parentage may be traced to that, wasn't it meant to run in families? Like pigeon-toes, and varicose veins, and warts and going prematurely grey. Though further conjecture was a waste of time – I'd never wished to know who the father was. It was enough that Bogey existed. He'd been granted to me by the group. A group baby. Like bulk buying – there was lashings of love to go round. And I had had no father figure whilst I was growing up, and hadn't seemed to suffer.

Bogey chuckled and wriggled around, increasing the width of absorption. I watched the advancing damp creep to the edge of the tiny bed. 'Naughty boy.' I tried hard to frown. His chuckling stopped. He sat up straight trying to gauge my reaction. 'Naughty,' I said and shook my finger, pointing at the sopping wet sheet. He looked down and laughed, then looked once more at me. I shook my head disapprovingly. His own small one now followed my action, copying it exactly so that we each of us must have resembled mandarins who communicate mainly by nodding.

I didn't smile, my eyes didn't soften, just the right degree of severity. Wasn't that how toilet training was supposed to be? Not too stern, not too much tension otherwise the problems occur in later life, wasn't that when they surfaced? Something to do with retention. The retention of turds, later translatable into the accummulation of possessions. Possessions and property and a general hoarding. I should have to watch it with Bogey. With the girls I'd never given it much thought, but they were never quite so incontinent. Or if they were I perhaps placed their dying father rather higher on my list of priorities.

Bogey was finally getting the message. His expression was heart-breaking to watch. The soft lower lip was starting to tremble, he puckered it up in a pale pink bunch like a tightly packed bouquet of rosebuds. At the top of his face his small forehead was knitting, converging in a criss-cross of scribbling lines above the pale smoky globes of his eyes. Rain clouds were starting to gather in these. As I blinked, he blinked. Tears fell. Just two of them first, then the others followed over the tight little scrunched-up shape of his cheeks. I couldn't bear it. I picked him up. 'There, baby! There, there it's all right!'

He flung his small hands around my neck and buried his head just beneath my left ear. I could feel the sleeve of my negligée, Hollywood Thirties from Portobello, dampening now like his bed. What did it matter? My little boy was cuddling up to his mother. Wasn't that one of the primary functions of Woman? To exude warmth when it was required?

He kissed my ear, I kissed his back. And then I kissed it again. And it was in this way entwined and embracing, exchanging our tokens of love, that Auntie arrived and discovered us.

She'd had a very good night's sleep, a full twelve hours in fact. 'What's the time then?' she asked, as bright as a button. Clearly the unpleasant events of yesterday would not impinge on today. Bogey, happily reinstated in my good books, cooed and stretched out to touch her. 'Hello, Bogey – and how's little boyo today? Oh, an accident, is it, in bed? Never mind, Auntie will change it now – or shall we have tea and toast first?' She turned to me enquiringly.

'The kettle's just boiled, but you go on down, Auntie. I'll just change Bogey, and look at the girls.'

'I've just looked, love. They're still both asleep.' She smiled. In her quilted dressing-gown, bright shiny purple with a waist-cord of curdling cerise, she put me in mind of a kind of tea-cosy. Rather risqué, and made in Hong Kong. But the comfortable countenance reassured, her cheeks looked like sweet orchard apples. I was sorely tempted to take a bite.

The thought must have transferred itself to Bogey, because now he was expressing the wish to be held by her and not me. What diplomacy and charm this child possessed. What a way he had of making all of us feel needed. 'Come to Auntie, then, now is it? Ooh, there's a boy you are! You dangle us all, you do!' Auntie took him and, tutting away, proceeded to take off his small, stretchy towelling sleeping-suit. His stomach curved smoothly in an egg-like shape, like a cupid, straight from his chin. And beneath the shell-like structure of his circumcision, the legs fell away, still with baby-folds of flesh at the top of his thighs. Before very long, the frame would emerge and he would begin to look more like a child instead of a cuddly doll. It had happened before, I'd seen it with Tallulah and Zsa-Zsa, hard bones replacing the softness. A magical metamorphosis. And soon, of course, the girls themselves would undergo another.

The subtle process of bodily change, of transformation into young women. I couldn't remember how mine had occurred. What had come first – under-arm hair? A shy down, anxiously studied, a shadow cast between the legs in the shape of a straggly triangle. And the sensation of sweating, I could recall that, of steaminess and sudden, inexplicable, lickety lubrications. It was as if a dry suburban house had turned into a damp sub-tropical cave.

'I'll wash him, I'll powder his little bots. We'll go and dry your dangle, won't we, Bogey—' I could hear Auntie musing away to herself and Bogey's answering chirrups as I went down the stairs to the kitchen. Had she forgotten completely, or what? Would the theft not be mentioned at all? I considered it carefully. This was all quite in character. Auntie had a built-in protection, whereby all that was deeply unpleasant to hear was deliberately put to one side. Not head in sand exactly, nor head in clouds – but something more child-like between the two. It was an enviable trait, it meant that she was more able to weather the storms of emotional and mental stresses. And in later years, I'd noticed she'd become even more of a safe, calm harbour despite several hazardous passages.

She came into the kitchen now, carrying a fresh, fragrant Bogey. 'There's a lovely day it is outside. Look at the sun, it's shining! Shall I take them out to the Park this morning? For a picnic and then to the Fair?' By Park, Auntie meant Battersea Park, the only park she acknowledged. Like shops and large stores, the less smart the better. She equated Hyde Park, say, with Harrods. And St James's with Fortnum and Mason, and Kensington Gardens was probably Simpson or possibly Debenham and Freebody. But Batterea Park, like Clapham Common and at a pinch perhaps Primrose Hill – they were more in the mass-production mould, the chain stores, the Tescos and Woolworths, and therefore earned her approval. And of course Battersea possessed the bonus of swings and roundabouts, the fairyland of Battersea Fair. It was hard to tell who enjoyed it more. Auntie or the children, their degree of delight was the same. At the mention of Fair, Bogey clapped both his hands.

Auntie had placed him in his high-chair, a childish throne which he refused to relinquish, battered by years of harsh monarchy but still surviving through the reigns of Tallulah and Zsa-Zsa. It had been re-painted several times in an effort to restore its appearance, but constant scratchings with small spoons and pushers had reduced the surface to a piebald effect of Pillar-box Red overlaying Leaf Green, which in turn overlaid Lemon Yellow.

Auntie considered it critically now, her hair-curlered head on one side. 'Am I to buy a bit of Fablon from Woolies and give this a nice new covering? Tartan, I thought for a bit of a change, though I might well be lucky and find Leopard-Skin.'

'Are they doing adhesive Leopard-Skin now? In plastic, I mean, by the sheet, Auntie?'

'Well.' Auntie looked vague. 'I don't know that they are, but they could be. I'll ask in the shops.' Her quest of the week, she enjoyed a good quest, a purpose, tracking down treasure.

'It could be quite smart, Leopard-Skin Fablon, for the restaurant I mean, on the tables.'

Auntie nodded. 'Nice and clean.' The reminder, restaurant, hadn't ruffled her sanguine approach to this sunny day. 'Are you going in there this morning? Are you doing the dinner? I can see to the girls and boy—'

I thought hard, I didn't quite know. Did they really require my presence at lunch-times? Zoë had decided to do it, to turn up in the mornings as well as the night for the welcome additional income. 'I'm saving up, you see, for some sort of decent holiday. Greece I'd thought, or maybe Tangiers, though I have a hankering for San Francisco. One of those cheap charter flights you can get that take off about two in the morning.' I'd warned her not to expect the same tips or even the same team of people. 'No, I know, Vince was saying they're miserable sods – the mid-dayers. But I don't mind. As long as you're paying me I may as well work. It keeps me off the streets – just.'

They could surely manage without me being there, then I'd go in this evening all fresh. Didn't my first and foremost duty and pleasure rest with my family?

I walked out to the garden to study the sky, to see if the sun would remain for the day. It glimmered through, clear and untrammelled by the traffic of gathering cloud formations. Promising hours of delight on the skin, the tinging of pink into biscuit, blushing pale flesh into beige.

'What about Brighton? Be there in two hours, if we wake up the girls and get going.'

'Brighton, oh Brighton!' Auntie beamed. If there was one place she enjoyed, it was Brighton. Even marginally more than Battersea Park and almost as much as her weekly treks over to Tescos at Brixton. 'What, driving do you mean? In the Rolls?'

'On the train, I think. That much quicker.' She tried not to show her disappointment over not going there in the Rolls, a nice chance now missed to bask in the admiration of the populace out on the prom. 'The Rolls is slow, Auntie. It would take us all day. Even going there in the Morgan is twice as long as taking the train. You want to be there as long as possible, don't you, to make it worth while?'

'I do. Yes, indeed. Will the shops be open, not half-day closing in Brighton on Saturday? There's a very good Woolworth's not far from the Clock Tower – we might find the Fablon we want.'

I'd ring Vincent up, I thought, from the station. At a little less ungodly hour. It was still only half past seven or so. He was having a lie-in this morning, sleeping till at least nine o'clock, so he'd planned. Not going to market for food. He and Dick had done all that yesterday. And in any case from what I could judge, our menu didn't require the refinements of fresh vegetables or daily sojourns to Smithfield and Billingsgate. I packed up our swimming costumes, including the one used by Auntie, her favourite, a two-piece covered in sea-horses interspersed with white spray. The bottom half was as big as her knickers, it reached to her knees like Bermuda shorts or a gentleman's Victorian swimsuit. The top had fierce reinforcements, ice-cream cone in shape like a fifties-style sweater girl. It cut Auntie's bosom in two so that in it she boasted four breasts before you even got to her midriff. 'Did you pack my bathing cap?' She wanted to know. Her bathing cap was actually a wig, a waterproof wig, an American Import from Peter Jones, pre-curled and pre-tested, and pretty. Very pretty in fact, the shade Auntie had chosen, a very pale platinum blonde. Curled up in the manner of early Mae West. Auntie wore it sometimes in the bath. She'd bought it in the depths of winter and as yet hadn't tried it out in public; this would be its first spring showing – her Easter bonnet.

Tallulah and Zsa-Zsa were very subdued, they'd stayed up late the night before, involved in a game of Monopoly. Tallulah had ended up owning Park Lane and all the adjoining properties, including the four major stations. But Zsa-Zsa had capital, more in the bank. The resulting friction had ended in blows, a physical fight all the way up the banisters. Tallulah's glasses were broken. She looked now at the world through a strip of clear Sellotape which Auntie had stuck over the cracked lens. Another small task for Monday morning, a further trip to Tallulah's Optician.

Zsa-Zsa had bitten her own lower lip, when a sharp right-hand swing aimed at her chin by Tallulah had trapped the lip in her long upper teeth. The gash almost, but not quite, needed stitches. They'd arrived down at breakfast like two wounded warriors; Bogey had found them most comical. His reaction in fact had so angered Zsa-Zsa that she'd bared her fierce teeth in a frightening snarl and had menacingly approached his high-chair, as if to inflict a similar wound on his quite undeserving person. But Auntie'd forestalled her. 'We're going to Brighton, Brighton Pier! On the beach, girls! And paddling – now eat up!' And she'd passed Zsa-Zsa's Weetabix straight into her hands, with the milk ready poured in the bowl.

They were all excited, though the girls couldn't show it. Zsa-Zsa claimed that it pained her to smile, and Tallulah had trouble selecting her clothes through suffering from multiple vision.

'Oh come on,' I said, 'it can't be that bad,' as she tried to get into her jeans. 'Put your leg here – in here!'

'Where? In there? Is that right?' She lunged one foot into my lap, losing her balance completely, almost tearing the denims in two. In the end she decided to wear a dress. The one she chose was long, to the ground, sprigged with daisies. It came with its own frilly pinafore. In it she looked like Little Bo-Peep. Peeping through a pair of cracked spectacles.

Zsa-Zsa was going in full riding kit, wearing jodhpurs that she'd swopped with a girl at school in exchange for a second-hand Scotch kilt. And the strange thing was that the jodhpurs suited her. There was really no need for the horse, Zsa-Zsa's own small profile was the perfect substitute. The blend of human and beast. We made a strange mix. The girls had dressed Bogey. He came as a carpenter's mate, in a set of minute striped dungarees, but with a tulle poke bonnet on his head. Auntie's touch. 'To protect his head and the back of his neck from the heat of the sun,' she'd explained. We didn't demur, it was scarcely a scorcher, not this early in the season. But Bogey was bedazzled by his poke bonnet, he couldn't get over the bow. And he knew it already; he'd seen it for years being worn by Tallu-lah's large teddy. The bear was about the same size as himself, a friendly but deaf and dumb buddy. Hugged to death, smoth-ered by love and now hatless into the bargain. The bow of the bonnet had been tied at the side as if on a grand box of choco-lates. It flopped from the level of Bogey's ear, obliterating a full half of his face. He peeped over it teasingly like a Gaiety Girl, with the air of an innocent flirt.

Auntie had foraged and managed to find a very old pair of Clarks sandals. The flat sort with a tee-strap sported by Boy Scouts and cross-country hikers. She wore them with her thick lisle stockings and a pair of fluorescent pink ankle socks rolled very low over the ankle in the manner of golfing ladies. She felt the sandals to be more suitable for shingle than her usual bed-room slippers. She wore what appeared to be an Institution dress but was actually an Orderly's overall from a Uniform Specialist shop that she'd chanced on along the Edgware Road.

They'd all of them groaned when I'd appeared in my jeans.

'Is that what you're wearing!' They'd pointed. 'But this is an outing – a special event!' I'd been forced to go back and change, and now emerged as a cricketing umpire, in white from head to toe. As unsuitable for a trip on a grimy train as anything any of them were wearing. They chorused their approval.

We drove in the Rolls to Victoria Station. Two exhausted Champagne bottles lay in the back still, and countless stubbed-out cigarette ends as evidence of last night's carousings between poor old Nutty and Stuffy.

I parked off Buckingham Palace Road, just at the Brighton train platform. 'Stay here, all you lot,' I ordered. 'Don't move. Auntie, keep your eyes on them. I'll run round and get the tickets.' The train was in, we'd arrived on the hop, not knowing what time it went.

'If you run quick, Missus, you might catch this. It's due out in under five minutes.' The ticket collector smiled at me with a special degree of sympathy. People often did that when I was out with my lot, as if they were not quite all there, and I was the kindly Voluntary Worker who was taking them out for the day. I ran. The crowds parted, the people sprang back at this pristine fluid white figure fleeing a would-be assailant. I barged in at the top of the ticket queue. 'Do you mind very much — two tickets, three halves to Brighton, oh yes, please — all Day Returns!' Then, 'So sorry!' I gasped to the rest of the queue. 'But my train, it's just leaving you see!' Theirs might just as well have been leaving too, I afterwards thought guiltily.

Telephoning Vincent was out of the question, we just managed by seconds to board the train. We did so despite Auntie's flapping Clarks sandal. She'd stored them so long, some twenty-two years, that in daylight they were deteriorating fast. 'It's the sun, I expect it's melting the rubber, it can have that effect — we've done it in school. In science—' Tallulah expounded. 'No, it's not, not the sun — it's the storage—' Zsa-Zsa rejoindered. Auntie's feet fell apart. Not completely but almost, they joined at the heels, soles and uppers. Each time that she lifted her legs in a step she left half her footwear behind. I bundled the kids in and then hauled her up.

'It's going,' she wailed.

'I know, Auntie. Come on, you must hurry, he's waving his flag—'

'It's gone now, my sole – I can feel it.' The guard slammed the door, barely missing her skirt. She hung on me heavily. 'Oh dear, there's a do. It's dropped off – look, see, from the window.'

I squeezed past her whoofing and phewing figure, and poked my head out of the window. As the train gathered speed and curved out of Victoria, the small shape became smaller and smaller. The shrivelled sole of her old Clarks sandal already collecting dust.

Much of the journey down was spent in to-ing and fro-ing from the buffet. I'd forbidden that Bogey should have anything to drink. The girls supplied him instead with nuts. He was sneezing them out through his nose. Zsa-Zsa held one up. 'Look at this – it's been in and come out, exactly the same!'

'It could be different.' Tallulah looked serious. 'Bogey may carry a collection of nuts up at the top of his nose. Like a camel with water, couldn't he, Mum? And be firing them like little cannon-balls.'

'Don't be silly,' Zsa-Zsa said shortly. 'You say stupid things.'

'I'm stretching my imagination. You're meant to do that, aren't you Mum—'

Auntie was listening with interest. 'Not tell lies though, Tallulah, not fibs, I don't think.'

'Well, Auntie, it's quite hard to tell the difference.'

'It isn't.' Zsa-Zsa had decided to argue.

'Yes it is,' Tallulah joined in.

''S'not, so there!'

''Tis, 'cos I know. And you don't!'

'Do!'

'Don't!'

'Yes!'

'No!'

I put my hands over my ears. Bogey laughed and did the same, first lifting one hand of Auntie's to show that she should too. We sat there like a trio of monkeys. I'd had a small brass trio once. Hear No Evil. See No Evil. And Speak No Evil. Perhaps not exactly in that order, and we weren't the same as them, we were all the Hear No. Tallulah and Zsa-Zsa stopped abruptly.

'Sorry, Mum,' they each said in turn.

'That's all right. Let's be nice though, the rest of the day. It's depressing to hear all that quarrelling.'

They fell silent and started to look out of the window, and before very long were engrossed again in intense and whispered discussion. But this time on far friendlier lines. That's how it went with those two. Auntie was playing happily with Bogey, This Little Piggy Went To Market, with his fingers as well as his toes. She'd removed his small plimsolls and spotted blue socks in order to play the game properly. Her own plump toes curled up and out of the tattered remains of her sandals. Our first task on arrival at Brighton was the purchase of suitable shoes. I knew perfectly well which ones she'd choose. The beach shoes in transparent plastic. The sort they sell specially for shingly shores. As flat as her Clarks and her slippers. A day of delights stretched before us in Brighton. I shut my eyes, and arrived there still sleeping.

The first thing I did was, of course, to ring Vincent. He answered the phone right away.

'Hello, Vince!'

'Oh, it's you.' I thought he sounded disappointed.

'Yes, were you expecting someone else?' I could hear his hesitation. Oh dear, an emotional matter? Another affair of the heart?

'I was expecting, yes, as a matter of fact. Look darling, let me ring you back.'

'Well, Vince, I'm in Brighton—'

'Who with? How bizarre!'

'With the kids, and with Auntie. To take her mind off the money, you know. Just for the day, is that all right? Can you manage?'

I don't know why I was feeling so guilty. He didn't answer for a moment. And then he said as if thinking carefully, 'What a terribly good idea. No confrontation this morning then?'

'No confrontation at all. I think I shan't bother, we won't get

165

it back. It would just cause a lot of embarrassment. I shall give it, the money, to Auntie myself—'

'You're a saint—'

'No I'm not.' I looked out of the telephone kiosk window towards Auntie and the three children. People were turning in an amused fashion to stare at their odd attire. Auntie's socks were so shockingly pink that they seemed to light up the whole station. Her sandal uppers were still strapped to her ankles. I could see a policeman approaching.

'Oh, Vincent – I'd best go I think! There's a copper accosting old Auntie. I'll see you tonight – be about seven I should think. Is that O.K.?'

It was hardly a question, I didn't wait to see if it was O.K. or not, but put the phone down hurriedly just catching his 'Have a good day!' I could see Auntie's bewildered expression in the face of the policeman's first words. Tallulah had taken it upon herself to answer him. She was turning now and pointing in my direction. The policeman followed her fingers with his eyes.

'Can I help you?' I said, approaching. He regarded me with respect, as his gaze flickered over my finery. My whites had survived the grime of British Rail remarkably well. In the dingy gloom of Brighton Station I might have been Isadora Duncan dressed for a day at Deauville.

The policeman now appeared to be tugging his forelock. Or was he merely scratching his forehead? 'All in order, Miss.' He spoke flatly, with old-fashioned formality and a very strong Sussex accent. 'I thought for a moment that this little lot were lost, but I can see that they're clearly in good hands.'

Auntie had recovered her composure and confided, 'We're off to the sea-front for a paddle.' The policeman bent and tweaked Bogey's cheek. 'Will this little lady be paddling?' Bogey's bonnet was sadly skew-whiff so that now the bow sat high up on his ear, and he looked like a beribboned debutante at her first dance. Zsa-Zsa giggled, she'd been put in charge of his collapsible push-chair. It lay still folded at her feet. I picked it up, it unfurled like a brolly, striped nylon, clear red and white. Bogey started jigging and swinging his arms to show that he wanted

166

to sit in. He looked like a baby chimpanzee, like the ones they dress up for television commercials.

The policeman bent from his waist again. 'Let me help the little lady into her chariot.' And he picked the writhing Bogey clean off the ground and manoeuvred him unsuccessfully into the push-chair. He sat uncomfortably, two little round legs squashed into the hole meant for one.

Zsa-Zsa continued to giggle. Tallulah blinked up at the policeman. 'That's all wrong. He doesn't go that way.' Bogey stared down at his legs, mystified. It was time to be moving on. Passers-by were beginning to linger, intrigued as crowds are by the sight of others engaged in confab with policemen. A curiosity not untinged with malice, the hope that someone else is getting it in the neck, being found out, landing in a whole load of trouble.

Tallulah brutally tugged one of Bogey's small knees, trying to bend the whole leg back up double. He screamed. The sound was high and clear like the top note of a soprano. He held it inordinately long as if he'd embarked on an aria.

'Bloody hell, some people don't deserve to have children! Look, the Law has arrived. Damn good thing. Who are they anyway, an odd-looking crew — gipsies d'you suppose?' The voice seemed immediately behind me. I swiftly picked up Bogey and replaced him correctly. We moved, all five of us, away from the scene and majestically out of the station.

We took a taxi from the station to the nearest shoe shop, on the way passing a store that sold sports clothes.

'They've got shoes, look there! Those are shoes in the window, lace-up ones.'

'They're for football, Auntie,' I said.

'They look strong enough,' Auntie persisted.

'Not for walking though, Auntie.'

'Why not, nice long laces.' Once a notion took root, Auntie could sometimes turn stubborn.

'They've got studs underneath—'

'You could saw them,' she said. We'd arrived now at a quite

normal shoe shop, double-fronted, with plenty to choose from. The taxi slowed down. 'Will this do? Shall I stop?'

'Thank you, driver. This seems to be perfect. We're here, Auntie.' Her whole face lit up. 'Freeman, Hardy and Willis!' she exclaimed. 'Oh good, I prefer them to Dolcis.'

The buying of the shoes took over an hour and a half by the time Tallulah and Zsa-Zsa had decided they should have some as well. Bogey fell asleep in his push-chair, a boiled sweet bulging out of one cheek. The motherly assistant had given it to him; he'd enslaved her with one of his smiles. Auntie had bought the exact shoes which I'd predicted, the very pair of transparent plastic.

'Now, my dear, that's all settled. You've got your beach sandals, now how about a pair of nice shoes to go on top of those lovely pink socks? My choice, personally speaking, would be red. I always think pink and red go lovely together, a real treat!' The assistant beamed, she'd taken to Auntie. 'Do you ever wear heels, dear? No? Well now, that seems a shame. They do lengthen the leg, you know, heels. Here, just try on these – the shade's called Carnation. You prefer the Fire Engine Red? Well, isn't that strange, because I do myself! But not everyone understands colour. They think we old souls should be dowdy and grey, them dark browns, all them fawns – I can't stand them. You're like me, dear, you go for the bright. Well, you have to. It keeps you so cheerful.'

Auntie agreed, she kept nodding her head. Whilst she nodded, the assistant slipped on the shoes, then stood up and taking Auntie by the hand, she led her like a child to the mirror. I was quite amazed. These were the first high-heels Auntie had ever had on.

'Gosh, they're great, Auntie!'

'You look taller! Are you having them? Oh do, they look lovely!'

Bogey was still awake at that stage; he regarded the proceedings with rapture. Auntie chose to refer to him for the final judgement. 'What do you think then, Bogey – boyo?' He clapped his hands in approval, as enchanted by bright colour as

Auntie herself. She studied the mirror reflection. 'Well, I have to say they feel strange. Will I be able to actually walk?' she asked anxiously. Her feet were slightly pigeon-toed, but the fact of the heels was forcing her now to stand in a different way. To splay the foot at a different angle, outward instead of in. She took a few uncertain steps.

'That's it, dear,' the assistant encouraged. 'You'll get the hang of it, in no time at all. And when you do, you mark my words — you'll throw away all your old flatties. Won't she though?'

By the time we emerged, as Auntie announced, it was well after opening time. I had managed, by a mulish determination, to resist the sales lady's advances. She would've very much liked to complete the full set by selling to me and to Bogey. But Bogey was by then fast asleep. I'd suggested that it seemed a shame at this point to disturb him.

The other three were all wearing their purchases. Tallulah's striped baseball boots looked strange with her sprigged gown and pinafore. But possibly not as outlandishly odd as Zsa-Zsa's striped boots did with her jodhpurs. Auntie, entranced by her feminine feet, was very afraid of falling. I suggested she push Bogey's pram for support. She did so, staring spellbound at her shoes. I could see the crash coming, but was unable to swerve Auntie or the push-chair in time.

'Can't you look where you're going!' Auntie'd managed a head-on collision with a large collie dog and its owner. 'So sorry!' I said, hurrying on, holding Auntie's arm with one hand and steering the pram with the other.

Auntie decided she could do with a drink. The children wanted to go on the Palace Pier.

'We can do both then, you can drink on the Pier. In the bar at the end—'

'By the Ghost Train!' the girls clamoured. 'Can we go on the Ghost Train today?' We saw them in, Bogey squeezed tight between them. They had money for more than one trip. 'I'd like to stay on all morning!' I heard Zsa-Zsa confide.

Auntie chose to start with a lager, following my example.

Just a half. It wouldn't have done to get too drunk on a day like today.

'What a lovely day indeed we're having.' She smiled and beamed round the bar. We'd sat in the window in order to watch when the children emerged from the Ghost Train. I could see in the distance the coastline of Sussex curve round the cliffs of Rottingdean. And, closer, I could see the seafront of Brighton itself, iced white like a wedding cake spiced with pale fondants. And in the middle I could see the Hotel. The Grand Hotel, the first Grand Hotel that I'd ever slept in. And the first time too that I'd been to Brighton or been away anywhere with The Old Man.

'I shall take you,' he'd said, 'for a dirty week-end. People will know perfectly well what we're up to. I shall take you from Friday, returning Sunday, to Brighton where everyone goes. It's tremendous fun going down on the train and coming back with the same couples. One's able to detect the subtle changes that the week-end has wrought in relationships. I shall teach you how you can tell.'

And he had. He'd pointed them out to me, travelling down and then travellling back. One pair in particular stayed in my mind, the man was so obviously married, and the girl so obviously not. They'd held hands on the Friday, he'd kept kissing her ear, she'd wriggled seductively close to him. But on Sunday they sat separately, not side by side, but stiffly opposite each other. And she'd yawned whenever he started to speak and was consulting her watch all the time.

'What will you do this evening?' he'd asked her bleakly.

'I shall go out, of course,' she answered. 'And what will you do, watch television, with your wife?' she'd cruelly added.

Their week-end had quite obviously not been a success. The Old Man had smiled into my eyes. I'd smiled back with no worries at all about ours. It was the week-end we'd fallen in love.

I hadn't been certain up until then, I'd found the sheer difference between us divisive. Not just of the age, but of outlook as well. All this knowledge and my limiting ignorance. The formidable force of his life's experience humbled me into servility. It was not his intention to cause this effect; before Brighton he was quite unaware that this was the case. Before Brighton I was still inarticulate and shy. Before Brighton I still dreaded my periods.

I'd been with The Old Man for just on three weeks when he'd suggested our week-end in Brighton. I'd taken my Personal Pocket Diary, a self-present from Smith's, to the bathroom. It contained, in its binding, a slim, gold-tipped pencil. The tip to prevent it from being lost. I eased it out, and leafed through the pages. My periods were due That Week-end!

Three days to go, and each day, every hour I tried hard to break the bad news. But as each opportunity presented itself by a silence in our mutual accord, or a moment of vacant emotion, or a chink which could have been filled, I shuddered away, I just couldn't.

If it should start, the curse – how aptly called – as we approach Brighton Promenade, I would divert his attention to the other direction. And slyly slide into the sea. 'The girl has gone! She's not here any more!' I could hear his loud roar of alarm. And he'd trace my path with his keen hawk-like eyes over the trail of fresh blood till he came to the edge of the sea.

It started, it must have, going up in the lift, the opulent lift of the Grand. I'd known because I'd slipped into the Ladies Powder Room to avoid the embarrassment as The Old Man signed us in. 'Mr and Mrs Cecil Clotworthy! That seems a good enough name to choose. Where can we be from – Chipping Norton?' The Old Man had chuckled to himself. And that had been just before the luxurious ascent to our suite. It was all clear then, not a spot to be seen, the slide upwards must have started it off.

Our suite boasted a brilliant sea-view. I crossed the room to the window, drawn as if by a magnet, like all children are by the powerful pull of such a vast amount of water. And not merely static stuff at that, but the relentless and fearful life-force that oceans contain. The Old Man had followed me silently, I could sense the bulk of him near. He came closer and lifted a wing of my hair and slid an insidious tongue in my ear, then stood back.

'These ears are like sea-shells, a cliché,' he said. 'But certainly true in your case. You are a creature of the deep. The sea is female, she claims her victims. You two have much in common. And, too, those accumulative waves resemble the womb in a sense. It's understandable why men in frail and destructible craft are drawn to return again and again knowing that death may await. The meaning is deeper than mere economy.'

I felt myself seizing up at his words. Did he wish for a deeper discussion? I swallowed hard, I didn't know then that he expected no such thing. Nor ever did in fact. Not from me or from anyone else. He thought aloud; it was simply that he pursued his own reasoning logic. During the years I accepted all this, and ceased to worry when sometimes at night I would wake to his voice next door in his study debating aloud with himself.

'Are you cold, child?' The Old Man lifted my hand, it seemed as blue as the sea. That must have been quick, the sudden withdrawal of blood from my outer extremities. The swift results of my seizing up?

'Not cold, no I'm not. It's lovely and warm in this room.' I glanced around shyly. 'It's nice and big.' Then faltered. 'Is that the bathroom?'

The door had no lock, rather bad I thought, that: you'd think money might buy some privacy. The Honeymoon Suite, The Old Man had said. Was this how honeymooners behaved then? Completely abandoned and able to walk in and out as the mood and curiosity caught them? Stephen and I had had no honeymoon, but apart from getting dressed up together, we were both highly circumspect regarding each other's toiletries. I'd never seen him swilling himself, nor he me. Our privates were private. Which made the discovery of his corpse that more shocking. I'd never seen him before in the bath.

I knew what to expect, before I took down my knickers, but the scarlet gout still shocked. I stared down at it dully. Small clouds of pain were starting to ache in the curve of my spine, my legs felt as leaden as water-logged pillows. My lower lip started to quiver. Would we go back? Would we catch the next train, our dirty week-end a fiasco? Would The Old Man start scolding for wasting his time, or simply sustain a cold silence? It was my fault, I knew perfectly well that this clearly was what would of course happen. Now all that was left was confession. I swallowed hard, it was quite difficult, there was a tennis ball stuck in my throat where my Adam's Apple had only just been.

As I stood there, in shock, a further spurt as if from a faulty faucet bubbled brightly through my long pubic hair. It was time, I reflected, for a trim. After all, pubic hair just like privet hedges looked better when pruned up a bit.

'What on earth are you up to?'

The Old Man held me by the shoulders, we were both tall but he was much taller. Blood trickled quite swiftly, like a thin mountain stream, down the inside of both my thighs.

'Glorious gore! Well, thank God for that! Quite a relief – I'd really begun to think that this old boy might quite well have inadvertently impregnated you, child! Next week, when this is over, this sweet menstruation. I shall organize safe contraception, my little one. You must forgive me for not having done so already. But I couldn't be sure until this period had come. Take a bath, I shall call for champagne!'

Auntie had already drunk up her half. 'More lager, love? Shall I get it? Or will you?' Her cheeks were already pink with excitement.

'Not another, I don't think, Auntie. Do you? We'll probably eat before very long, you know. A nice lunch—'

'Oh, some wine—' Auntie brightened, my denial of lager had disappointed.

'Well, why not champagne?' The Old Man's memory still lingered at the back of my mind. Auntie brightened still further.

'Oh, well then, we'll go.' She stood up a little unsteadily, the fault of her footwear and the unfamiliarity of wearing high-heels, rather than the effects of her half. An extremely old fisherman, like the Ancient Mariner, stared with what seemed like approval and gave a strange bird sound high up in his nose before taking a puff on his pipe. As we passed him in walking towards the door, I could have sworn that one hooded eye winked. Not at me, but at Auntie who'd moved on ahead. It was certainly the first time in my living memory that I'd seen Auntie arouse a man's interest.

She wanted, she said, to eat at English's.

'Oysters at English's, it's just taken my fancy. I've never been there, have I, before?' Auntie frowned in the effort to remember. She hadn't, she'd always when offered the choice chosen under the Pier. Or fish and chips straight from the paper. Or Wimpys, or The Golden Egg. Why then this sudden switch of Auntie's? Could her new shoes have made such a difference?

Tallulah and Zsa-Zsa were alone at the Ghost Train.

'Where's Bogey?'

'He's inside.'

'What? Alone?'

'Not alone,' Zsa-Zsa answered baring her teeth. 'With the ghosts.'

'He's perfectly safe.' Tallulah looked serious. 'We tied him, you see, with the bows of his bonnet. He won't fall. Look, here he comes now, the car's coming out!'

I looked with concern at the Ghost Train Exit. The push-to gates were opening out, the front of the heavy vehicle emerged. Bogey sat, strapped and stuffed like young poultry, high up in the second compartment. On seeing us his small round dazed face broke into a smile of pure sunshine. His dimples bored deep into each of his cheeks. His eyes became slits in his happiness, they glinted like splinters of flint. The reproaches I'd formed on my tongue towards Tallulah and Zsa-Zsa's gross cruelty – those reproaches died still unsaid. There probably wasn't anything much that could swerve Bogey's unerring nature. He was born to be pleased and unsullied and safe, in the same mould as Auntie, but smaller.

I rang English's Oyster Bar from the telephone kiosk.

'Best to ring first and book a table. They might not accept us otherwise. As it is, even with booking, they could turn us away at the door.' I thought it wisest to prepare for the worst.

Auntie became highly indignant. 'Not accept us? Well, why not?'

Tallulah was matter-of-fact in her reaction. 'Unsuitably dressed,' she said briefly as if the matter of whether we got in or not was of minimal importance.

We all looked at each other critically. Auntie, perhaps, looked most eccentric. Mine was high glamour, with a theatrical twist. And the children were just fancy-dress and amusing. A snooty head-waiter might tolerate them, permitting his own self-indulgence, but the two girls and myself could see without saying that Auntie presented a problem.

We made our way slowly from the Pier, past Old Steine and through to the corner of East Street. 'Ughavee, Jaegers,' Auntie said crossly.

'Let's look in the window.' An idea had formed in my mind, but it had to be carefully presented. 'Just for a laugh—'

The window featured a flowing cape in a gloriously sharp tangerine; whoever had dressed it had certainly known a thing or two about window-display. And more than that, an eye for colour that even Auntie couldn't fault. 'Well, I never, my goodness. Who would have guessed!' The girls pressed their noses on the glass and misted it up with their breath, in order to write their initials. Bogey leaned from his push-chair to do the same. Auntie was completely entranced, not just by the cape, but also what went with it. My plan might possibly work.

The cape was artfully arranged to reveal enough of the patterned robe underneath, a rococo print based on old wallpaper, a jungle of riotous roses. Pink ones, crimson, scarlet, puce and a particularly singing yellow, which was picked out tonally by the tangerine cape and the choice of small beads round the neck, and as well by the slick matching beret.

'It's nice,' I said, 'Auntie?'

'It is. How much is it? I can't see the price. Is it there?' She peered through the glass. Beneath us the children had managed to fog up the width of the window. 'Don't do that girls; no, Bogey, be a good boy – we're just about to go in here.'

'Are we, love?' Auntie looked very uncertain.

'We are.' I dismissed her reluctance.

'But they won't have my size—' Her voice wavered and fell.

'They go up to Size 16, I think even more. Besides these sort of clothes always fit, cloaks and capes – the fit's unimportant. And the same with the dress, see, it's more of a Grecian tunic—'

'I don't look too fat? You're sure now, you'd say?'

'You look gorgeous,' we all chorused in turn. The cape was too long, and so was the gown. Both were meant to end lower mid-calf. But on Auntie they reached down right to her ankles, leaving just room to show her new shoes. The pink socks, though much brighter, picked out the pink rose, and fought fiercely with the brave cape. But it didn't matter, the whole thing was so brilliant, like a walking herbaceous border or a Woolworths seed packet of bright, dashing dahlias. Auntie's face glowed a pretty pink pearl. She still looked eccentric, but reminded me now of marvellous Margaret Rutherford who I'd once seen in Pall Mall, flying along in a similar cloak, covered in amber.

They placed us downstairs in the Oyster Bar, in the Banquet facing the door. So that when people came in they could instantly see us. It was like being on permanent show.

Auntie was thrilled; we studied the menu, as everyone else studied us.

'Do you mind if I smoke?' Auntie asked the next table, lighting up before the man there could answer.

'Not at all, madam, no. Here, allow me to light you.' Auntie's match was refusing to strike. The man arose and flicked his lighter, his eyes flickering warmly to me. I smiled. He smiled back.

'There's nice, ooh, that's kind. The silly old matches must be damp. I'm hopeless with lighters, I have them, then I lose them—'

The man dropped his lighter in her hand and enclosed her fingers around it. 'A small present,' he said smoothly.

'But—' Auntie was astounded.

'No buts, madam. My pleasure, I assure you. And if you

should lose this one in your usual fashion, it's hardly a tragedy
– the lighter is only a throw-away one, an inadequate offering
in exchange for your brightening my view.'

Auntie couldn't get over her gift. 'It's like Christmas today.'
She glanced down. 'Shall I tell him that we've got a restaurant
as well? Why not write down the address, in case he's passing?'

'What, passing from Brighton? He probably lives here. Not
everyone goes up to London.' Tallulah had decided to join with
the adults and give us the benefit of her opinion. 'In any case,
he'd probably consider Mum's restaurant to be pretty rotten,
compared to this I mean.' She glanced round. 'Look at that!' A
waiter near by was engrossed in a flambé, pouring Brandy and
making it burn. 'Could you do that? Could Soc or Ari? Could
Zoë, could Vince, do you think?' Tallulah's tenacity could be
very tiring.

'No. Now, decide what you want.' Her questioning reminded
me of what I'd forgotten amazingly enough, yes – the restaurant! I looked at my watch. Half-past one. How were they
doing?

'How are they doing, do you think?' Auntie said.

'That's funny, that's just what I was wondering.'

'There's a name for that – Extra Sensory something,' Tallulah
stated importantly. 'We've done it at school.'

'That's something different, that's not the same thing.' It
was Zsa-Zsa's plan now to quarrel.

'It is the same, so there!' Tallulah flared quickly.

'No, it's not.'

'Yes, it is, so shut up. There, take that!' Tallulah lifted her
fork like a spear, ready to impale Zsa-Zsa's left thumb. Auntie
just managed to move it in time and the fork fell to the floor
with a twang.

'Allow me.' The man from the next table bent swiftly to
retrieve the fork. His gaze had barely left our small group since
Auntie had last exchanged words. 'Waiter!' He raised his voice
imperiously, subtly stressing their difference in station. If fate
had been different, I found myself thinking, the roles might
have well been reversed. The hurrying waiter was about the

same age. 'Sir?' he said in a tone of respect. The man lifted the fork. 'A fresh one of these.' 'Certainly, sir! I am so sorry! Of course, I shall bring it at once!'

'Christ Almighty, he'd have been lucky here not to get a boot right up his bum!'

'Whose bum? What are you saying?' Zoë swayed in. She was late arriving this evening.

Vincent enlightened her. 'We're talking,' he said, 'about the wonderful restaurant she went to, down in Brighton. Dick was saying this guy who was bollocking the waiter would've had a big boot up the bum if he'd spoken like that to one of us!'

'It's not the same though,' I chimed in quickly. 'We're amateurs—'

'I'm not,' Dick said sourly.

They'd all been there already, except Zoë that is, when I'd arrived. They'd all been in there slaving. Midday had been hell. They might not do it again, it was just too miserable for words. Soc and Ari had welcomed me with deep grunts of relief and high squeals of unparalleled pleasure. 'You no go again? Is terrible here, you no here and that Dick he come bossin'! He hit my head with a box of eggs—' Soc couldn't get it out quick enough. 'And then he spill oil and I slip and I fall, see here bad, bad graze on my elbow—'

'You happy, boss lady? Your Auntie, she fine?' Ari interrupted Soc's hysterical saga. I had come dressed in black. He had clearly mistaken it as an indication of mourning and grief.

'She's fine, yes of course. She's at home, she's quite well,' I reassured Ari and glanced at them all. Vince stood with his face to the wall.

No one looked ashamed at the mention of Auntie – after all any one of them could have caused her a coronary.

Vince continued to study what it was he was facing. 'We're full up,' he said. 'Every seat's taken. From eight until twelve – no free tables at all. Look, it's here on this seating arrangement. Their names and everything, how long they should stay, when I'll ask them to go – what do you think?'

There were several familiar names on the chart, including Stuffy and Nutty, I saw. And also a note: 'Rufus rang.'

'When did he ring?' I wanted to know. Dick had taken the call.

'I dunno, what's it matter? He rang that was all. I told him you were off with some geyser—'

'You said what, Dick?' I demanded.

He shrugged. 'Eh, what? You heard!'

'Why say that when it wasn't even true?'

He grinned and turned what had just looked like a sneer into a smile full of mischievous cunning. 'Well, perhaps not this time but it might have been. We're two of a kind, me and you. It takes one to recognize one, they say! Box clever, you'll get round poor old Rufus—'

I ignored his attempt at intimate charm, though I could see it might well work with others. 'Did he say he'd come in tonight?'

'There's no room if he does, darling.' Vince sailed past as I asked Dick the question. 'Not a single seat left. Really, your lovers will have to learn to organize themselves if they wish to see you. I've put Stuffy and the nauseous Nutty both together as they've requested. But is that wise? I didn't know they even knew each other.'

'Nor did I, not until last night.' Was it only last night that I'd seen them? And was it only this morning that Lionel had made his cock-in-hand call from New York? 'Lionel rang, Lionel Striving, from the States, at about five o'clock this morning. You remember him, Vince—'

'I do indeed, darling. What did he want at five in the morning?'

'A wank I believe, but one in my hearing.'

The menu tonight was the same as before, but with several slight refinements. 'Hot sossage roles' replaced 'Cold Pork Pie'. And 'Corned Beef Fritters' came instead of 'Cauliflour cheese'.

'What's this here, Dick? I can't make it out—' And I couldn't. The word had been crossed out three times until now there was hardly space on the crowded, rewritten menu to barely decipher a thing. It looked like a lavatory wall. The sort of graffiti done by under-fives, as badly spelt and confused.

'That? Oh, that's 'Bubbole and Scweek,' Dick replied.

'No, Dick – there – what's that word?' I asked. Vince bent forward to take a guess, as Zoë came up to join in too.

'It's "Riddles",' Vince said.

'No, it's not! No, it's – "Noodles",' Zoë declared.

Dick frowned. He was having as much trouble as us. 'It's – it's "Rissoles",' he finally announced.

'Rissoles? Spelt "Rizholes"! You'd have fooled me!' Zoë struck home with a vengeance. 'You're dyslectic, Dick, surely! Completely word blind, I swear it. Your spelling is out of this world—'

'So's your snout!' Dick said cruelly. 'What happened, darlin', did the surgeon slip with his scissors?'

Vincent intervened. 'Oh, don't be so childish, you two. Zoë, get ready. There's still all the tables to lay. And the candles to light.' He turned to me. 'We're using candles instead of these lights – better, darling. The lighting's atrocious in here – it puts ten years on before you've bent over! Last night I felt ancient, I honestly did, and there's nothing like candle-light for flattery.'

'There's complete darkness in your case. That would be an improvement.' Vince looked cut to the quick at Dick's deliberately wounding words. We could have done with old Auntie and her brand of sane wisdom. I stepped in.

'A small drink first, I suggest – to start our second night off with a nice swing!'

Zoë confided afterwards that it was the first thing all day she'd allowed to pass through her lips. 'I'm not only saving, I'm slimming as well. Two pounds I've lost since this morning. I think all that rushing at lunchtime lost one. I hope to lose one more this evening!'

Stuffy had called in on her late last night. 'Completely arse-holed of course! And he fell asleep when his face touched the pillow – but—' Her expression softened at the memory. 'It was great in the middle of the night. Except he kept muttering that I seemed much plumper. I think he thought I was someone else.' A thread of disappointment ran through her last words. But then she brightened and added, 'I don't care though. I don't really honestly mind that much whoever he thought I might be. I shall get him in the end, I'm quite sure – simply by being around.' I looked at her. Was she in love? Was she simply a 'one-man woman' as those stories I'd read in my teens used to say? Suggesting subtly that this was the best. And yet of course that's what I'd been both with Stephen and The Old Man. But he'd grown sad and concerned, The Old Man, towards the end over my love and loyalty. 'I appreciate your fidelity, child—' Still 'child', though by then I'd borne two. 'But I question the right of any human to demand such sacrifice from another. My body fails me, it is no longer capable of arousing or satisfying your own. And you are at your peak and will be for years. It's the waste that is more appalling, even than my constant frustration.' And he'd turned his tear filled eyes to the sheet to hide his deep and obvious distress. The situation was unfamiliar. He was Knowledge and Strength. I was Ignorance. He'd been teacher and tutor to my student so long that the reversal of roles seemed impossible. And yet it happened. In those last few years, from the time he'd become totally bedridden, I emerged as the sexual leader.

'Is it permitted,' I'd enquired of the undertaker, 'to place personal possessions in the coffin?'

'Not only permitted, but indeed quite customary,' he had assured me gravely, then adding, 'providing, of course, the possessions in question are in scale and in keeping with the width of the coffin. We cannot accommodate three-piece suites or more than a full suit of clothing.' He had allowed himself a thin smile at his jest, more a maiden aunt than a man.

He would not have approved the possessions. I placed them carefully under the pillow, beneath The Old Man's great head. We'd spoken of it before his death. 'I'd like to be buried with these,' he'd one night announced. 'Just like this, just under my pillow. The idea amuses me that in years to come when they dig up my withered remains, scholars and wisemen will be scratching their scalps trying to figure out what these things are. Should one label them, do you suppose, '*Prosthetic with scrotum for simulated ejaculation – price £16.50 inc. V.A.T.?*' He had stroked the soft beautifully modelled male genitals that I'd helped to strap on his frail body. A narrow tube led from the tip to the hollow scrotum behind, which was now at this moment filled up with warm water for 'Realistically Simulated Ejaculation' to occur. It was The Old Man's favourite toy. Along with my Angel's Delight. 'A New Treat for the Ladies', the pamphlet had read. 'You have had the Vibrator and the Love Eggs – now the two are combined in one erotic package. Complete with tiny motor, batteries and strength-tested lead. This ultra-smooth beautifully moulded pleasure egg is the ultimate delight. The vibrations can be controlled to your own desire.' I'd ordered both, through the post, out of interest. The climactic cock to see if it worked – and the Angel's Delight, for its name. 'Take off your clothes!' The Old Man had commanded. "Or better still, no, keep them all on. And sit like that with your legs apart. Just slip the egg in past your knickers. I like to see the flex emerging, it's as if you'd devoured a rat – sucked it, straight in, unmercifully between those strong labiae of yours.'

The sight had excited him, so he claimed, as much as anything since he had loved me. His one regret was that we'd left it so late. How our sex life would have benefited before! I'd smiled at his enthusiasm and had moved in much closer, the Angel's Delight in my vagina. 'Would you care to control my vibrations?' I said, and offered him the small switched-on motor. He twiddled the knob. 'This knob twiddling suits me – it is so reminiscent of your nipple. Would you unbutton your blouse, child, and pass me one breast – we could embark on a fine duo-action!'

I hadn't expected to become so aroused, it seemed years since I had felt quite like this. The Old Man's failing strength and, worse, his failing spirit had occupied all my thoughts and channelled attention away from the sensual needs of my body. And, as well, the two girls were still very young. The last lips on my breast had been Zsa-Zsa's.

He tuned the motor down to low, a small wave invaded my vagina and set off a wash of rippling currents which seemed to extend to my womb. What muscle control I must be achieving! The Old Man gently turned the switch, manoeuvring it up to high, and adjusting the egg by easing the flex to the outermost stretch of my opening – my vulva? Or not? I was always confused on the accurate labelling of myself.

'If you bend over, child, yes like that – you can see, actually see yourself swelling.' I'd shut my eyes, but at The Old Man's words I'd opened them and bent as he'd said.

'Here.' The Old Man had shifted his hand from my nipple. 'See, your clitoris has a life of its own. Look how swollen it is, almost crimson and bruised, engorged like an insect with blood—'

He held it carefully between finger and thumb and rolled it as if rolling a joint, tenderly so as not to spill the precious contents within. I'd seen Brad do the same so many times since, though it seemed to me that Brad's greater reverence was reserved for the weed rather than for me.

The Old Man's hand was trembling now, I'd have to be careful of course. I would certainly have to consult his physician as to how much excitement he could stand. But the look on his face dispelled any doubts regarding these sexual aids. The lift to his spirit, the new life they presented exonerated possible risks.

'It's working!' he quavered. 'I see by your face. You're transported, my child – I've achieved it. Come closer to me – I shall enter you now with my sturdy new, ready-made weapon!'

I slid the egg out, and switched off its battery. No need to waste it, they cost money.

The ready-made weapon was so like real flesh that it made my own flesh crawl to feel it. I'd fitted the penis as the pamphlet suggested with a sheath of fine Fourex Skin – price 82½p per packet of 3 inc. V.A.T. The sheaths were made of a soft natural membrane, actually obtained from young lambs. If I shut my eyes, I could easily imagine I was being fucked by a whole flock of sheep.

I cuddled The Old Man carefully, kneeling above him, as he'd once kneeled above me – so towering and strong in those days. And I kissed him gently over his face, closing his eyes in their deep sunken sockets with the touch of my lips on his lids. How like a corpse he looked for that second, so much so that I shuddered. The tremor, misunderstood as one of pleasure, inflamed his state of excitement. He gasped as I eased my haunches down, then up, then down again. Oddly enough the terrible tension of the ludicrous situation, aided I had to admit to myself by the bulk up inside me – all these factors aroused me immensely. I'd never loved The Old Man as much as now in his moment of weakness. A sob arose from these mixed emotions, was I sad, was I happy – or what?

'You're right my child – you're ready I know. Your passion has reached its peak.' His bed was prepared with a rubber sheet. In those days I still gave him his bed-bath; it wasn't until later that a trained nurse was essential.

'Shall I help you?' I offered, my hand moving down.

'What, to squeeze my new scrotum? How dare you?' And with the delight of a boy who sets his first train in motion, he squeezed hard and released the water.

It flooded my passage, pervaded my parts, as sweet as a douche. It cleansed away the musty cobwebs of frustrated months when masturbation might have heightened misery, and intercourse was out of the question. I relaxed completely and let myself go. Was I passing some water myself? I couldn't tell, the release was such that I didn't know where it sprang from.

The Prosthetic with Scrotum was showing its age, it looked more worn than The Old Man's smooth corpse. But its battered appearance, the result of much ramming, had endeared it much more to us both. I kissed the old faithful, and lovingly fitted a fresh Fourex Skin on the rubber, then I lifted the pillow with its cold satin shine, and arranged the penis under The Old Man's left ear. The right, I reserved for my Angel's Delight. That still looked as good as brand new. I held the pink egg in the palm of my hand for the last time. Ought I not perhaps to anoint it?

The Old Man's hands lay crossed on his pubes, locked together in permanent prayer. He wouldn't have liked that, he refused to recognize Religion, it fitted so falsely with Logic.

I kissed the cold knuckles, it was like kissing stone. As I bent, I switched on my small motor, and with the other hand I slipped the smooth egg up inside me.

Grief fought with Sensuality, both wiping out Guilt. The Old Man would have been proud. I studied his face, I dwelt on his lips and reflected on how much Wisdom, through words, they had imparted.

'My child, oh, my child—' I said the words for him, as I tightened my thighs in a climax. Then I slowly removed my Angel's Delight and laid it to rest with its Master.

Soc and Ari were engaged in what seemed like discussion actually inside the deep freeze. The lower limbs emerged untidily, and an elbow belonging to each. Dick didn't seem to be anywhere around in the kitchen, unless he was inside the oven.

'What on earth are you doing in there, Soc and Ari?' Soc slid out. 'Am squeezin' him plackheads! Is much simple in the cold, Boss Lady. You have some, you have plackheads? I do, I do for you?' He nodded so genially, I hadn't the heart to confess that I did my own. When I could find them these days, that was. Are blackheads, like the dewy first signs of beauty, reserved exclusively to youth? Apparently not, if Ari was liberally sprinkled. 'Come out Ari, you can't do that in there!' What if Soc were popping these small encrustations straight into our vanilla ice-cream. Did they do currant ice-cream, sultana and such? We might pass it off as nut crunch.

Dick emerged from the lavatory and kicked Soc up the arse. 'One for good luck, you crass turd!' Ari protested on behalf of his brother-in-law who was whimpering now like a wounded beast. It occurred to me that Dick's uncalled-for aggression could be channelled and put to some use. Nutty, for instance, would swoon with pleasure if I employed the same brand of viciousness. But would he react with a man?

Dick was peering into a variety of saucepans, all boiling away on the gas stove. 'Taste this.' He plunged in a long wooden spoon and offered me the pale beige contents. 'What is it?' I said dubiously, the smell was quite nauseous. Dick frowned. 'Never mind that – enough salt?'

'A spot more sugar is called for,' I said carefully. 'It's custard isn't it?'

'Is it fuck! It's soup, bloody soup from a packet—'

'Ah.' I drew the word out, and nodded my head. 'So it is. I see it is now.' I picked up the empty soup packet. Chicken Noodle it appeared to lay claim to be. The Noodles had congealed, that was obvious. They clung together in a glutinous mass, much like home-made sticky-paste concocted by children from plain flour and water.

'They should be shot, the makers of these!' Dick said savagely, and poured the whole lot down the sink. We looked at him speechlessly, Soc, Ari and I. The sheer waste seemed somehow so shocking.

Dick moved over to the Dumb Waiter and bawled up to Vincent, 'Chicken Noodle off' I just caught Soc's muttered 'Is true. Is all off down here.' His first stab at original wit.

I steered my mind away from the sight of the menus and this latest defiling caused by Dick. There were now so many crossings-out that only a squint-eyed person with eyeballs in all directions could hope to decipher the contents. We might be called upon to issue spectacles, special ones like they have for 3D. On the other hand we could forfeit the menus and merely pin up a board which said MUCK. 'Madam, what would you like to drink with your Muck? Moët Chandon? A very fine choice, I myself quite agree, no expense should be spared with the booze you imbibe with this Swill. Pigs practise this same principle – oh yes, their palates apparently are impeccable!'

A stampede of footsteps up above our heads heralded the first of our arrivals. The sound was followed by Vincent's thin scream summoning me up to my position at the bar. The panic was contagious.

'Here arse-hole, hold this—' Dick nudged Soc roughly and passed a full frying-pan sizzling with pork chipolatas. The sudden movement sent the fat literally flying, it slurped straight from the pan to Soc's open-toed sandals followed in seconds by seventeen small sausages and Soc's intimation of agony.

'Pick 'em up!' Dick commanded completely unruffled. 'And run 'em under the tap. Not the cold one, you fool—' I moved to the door, I could imagine the comments. 'Tasty bangers, eh what! A very fine flavour – Athlete's Foot, if I'm not much mistaken!'

Our first arrivals were men, dressed as Boy Scouts, who had forgathered in London for a Conference. They seemed surprised that we weren't aware that this week was International Boy Scout Week, starting tomorrow with a rousing rally along Rotten Row in Hyde Park. And ending in seven days time with a Display of Tree Climbing on Barnes Common.

'Get a load of those knees!' Zoë murmured in passing. They'd all ordered Lemon and Lime, except one who felt safer on Coke.

'Lemon and Lime and what though, Vince?' I kept a tight rein on my patience. If he was going to start mucking me around, confusing orders as he had done last night, we'd have to make other arrangements.

'That's it,' he said bleakly. 'Not much of an order.'

'Charge them extra for non-intoxicants, I would.' Zoë tapped her high heel almost wantonly, and flung her full bosom towards them. The nearest blinked behind his glasses and smiled nervously in my direction. 'Jesus God, look at that one!' Zoë's lip curled contemptuously. 'Do they screw, or not, Boy Scouts? Do they take the vow, like priests?'

I gave the matter brief thought as I measured out Lemon. 'Baden-Powell poked, didn't he Vince?' Vince wasn't concentrating, there were two new arrivals. Both women, dressed up as Girl Guides.

'He was married I mean, I don't know about children,' I continued, pouring out carefully.

'There you are then!' Zoë beamed triumphantly, as if she'd just proved her own point. She'd not yet caught sight of the Girl Guides behind her. The place was beginning to look like a fancy dress do, all we needed was a nurse and two vicars and perhaps a miner with a lamp on his head.

'I don't believe it!' She'd seen them. 'Two more bloody perverts. The full moon must be bringing them out. Where are they sitting, Vince?' she hissed in a whisper. 'Oh, do put them on the next table to the other team!'

They knew each other, as it all turned out. The Boy Scouts were not too pleased to be greeted. 'I thought this was to be just buddies, us chaps all together this evening,' I heard one of them grumble. 'How did the Girls get wind of where we were. There's a traitor in our midst, that's obvious!'

The Girl Guides both ordered stiff Vodkas and Tonic, large ones with not too much ice. 'I've heard that before, that they're terrible boozers.' Zoë gave a satisfied smirk. 'All Women's Movements are much the same. Alcoholics Anonymous consists almost wholly of women who've become Winos with the Women's Institute. It's that knitting and sewing, it's thirsty work – they switch to spirits as a change from tea!'

The Girl Guides toasted each other loudly and drank the whole lot in one fell swoop. 'Did you see that! What gulpers!' Zoë gasped. 'I shouldn't care to see those two cock-sucking! They'd swallow the lot, balls and all, poor bugger wouldn't know if he was coming or going—'

'Zoë, love – less soliloquizing, more service, if you don't mind.' Vincent employed a note of weary sarcasm. He looked worried and grey, not himself. Or rather, quite himself – the himself which was surfacing lately. What was wrong? No doubt an emotional entanglement.

I consulted the chart of who was coming this evening. Nutty and Stuffy were due in an hour. I wondered if Zoë was aware of that. She was taking the order from the two Girl Guides, who were giggling together quite foolishly.

'They're gay,' I said on her return.

'That's what I think – both bloody Leslies.' Zoë winked as she said it. 'Not that you and I mind, surrounded as we are by homosexuals.' She turned to Vincent. 'That's right isn't it Vince! One has to be big in these matters.' And she accompanied her final statement by goosing him with a banana.

'Oh, for God's sake, Zoë! Cut it out, can't you see – there's a whole lot more coming now! And Dick's had a disaster, he says, in the kitchen. Ari's spilt strawberry jam on the Rissoles, and Soc's just burnt half the Corned Beef Fritters!'

'Rufus rang.' I made my mind go a blank, preferring to consider Rufus's call rather than charred Corned Beef Fritters. But mental escape was patently impossible, the restaurant was, quite suddenly, full.

'Bread! Where's the bread?'

'What?'

'The bread!'

'There's no bread!'

'Fucking hell!'

'Not my fault! We've run out!'

'You bitch!'

'Thank you dear! You bitch, back!'

Zoë and Vincent were having one of their rows, the evening had been one long bickering quarrel. 'Come on you two, go easy.' They glared, one on each side. 'It doesn't matter now about bread. Who wants it, this late?'

'That man over there. He wants it to mop up his gravy. And he's asked as well if we've got marmalade. I think he's expecting some toast.' Zoë looked lined, which she didn't look often, there wasn't enough slack on her face. Not with all they'd taken off when reducing the size of her nose. 'I don't want to upset him. I think he's good for a big tip. I can tell now which bastards are best. He's got a buttonhole you see – that's always a safe bet to go by.' Lionel Striving wore buttonholes and was as mean as all-get-out, quite embarrassing when tipping I recalled, on the rare occasion that we'd eaten out. Always asking if I had change of 5p.

Vincent looked disgruntled, he hadn't received a tip at all. 'You're too grand dear, too much major domo.' Zoë had tried to make up earlier on for the remarkable size of her tips. The two Girl Guides, both thoroughly drunk, had left more as a tip than the price of the meal. The Boy Scouts had left barely nothing, but a coloured couple from the Civil Service, celebrating his passing an exam which edged him up two extra increments and meant he now had his name on the door – they had bought Zoë a whole bottle of Daquiri, which she insisted on selling back to me before they'd even reached the door. 'Will you purchase my darkies' Daquiri?' she said. 'I'd much rather have cash in hand.'

I hadn't the heart to refuse her request, though Vincent claimed I'd pandered to her greed. 'Mercenary cow,' he'd muttered.

Nutty and Stuffy came late; seven minutes or so, Vincent accused them.

'I could've let your table go more than a dozen times—'

'What, in seven minutes? Remarkable!' Stuffy gave as good as he got.

Zoë had dropped two Jam with Rice Puddings the minute she'd seen Stuffy enter. I watched one splash the entire back of a vicar, yes one had come in after all, and wondered if I should tell him or not. The jam glistened darkly amongst all the white rice; if it continued to trickle in the way it was doing, he might find it in his pocket when he got home.

Stuffy reacted sheepishly to Zoë's obvious approach. I watched him closely whilst pouring his Campari, discreetly so, and noted that his slight discomfiture in the face of her adoration contained at the same time a degree of self-pride. Not exactly the air of a stallion, his stature and spectacles cancelled that out, but something much more insidious. You could tell he was getting his oats.

Zoë offered both cheeks in affectionate greeting, her hands suddenly free of rice pudding. The floor was awash with the milky substance, but no one appeared to mind, or even to notice come to that. The evening had reached a high note of hysteria, such as happens when for no real reason the crowd gets caught up in contagious pleasure – the smiles spread with accumulative force. I'd experienced it often in theatre audiences, in pop concerts, on picnics and New Year's Eve when each person indulges everyone else with an almost religious fervour, all forgiving and suffused with love. Anyone could have done anything tonight and found a favourable reaction. 'You say you'd like to stab my back? Here, old thing, take my knife – it's much sharper!' 'Do I mind that you spit quite so much when you speak? Not at all, dear – I find the spray rather refreshing!' 'What's that, you've been rogering my wife for three weeks? That's fine – I've been fucking yours for years!'

Nutty took the table intended for two, just to the left of the till, whilst Stuffy did his best to maintain his balance against the force of Zoë's embrace. The chair Nutty chose faced exactly my way with his back, as it were, to the kitchen. An ominous calm ensued from there.

'Everything all right, Vince, I mean in the kitchen?' I'd already declared last orders for drinks, though last night I'd taken terrible risks with our temporary licence and extended it far beyond time.

Dick had appeared at the top of the stairs, staring resentfully around the full tables. Meals, miraculously, were appearing and served barely before they'd been ordered. I had to hand it to him, Dick's decisiveness and direct frontal attack where food and brute force were concerned could have made him a very good man at Auschwitz. He'd have served up the Jews instead of starving them. Cooking by gas of course. In fact, now, all evening regardless of orders, stray dishes appeared in the Dumb Waiter – five Chips, seven Mash, four Boiled Carrots and six Shepherd's Pie left over from lunch time, re-heated and wrinkled on top.

'Who ordered these, this rubbish?' Zoë wanted to know. Vincent looked equally mystified.

'Not my lot, my dear. They must be all yours—'

'Shepherd's Pie? I thought that was off. It smells as if it is – what a bloody stinking mess – I'm not taking that to any of my tables!' Zoë flounced away. I came to the rescue. 'Nutty's always keen on Shepherd's Pie. They used to serve it at Eton – the best thing they had. You'll probably find Stuffy likes it too.'

Zoë blew a raspberry, the sound passed unnoticed by people on surrounding tables whose conversations seemed equally peppered with the same blasts of rude anal explosions. Didn't it take longer than that for wind to formulate, or was our food more ferocious than most. Did the true trencherman fart more than others? Or was that the distinction made between glutton and gourmet? The Old Man was drawn to making these distinctions. Food and Sex shared very much in common, that was his continuing claim. And it was from this basis, understanding the essentials, that he cooked so superbly himself. I was rarely, if ever, allowed in the kitchen, just as my role was clearly defined, those years, in our bed. But as his powers decreased and his potency waned, his cooking became non-existent. Until in the end his diet consisted of whatever it was Nurse decreed. A soft, milky diet it was for the most part. Not unlike that which I served to the children, his children – those small versions of him. In fact sometimes, spooning in variations on Farex, it was hard to distinguish his soft gums from Zsa-Zsa's. Both toothless, and pale as pink silk. Both vulnerable machines made to masticate food, but each missing the last vital link of the teeth. Hers were coming. He'd had his already.

I ignored Zoë's raspberry. 'Shall I ask?' I offered. 'If they'd like Shepherd's Pie? I don't mind.'

Zoë wrinkled her nose. 'But it's curdled, I promise! Just smell it yourself – I don't care to think where it's been!'

'Don't fuss-pot now, Zoë.' I spoke to her firmly. 'Both Nutty and Stuffy will love it.'

'But it's not what they ordered—' she objected afresh, looking past me at Dick who'd appeared up the stairs. She lowered her voice, but not very much. 'That bastard should be booted straight out of here. He's running this place, if you'd care to ask me. You and Vincent have been reduced to mere pawns—'

'Prawns? I'll have prawns, that is if I heard you correctly?' A heavily built man, sitting close by, tilted his chair towards Zoë. The back wooden legs squeaked in protest, he had already eaten two dinners, straight through from Starters to Pud, proclaiming our food delicious!

I couldn't understand it, the general reaction seemed to be that the food was exceptional! Flavoursome English! Top grade Transport Cafe, low prices with Very Fine Wines!

Of course, most of our clients — patrons? customers? —

were middle class, and most keen on a 'find', especially one with low prices. And we were a bargain, I could quite well see that. And I'd purchased the wine wisely and well, such that a connoisseur could have quickly recognized that this wasn't cheap carafe gut-rot. This additional bonus was paying big dividends, far more than if the wine had been inferior. Vincent approvingly noted this fact. 'More Minervois for Table Ten. One bottle – no, they say two! And a Côtes du Roussillon for Table Four, and three more for Six, in a sec.'

I was quite pleased with myself; Vincent originally had accused me of the utmost extravagance regarding the prices I'd paid for the wines. 'They're cheaper than that at the Liquor-Mart, a litre of Valpolicella costs something just over the pound. And Tesco's do Red, White and Pink Charbonnière for much the same, you've gone mad with these wines. It's not as if they're even going to notice the difference—' I remembered the warm eyes of the Italian who'd sold them. Soon I'd have to re-order again. Would he remember me? Probably so, once seen rarely forgotten.

'Any chance of a drink around here?' Dick's dry voice sliced through Zoë's sentence and the man's interruption. 'No prawns, sir,' I apologized and then turned to Dick. 'You're doing well, Dick, tonight! A.1. – plus service, so everyone says—'

'Yes,' Zoë sneered. 'You're even giving us what we're not bloody asking for! What are you trying to do, finish off all the scraps?'

Dick stared at her coldly with open dislike, and deliberately chose not to answer. She persisted however, she refused to give up. 'It's all right for you in the kitchen, not facing the customers – but I'm expected to serve it—'

Dick examined his nails and carefully picked a shred of cold cabbage from the half-moon of one of his thumbs. 'You can stuff it,' he said slowly, 'as far as I'm concerned, all the way up your own arsehole. And serve it from there straight on to the plates—'

Zoë seized her chance. 'I may do that.' Then she added, 'Certainly no one would detect any difference.'

She turned away and returned with the tray of Shepherd's Pie held in her hands. 'Here,' she said, holding it towards me. 'You can serve this, I refuse responsibility. If anyone's going to be poisoning Stuffy, I'm damned if it's going to be me. Better still,' she stared at Dick, 'you do it, you arrogant bastard, and just see how their faces fall in disgust at this puke-making sick you serve up!'

Dick looked laconically at the tray, and then all around the restaurant. 'Which cunt is it meant for, they all look the same?' He flexed both his fists, revealing long muscles up along both his arms. His tee-shirt today was even tighter, it seemed woven in one with his skin. The effect, with the truculent cast of his brow, was more than a little menacing.

I pointed to poor Nutty's table. He was already in a state of nerves, I could tell by the violent eye movements. He'd been trying to catch my glance since he'd arrived, I was aware of it but just that much too busy to bother. He was clearly enthralled by my cruel indifference. Dick's harshness might just tip the balance and shift him right over the edge. We didn't want an exhibition before all the other tables had completely cleared and gone home.

'Oh, do be careful, in your manner of serving, Dick.' I'd agreed to give him a bottle of our very best Claret, in exchange for attending Nutty's table. 'Yes, he has rather a nervous disposition. You go first, and I'll come and introduce you. Both those men are quite close friends of mine.' I couldn't bring myself to look at Nutty, as I introduced him to Dick. It was as if the chemical components of his flesh had changed gear and shifted to something completely different. Not unlike the bubbling substance some years ago in the television serial, *Quatermass*. Could Dick's wavelengths have wrought such a positive change in that second it had taken to introduce him? Without a doubt, these things did happen – hadn't I reacted similarly to Brad? Though our relationship was threaded with humour. Brad's eyes displayed light-hearted mockery, self-mockery too, which was always a winner. They teased, whilst Dick's clearly terrified. They terrified Vince, they antagonized Zoë, they dictated to poor Soc and Ari. What they did to myself was a little more complex, they reminded me of Stephen's final despair and the underlying fury that that had masked.

Was it irresponsible of me to have got them together, would I live to regret the final outcome? They fitted so well, shivering Nutty and Dick – the Rabbit and the Snake. Nutty was so hypnotized so that when Dick addressed him directly, his stammer rendered him speechless.

'Where do you live, Squire?' The 'Squire' held a sneer, a deliberately insulting accusation. It contained centuries of class hatred in one single word. 'What's that, Squire? I didn't quite catch it!' Nutty was struggling, not to utter a whole sentence, but simply to start the first word. 'W-w-w-wi! W-wil, will, will! Will. Will. Will!' I looked away, out of pity. Stuffy chose to polish his spectacles, but I saw that Dick was actually leaning forward to stare more closely at Nutty's poor mouth. Nutty's tongue seemed completely paralysed. 'Will. Will. Will,' Dick repeated with relentless cruelty. 'Shall I have a shot at finishing it for you? Our doctor back home had a shocking stutter – by the time the old sod had asked for your symptoms, you'd started a new fucking illness!'

Nutty's dud eye did a looping somersault, at the fair rate of fifteen knots. I wished that my girls, who so enjoyed Nutty's eye, had been there for the impressive spectacle.

'Yes, Squire,' Dick continued, quite ruthlessly. 'It's the scourge of the privileged classes, they say, this difficulty with verbal delivery. Yet the Conservative Party and this country's Government are crammed full of you stuttering twerps!' He leaned further forward. 'You'd be hard put, I tell you true, Squire, to find a milkman, or a miner, or a munitions worker with a similar affliction to yours! Now tell me why you think that is? Do those silver spoons you're bloody born with get tangled up with your tonsils?' He suddenly smiled. The effect was quite shattering. He looked, all of a sudden, like Puck. Completely beguiling, a beautiful boy. I thought, afterwards, that that must have been the precise moment that Nutty had fallen.

The evening had continued to climb quite steadily to the climax which later took place. The signs were all there, but I just didn't see them. In any case, separately they didn't mean much. Dick had repeated his original question. 'Well, own up, Squire – where is it you live? Will, you say – Will, Will, Will – I've got it – you live where I do! In Willesden!'

Nutty had managed to shake his poor head, squirming over his cold Shepherd's Pie. In a moment, I knew, Dick would force him to eat it, despite its congealing, chill greasiness.

'Do I take that as "no", that mute nodding of yours?' Dick demanded, enjoying himself. 'Well, Squire – Will, Will, Will, Will!' He stretched back in the chair he'd pulled up for the purpose, and raising both arms in the air he linked them insolently around the back of his head, displaying dark under-arm growth.

It was riveting to see, the tight curling profusion, especially since his arms were so smooth. Men, in the same way, found girls' crotches arousing. Pubic hair peeping around flimsy panties.

I glanced around, we'd been there mere minutes. The restaurant appeared in an uproar. Vincent approached, and now so did Zoë.

'Who's meant to be minding the shop down below?' Vincent tried to make his voice pleasant. He nodded in Nutty's direction; his dislike of him was quite obvious, and had been whenever they'd met. But this evening he'd been given a greater cause. Dick was his friend, despite Dick thinking otherwise.

Zoë was holding a muffled conversation with Stuffy, who'd been ploughing through his Shepherd's Pie, silently, not participating in Dick's and Nutty's appalling exchanges. Even now, at this moment, Nutty was still attempting desperately to say something. Vincent's intimation that Dick should return to his station of duty below, seemed to exacerbate matters for him. The most sought for sentence came out quite clearly, in his most charming and cultivated manner. 'Will you permit me to offer you a drink? I live in Wiltshire – are you ever down that way? If you are, you might care to pay me a visit.' He glanced down at his grey Shepherd's Pie. 'This dish, you know, is my absolute favourite. A nursery treat, I remember. Cook used to make me one of my own – then later, at school—' His voice trailed away, we were all gazing in surprise. I couldn't remember a single occasion when Nutty had managed to say so much, without one single stammer or pause. Dick, from the look on his face, appeared more surprised than the rest of us. But in that same look another one surfaced as if Nutty's small show of strength presented an unlooked-for challenge. His interest, I thought, had been roused. They could be locked in eternal combat, those two, neither ever quite winning.

I'd returned to the bar, two people were waiting to pay their bill at my till. They were arguing fiercely over who should do it. She said she should, it was her treat, they'd agreed that it would be before she'd invited him out. He'd replied that was cold-blooded blackmail. I looked at them both, between totting the bill and handing it in their direction. They both made as if to grab it from me. The woman's grasp was much stronger, her companion retreated, shrugging off his defeat. Were they married? Divorced? Or estranged? They were certainly that, whether married or not to each other. Both wore a wide wedding band, but in this light it was hard to see if they'd been cut from the same strip of gold. The woman smiled at me, but sadly I thought. I returned her smile, mine was quite effortless. 'Is this your restaurant? You're new, it's quite different. We used to come here in the old days.' She glanced towards the door, the man she'd been with had already left. Without her? Or would she find him moodily waiting to start up again, there outside?

The bill was quite small, they hadn't drunk much. Things might have improved if they had. I was pleased for her though, that she hadn't spent much, hadn't wasted too much of her money, on what had plainly been an abortive outing.

'Did that bastard let her foot the bill?' Zoë'd joined me; we watched the woman walking alone, wending her way to the door. 'She was his secretary, you know – I heard it all. Yes, he was her boss—'

'I think at some time or other, he was certainly more than her boss,' I said, sorting loose change. The till seemed to bulge with its contents. Could it be that we might make a profit from this daft venture of ours?

The sight of the notes, all those fivers and oncers, reminded me of dear old Auntie. I suddenly yawned, it had been a long day. I wondered if she was asleep. If I rang her now it would make no difference, she always slept right through the ringing of the telephone. And if she was awake, she might welcome the call, might even pop down for a night-cap.

I telephoned. 'Auntie?' She'd answered at once.

'There's funny, I was just ringing you! My hand, just this moment, was picking it up when it rang. It felt like an electric shock!' She laughed, in a particular way that I knew very well. I wondered what exactly she'd been drinking. I was faintly surprised, it wasn't like Auntie ever to imbibe on her own. She seemed in control, but suffused in the gaiety that spells several stages short of oblivion.

'Would you care to come here, to the restaurant, for coffee?' Coffee would keep her on her feet.

'Coffee?' she echoed. 'Oh, I've just had loads of coffee — Gaelic Coffee. It didn't taste very Welsh.' She giggled. I could tell that she wasn't alone. 'Guess who's here — shall I tell you — Brad is! Yes, he is. Just passing in his cab. I gave him coffee. He supplied the cream and Irish Whiskey—'

'Put him on, Auntie.'

'Can I still come? I'm still dressed up in my finery — Brad's being awful — he says I look lovely. You should hear all the things he's been saying. Oooh, he's terrible really, I keep telling him that — here he is. Shall I ask him to drive me?' Her voice was wavering with happy optimism. She was with someone she liked and trusted. It wasn't the first time they'd spent time together. Brad's habit of dropping in unexpectedly and the fact that we'd never stuck to a schedule, not once in our long relationship, rendered him really to be one of the family. Much more than my other Gentlemen.

'All right, don't put him on. I'll see you both in a minute. Ask

198

Brad if he wants something to eat—' But I could hear his far-away answering shout. 'Only her, tell her, Auntie – I'll eat her!'

The tables were gradually thinning out. The calm from the kitchen had commenced. It was at this point approximately that I'd made the query to Vincent as to whether all was well. He hadn't answered, he'd reached that point of exhaustion where he couldn't be concerned. The second I'd replaced the telephone after my call, it had rung immediately for Vincent. I'd answered the phone. The voice had been Irish. The Irish chippy from Willesden? Or had he been Welsh? I couldn't remember. 'It's for you, Vince!' Hearing the voice at the other end of the phone, he'd turned his back to me. He hadn't ever done that before.

Soc and Ari were singing the Greek Cypriot Anthem. Dick sat outside on the step, he was holding a languid conversation with someone ensconced in the lav. There was no mistaking the stuttering, Nutty had reverted once more from his position of dignity to that of a gibbering idiot. Soc and Ari stopped singing. I could detect on their breath the sweet unmistakable scent of Sherry. The cooking Sherry shelf was bare, two bottle tops poked out of the dustbin. 'Boss Lady, you lovely! Your Auntie, she no here?' They stood like two terrible trolls, grinning inanely from ear to ear, their arms linked in brotherly affection. Or rather, brother-in-lawly affection, if there was in fact such a thing.

'Auntie? No, she's not here – but she's coming in a moment.' I wondered briefly if they could be conscience-stricken, or were they as transparently honest as they seemed. I shut my mind firmly off from the subject; if Auntie could do it so could I. 'Yes, boys,' I continued. 'She's bought a new dress and a cloak to-day, down in Brighton. She'll be showing it off right here in a minute. You'll have to tell her it looks nice.'

Soc clasped Ari, as if Ari was Auntie. 'Oh, Auntie – you have the new dress! Is lovely! I like! You beautiful lady, like my mother. I love you, is good!' Then he turned to me and said seriously as if addressing a priest. 'In our country we love very much the women – the mothers, grandmothers and aunties. We

199

love them as much, we want them you see, as we want our wives and our daughters. Is good, no? Is right?' He nodded several times, and ended, speaking as if to himself, 'Is no wrong yes, is right.' Ari kissed him swiftly, hard, full on the mouth, as if he were stamping an envelope. Or placing the seal on an official document, one that was going to the Nation. I had an insane image of Soc, backed by Ari, lavishing lashings of love on their womenfolk. Claiming Droit de Seigneur from cradle to coffin, age presenting no barriers. Both sweeping the board of the generation gap, their generosity uniting the whole.

Upstairs something was happening, I could tell by the sounds of small cheering. Vincent and Zoë, and Stuffy it seemed, were greeting the arrival of Auntie.

'She's here!' I said.

'She am here – she arrive! Your Auntie, she come! We go, we go say hello—' Soc and Ari scampered up the stairs like two mice up a maypole, their front paws as active as their feet, slicking their hair and wiping their mouths in swift and excitable movements.

Auntie stood in the centre of the stage surveying the scene like a Queen, with all the graciousness of Royalty greeting her Senior Court Dignitaries. In the flickering shadows cast by one candle-light, her new robes assumed extra glamour. The sharp tangerine lines of the beautiful cloak throbbed with a new orange dimension. Her small bright yellow beret had slipped to one side and much more to the back of her head. It looked like a halo, a heavenly light such as you see round the head of Our Lord in luridly illustrated Bible stories. The matching beads that she wore around her neck glistened like freshly picked berries. You felt you could eat them, and eat Auntie too, the effect was so succulent and ripe.

An elderly woman of about Auntie's age, seated nearby all alone, dressed severely in silver and black, was regarding the scene with great interest. Her appearance spoke unmistakably of the restraint that she must have practised in life, in her attitudes and in regard to her relationships. The interest was tempered with faint disapproval and at the same time with unalloyed envy.

'Who's that?' I heard a masculine voice whisper at Auntie's arrival.

'Some actress, I suppose – could it be Sybil Thorndike?' an answering voice whispered back.

Only about three or four tables remained occupied – people lingering with their drinks. I followed as Soc and Ari threaded their way past them, whooping as they went. 'Auntie! Auntie! Is Soc and Ari come to see your nice dress. Boss lady, he ask us – no, she tell, is new! Ah, yes, we see, is divine!' Soc and Ari flung themselves like two fawning dogs on the floor, feeling the hem of Auntie's long gown and kissing the rim of her cloak. Her pink socks twinkled through, her high-heels curved down under her comfortable instep. Soc saw them first. 'She have new shoes!' he shouted as if pronouncing a ship's maiden voyage. 'New shoes – she have!' And he proceeded to slaver, almost licking each toe-cap in turn.

The elderly woman rose in distaste, the scene had become too Bacchanalian for her to bear. Auntie smiled as she passed her. The woman seemed temporarily blinded, but managed a stiff twist of the lip before leaving.

'Hello, Auntie.' I went forward to kiss her. I could smell my perfume on her neck. Shalimar, a scent The Old Man had first bought me in Paris, the time he'd taken me to Balenciaga and dressed me completely in black. I was barely nineteen. The Master himself had approved The Old Man's final selection. He'd sighed with deep pleasure and conversed with The Old Man in his native Spanish language. Afterwards The Old Man had told me what he'd said, that I'd looked, in the black, like a lovely girl-widow. The reverse of a white-clad child-bride. I don't think that he knew that in fact I'd been both, before I'd met The Old Man.

The Old Man had taken me that first day, in my black, to dinner at the Coupole. Picasso had been there, he'd done a drawing of me on a food-stained linen napkin – which The Old Man, by mistake, later in London sent to be washed at the laundry. When it came back the drawing had vanished. The Old Man showed me how not to mind. And on our last night in Paris, we'd dined late at Maxim's. Mistinguette sat two tables away, surrounded by fawning young men. 'You'll be like that when you're seventy.' The Old Man had smiled. 'But your admirers won't be all homosexuals.'

After Maxim's he'd taken me on to a night-club run exclusively by women. I wouldn't have known, I'd thought they were men, immaculately suited and coiffured. After five minutes, one had asked me to dance, first asking The Old Man's permission. He'd given it roguishly and pinched my behind as I was led firmly to the small dance-floor. The youth, it was hard for me to think of her as a girl, had held me tightly against herself. I could feel no swell of breasts, and when, at one point she guided my hand to the small of her back, the lean buttocks felt just like a boy's. The record we danced to was 'La Vie en Rose', sung by Edith Piaf, but after that first song I lost concentration. I couldn't have said what it was that they played. I could see The Old Man watching us and at the beginning, each time we'd danced past, he'd winked and I'd grinned gratefully back. But, as the music continued and the sinuous body against mine moulded itself cunningly to me I was aware of a change taking place. The youth clasped my hand more tightly in his, hers — and dropped both our arms to our sides. So that now, not only did the entire front of me touch his, hers, but by subtle pressure on my thigh his, her, own snaked between my two legs. We swayed, barely moving, in one spot on the floor. I couldn't have greeted The Old Man if I'd wished, he belonged to a far distant world. I hoped for his own sake that he couldn't see, because now the youth was kissing me passionately. And I was returning the kiss. And the hand which just a second ago had exerted pressure on my thigh, had sneaked slyly around and in between us it was stroking my pants like a thief. Straight through my glorious Balenciaga, stroking until I could have cried. And would have done, if his, her, lips had let me. There was no room for tears on my face.

'Ma cherie.' The voice was hoarse and thrilling, murmuring

in my left ear. I could smell the powder on the smooth skin and the impression of scent in the curve of the neck. The effect was unbearably moving, it reminded me so much of Stephen, of his fragrance and fragile strength. But this youth had a purpose, she, he, wanted me badly.

'*Ma cherie,*' the voice murmured. I made no reply. I couldn't speak French anyway.

But now she – strange that, how quite suddenly I regarded her as she! Was it the scent? Or the voice, so low but so feminine? Yes, she was now suggesting very much more. The words were ones that far exceeded my flimsy knowledge of French, but even so the way they were said, from the ardent delivery to the quickened breathing and suggestive movements she made, left me in no doubt as to what might be their meaning.

The situation distressed me. I didn't dare to look in The Old Man's direction at all. I hadn't looked, not for a full five minutes or more, so that now as I did and saw he wasn't there, stark fear sliced across my emotions. Stranded in Paris! With no place to go, except into the arms of this exquisite creature – the idea both thrilled and appalled me. This wasn't what I wanted, not without The Old Man to tell me if I should, or I shouldn't. Would it count after all, with her being a girl? Would it be viewed as the same, infidelity?

I felt a new pressure on my elbow. Was this an Excuse-Me Dance? The pressure increaed and my dancing partner gradually released her hold. A hopelessness bordering on despair and panic surged through me at the thought of losing her. We stared at each other, unwilling to part. I turned my head towards the unwelcome intruder. The Old Man's hand released its pressure. 'Come children.' He was addressing us both.

We didn't go to where we were staying, not to our hotel at all. Though it wouldn't have mattered what we did there, tonight was our last night in Paris. And they were worldly enough to have accepted anything. Neither did we go to the girl's own place, as I'd hoped. Long after, The Old Man had told me why not. I'd been surprised when he did, that it hadn't caused me more pain, the fact that she lived with a mistress. Mistress?

No, that wasn't the word. With her lover, a girl much like me. And I'd been surprised as well to discover, when The Old Man had told me, how old she'd actually been. In her early thirties, according to him. They'd known each other since she'd been my age.

I didn't go further in that discussion, I shrank back, not wishing to know the exact ins and outs of their relationship and whether I'd been the first that he'd watched with her, or not. Because though my feelings may have faded for the girl, I felt fiercely possessive over him. And it was this dangerous jealousy, if that was the word, that spoiled at the start my full enjoyment of our bizarre arrangement as the three of us approached the ambience The Old Man had selected.

It was within walking distance of where we'd just been, but I had no idea of the district at all. Saint-Germain, Les Halles, the Champs Elysée? It made no difference, because I was obsessed whether or not The Old Man was holding her hand, she on one side of him and me on the other. He was holding mine tightly, as he usually did. But he spoke all the way, rapidly to her in his unfailing French – he spoke eighteen languages. She'd answered him lightly and laughed several times. Were they talking of me, both, between them? Were they plotting a lurid and mutual seduction? I clung miserably to his tight hand and wished we were back in our hotel bedroom packing for our morning departure. I wouldn't have minded if I'd been in the middle, sandwiched between them, the succulent filling. But The Old Man stage-managed it all. He strode us along, until we suddenly stopped outside a tiny patisserie. A powdery smell of choux and puff lingered around the entrance which appeared to lead past the shop itself straight through to the bakery behind. And still further behind – Paris like New York was like layered cake, always more underneath – still further behind was a minute garden. We crossed it and reached a locked, shuttered building, which resembled a Bohemian studio. But it couldn't be that because the light wasn't right, which was why working painters used garrets. This one was low and overpowered by all the surrounding buildings. I wondered now who it might belong to, as

The Old Man produced the right key from the large bunch of keys that he always had with him in the inner pocket of his cloak.

It was quite dark inside, but not for long. A small torch hung on a hook just inside the door. The Old Man must have known the place well, his hand sneaked instinctively for it. The place couldn't have been wired for electricity. Wide church candles shone waxily in the light of the torch, as The Old Man flashed it around.

'Hold this, child,' he said softly, handing me the torch. 'And shine it as I light all these up.' My senses thrilled that I'd been chosen, and not the girl, to do this small task. But as I watched him move away, leaving swaying pools of light in his wake, I realized that that had been part of the plan; the girl had moved closer beside me. We were already kissing each other.

It was she, and not he, not The Old Man at all who stage-managed proceedings from there. It was she, who even without moving from the original spot where it was I'd been handed the torch, had undressed me. Had removed my black dress. It had slithered, my beautiful Balenciaga, from my shoulders straight to the floor. I'd shivered as her hands had followed its flight and come to rest on my thin flimsy panties.

She'd led me, still wearing them, but now nothing else, through what seemed like a forest of small flames. I couldn't tell, the images blurred. Was that person over there The Old Man?

I was lain upon what felt like very smooth velvet. The girl, for a second, had gone. I shut my eyes, it was so like a dream that I couldn't be sure she'd been there at all. Then I felt her return, as naked as me. She slid her hand into my panties, those same fingers that had searched in that space once before on the dance floor. She withdrew them, the tips were quite drenched.

I fell asleep, and woke all alone. The body, her body had gone. I wasn't afraid, somewhere quite close I could hear the drift of familiar voices — The Old Man and the girl were conversing together in an unmistakably intimate manner. But now I didn't seem to mind. The flickering candle flames reflected my own bodily sensations. They may, quite easily, have darted like that all over my skin for all I knew – the effect now seemed much the same. She had kindled me gently, applied her own light so skilfully to mine that I progressed from the smouldering start to the state of the candles around me. They waved and faltered, weakly like wands appearing to fall in the wind.

And there was wind now, or a chill gust of night air had entered the place. And in seconds several candles were extinguished. I shivered again, but not this time with pleasure as I had when her hands were upon me. And I shut my eyes tightly. The voices weren't there. For the first time I did feel that I was quite alone, and fled from the fear far away, once again, into sleep.

Shalimar, that same scent sat on Auntie's soft neck as happily as it had, all those years ago, on the smooth boyish neck of the girl. My brief embrace must have lasted fractionally longer than normal welcome merited. Auntie withdrew and looked at me anxiously.

'I put on a little dab of your scent, only a bit, love, at the back of my ears. Not wastefully, not even a dab on my wrists – in case Soc and Ari needed a spot of help with all this old washing-up. You don't mind, love? It's just that, somehow, this French perfume seems to go that much better with these clothes. Rather than my old Californian Poppy or the Juice of Dew Violets, you know?'

I laughed and gave her another kiss, one unconnected with memories. How strange that those memories had surfaced tonight.

'Where's Brad, Auntie? Didn't he bring you?'

'Oh yes, Brad! He did bring me, but on the way here he had a call to pick up a fare. And the funny thing was – do you know who the fare was? It came through on that speaking machine – a gentleman they said called Mr Rufus Justice! And do you know where he's to drop him? Yes, here! But I didn't let on, love, that I knew the name. I just sat there. Mum's the word!

Brad said to say that he'll pick up this chap and deliver him here, then come in himself for a night-cap.'

The momentary panic must have shown on my face. Vincent, watching me, laughed and, in a voice of mock horror, exclaimed, 'Oh darling, your past is catching up with you!' It was a rare and, because of that, a welcome return to the easier days of our former intimacy. He never, if ever now, relaxed in the same way. Had the arrival of Auntie anything to do with it? He was holding her arm with desperate affection, hanging on, as if for grim life. Or was it grim death? I couldn't remember how the saying quite went. But it didn't much matter, one way or the other. He took her hand. 'You look absolutely divine, darling Auntie! Where have you been? I've missed you so much!'

It was of course the very first time Vincent had seen Auntie since her loss. He wouldn't mention it, I knew, if she didn't mention it first. Perhaps this ardent welcome he gave her was a show of unspoken sympathy. She beamed at him. 'It's new, the whole outfit, it's new – top to bottom!' She pointed a matronly toe. 'New shoes, look, high heels, Vincent. Nearly as high as yours.' She glanced down at Vincent's stacked King's Road laceups. 'Well, p'raps not as high, but nearly. And d'you know what, Vincent – there's not a thread of Man-Made, no Acrylic, Synthetics, not nothing in this frock of mine, nor in the cloak, nor the beret! See, look on the labels, ALL WOOL!' She strained around to yank forward her labels, scruffing the back of her own neck. Like a rabid terrier attempting to produce evidence of its own identity.

'All Wool! No, Auntie dear! But why?' Vincent's voice contained genuine horror. Auntie's dress sense up till then had actually tickled his fancy. The fact of Tesco's Brushed Nylon and affiliated fabrics from all her other chain stores, had seemed to him the height of camp chic. All Wool was a different matter.

Soc and Ari sensed the drama, something serious had obviously happened. They took up the chant, wearing woebegone faces. 'Hall Wool! Hall Wool! Why, why? Why, Hall Wool? Why, Auntie, why Hall Wool?'

Auntie looked now as alarmed as they. 'What's the matter?' she said to me. 'What's the matter, Zoë? Was All Wool all wrong—?' Zoë had joined us, she was looking contemptuously at the swooping, gesticulating chorus, performing as if from Cole Porter. Or an amateur performance of Gilbert and Sullivan. 'They're pissed!' she said. 'Auntie, pay no attention. Those two have been on the cooking Sherry.' She nodded towards Soc and Ari. 'And he—' She bent forward after glancing at Vince, 'He is so bloody neurotic, he doesn't need anything to send him over the top! They're crackers, the lot of them. Auntie old love, I don't think I could stand another night of it. Have you met Hitler yet, he's in the kitchen dishing up all the shit? I tell you straight, Auntie, I'm scared stiff to serve it. I keep seeing this powdered glass!'

'Dear oh dear, it's like that, is it? Never mind Zoë, love. You look very nice, I must say, tonight. Less make-up on than usual?' Auntie meant it kindly, but had touched a sore spot. Zoë's nose shone out like a beacon, unpowdered and filmed in a shroud of chip-fat. Soc's and Ari's looked much the same. But perhaps Zoë's looked worse, her nose pores were much larger from where they'd been stretched with her Op. She herself was the first one to point it out. 'Save's carrying a handbag.' I think I'd said to lighten her obvious gloom. 'You could pocket it all in your pores—' She had, mercifully, managed a small smile.

Her hand now flew up to the centre of her face. 'That's what I mean, you see! There's no bloody time to think of your looks. Though I must say—' Her face quickly softened as she looked behind her towards Stuffy. 'It has worked quite well with Stuffy, cross fingers. There's talk of him taking off for Hamburg—'

'Hamburg?' I echoed. I couldn't imagine Stuffy anywhere other than England.

'The home of the Hapsburgs.' Zoë explained, importantly as if sure of her facts. 'It seems that in his thesis, indications are emerging that the Krauts are responsible for more than just the last two World Wars – in medieval poetry, I mean.'

'Oh dear,' Auntie said sympathetically. 'Poor Stuffy.'

'Oh, not Oh dear, Auntie. It's good!' Zoë glowed. 'Good for me, my German is fluent. '*Guten tag*' – that means "Good day"! And it means as well, that there's a bloody good chance of little me going with Stuffy to Hamburg.' Zoë winked in my direction. 'He's giving me a Reading tonight!'

Soc and Ari had clearly not followed this side conversation of Zoë's. They'd been gazing adoringly up at Auntie. She patted them both on the head. And when her 'Oh Dear' to Zoë was so patently not the right answer, she'd given the boys her full attention. Vincent had withdrawn into a strange worried state, even Auntie it seemed couldn't reach him. 'How's it going, then, boyos?' She addressed them like Bogey. And like Bogey they answered by sniffing her first and slyly poking and prodding. She lifted the wings of her cloak like a bird and enclosed Soc and Ari, one on each side. Their craggy brown faces and dull crooked teeth displayed like discarded dentures, the full set top and bottom, looked at odds in the folds of her magnificent garment. But at the same time strangely at home, as if they'd replaced something else that was missing. Of course – she wasn't carrying Mock Croc!

'Why not sit down, Auntie – and have something to drink?'

'Ooh, something to drink! Soc and Ari, would you like something nice with me?' Auntie gazed fondly down, first to her left and then to her right, as if addressing two small Pekinese. They both nodded, tongues hanging. All three repaired to a corner, the darkest without any light. 'Well, I don't know about that!' Vincent said sourly. 'Kitchen staff fraternizing with customers!'

Zoë sailed past, undoing her pinny. 'Have you been in the kitchen, lately? Our Chef is fraternizing like mad with old Nutty, no need to spell it out further? Oh, is it all right, I'm shoving off now. Stuffy's going. Sunday tomorrow, we're not open are we? Monday? Well, I don't know, I'll see. In any case I'll let you know, I wouldn't just leave you in the lurch!'

We watched them go, Vincent and I. 'What does she mean, in the lurch?' Vincent looked irritable.

'I think it means, Vincent, that we're going to need a new waitress.'

'And a new chef—'

'New chef? What? Dick's—'

'Chucking it in! Yes, latest development! Dick's going as Nutty's new butler! He told me now, ten minutes ago—'

'Has he told Nutty yet?' I said calmly trying as best I could to control my amusement. But Vincent didn't react, his mournful face remained exactly the same.

'Dick does as he likes, it doesn't matter what anyone else thinks with him. They go along with everything.'

'Only if they're a certain sort of people, Vince.' I spoke gently now, he seemed so lost.

'Oh I know that someone like you would withstand him. You've never been manipulated though.'

I didn't answer, it wasn't true. I thought above all of The Old Man. Had he manipulated me? Or could his influence be regarded as education?

Vincent stared ahead. The lines around his mouth began knitting together uncontrollably. I could feel one shoulder lightly lean on my own. 'I've done a terrible thing,' he said brokenly. 'So dreadful, I daren't even tell you I've done it. But I have to, or I can't go on living.'

A table was clearing, the last, near the door. I looked at them, and smiled my 'Good Night'. They'd long since paid their bill, we'd been serving them coffee for over an hour it seemed. Vincent's words set up such a terrible chill, I wished the table would stay. But they'd gone now and we stood there together, Vincent and I, with the silence growing between us.

What had he done? Whatever it was, now was not the moment to be told. It would have been, but even as his quivering lips opened and started to speak in low explanation, the sound of doors slamming as from taxis and cars arriving outside our establishment, wrecked the sensitive timing. I dreaded to look, recognizing the voices, not just of Brad, and of Rufus – but also of Lionel!

'Lionel Striving! Christ – Vince—!' I knelt down on the

floor, cowering beneath my frail till. Vince looked down in surprise.

'Wasn't he in the States – Lionel Striving? You said he was there.'

'Well, he was,' I said desperately. 'But he's not now is he – he's here! So is Brad. So is Rufus. I can hear them—' The door opened.

'I can see them,' Vince managed to mutter. He bent down as if for a bottle.

'Jesus God!' I whispered wretchedly. 'There's bound to be blood! Any chance of some sort of an escape route?'

We both looked despairingly at the open Dumb Waiter, me still on all fours and Vince folded from the waist, his neat buttocks high in the air.

'What the hell are you two doing?' Zoë's voice rang out clearly, facing us as she rose up the stairs. She was wearing her coat, her pinny in her hand about to be stuffed in her handbag. 'There's more buggers just come in – shall I tell them to fuck off—? Bloody hell! Just look at that—' Her voice stopped short, her jaw dropped down. 'They're fighting now!'

The Dumb Waiter was quite large, the width of a window-sill, a deep one. The sort used by children on snug wintery evenings, when, accommodated on cushions, they'd fit themselves in to study slow snowstorms, entranced for hours by the swirling flakes. Warm and secure, and safe. Feeling quite the opposite to how I felt now, suspended half-way to the kitchen. Above, a storm of a different sort was raging far more fiercely, whilst below the startings of another, less furious but with almost equal vehemence, was surfacing between Dick and Nutty. I could have done with a cushion not just for my coccyx, but to hold tight over my head.

Brad's voice was the loudest. 'You'll get this straight up your hooter, mate – overtaking on the inside!' I could see his clenched fist, though my eyes were shut tight. Vincent's thin voice wavered. 'Please, lads—' Lionel Striving was coughing, offensively so; it went with a dismissive sneer. 'Old chap,' he was saying.

'Yes, my man,' added Rufus, calmly. The sort of calm and air of authority to rightly infuriate everyone. 'I was probably, as passenger, the very best person to judge accurately who was to blame—'

'Blame! Bloody blame!' Brad's strong voice rose, stronger. 'This four-eyed fart nearly ripped off my bumper!'

'You exaggerate, you weren't even scratched. In the States, where I've come from—' Lionel's words were now drowned by a crash like an exploding bomb from below in the kitchen. The Dumb Waiter gave a dangerous shudder. I prayed that I shouldn't be sick. A small sticky glass of discarded Chartreuse and the sour ash of someone's cigar tainted what air I was trying to breathe. I hoped Vincent wouldn't forget I was here. If I screamed now I knew no one would hear me. The violence was catching. The uproar below had spread without doubt to above. Everyone shouted.

'You bastard!'

'Ye Gods!'

'Now look here!'

'This aggression, you know, is uncalled for—'

'Chaps like you—'

'All you lot—'

'Yeah – your fuckin' class—'

It was hard to tell Brad's voice from Dick's. Or was it that what they said was the same. Dick's was closer, that was all I knew – mere inches away on the stairs.

I dipped my thumb in the tacky Chartreuse, and licked as I listened, all ears. Two new voices entered now, female. One shrill and one soft. Zoë's first, followed faintly by Auntie's. 'Stuffy's glasses – they're broken! You buggers – take that and that and that. And that!' A regular beat, beat, beat accompanied Zoë's words like the rhythm employed by a drummer. She was wielding her handbag around numerous heads. I could tell by the shrill yelps of pain. A crescendo of voices, joint victims, joined in.

'Hell!'

'The bitch!'

'My eye's bleeding!'

'I'm cut—' 'Serve you right – look at me!' 'Hey, look out boys – she's heaving that table!' Zoë, amazon-like, took on all, avenging Stuffy's poor spectacles. She needn't have bothered, I knew he had more in reserve. Five or six pairs at least, from what I could remember, for deciphering rare manuscripts.

There was a terrible scraping, as of wood upon wood – then a thunderous rumble and roar. A table was going, there was no doubt of that. It fell heavily just short of the window. I guessed this was so by the shimmering tinkle of shattering glass. That small case to the left-hand side of the door which contained decorative objects of Vincent's. Quite unsuitable, I'd warned at the time – they were bound to get smashed in the end. Lots of Babycham Bambis batting their lashes, doing very coy things with their legs. Very kitsch, so he'd claimed – and good for a laugh. Someone was having a laugh now – a high-pitched hyena soaring hysteria which I recognized as belonging to Soc. Ari joined in. They must have both surfaced, believing it to be a big game.

'I chuck now!' chuckled Soc. I heard the sound of his chucking as a plate made contact, closely followed by others from Ari, blended with a bouncing from my side of the stairs. Dick and Nutty were involved in a ball game. They ricocheted from wall to banister, quite often banging shoulders with me. I wondered exactly how many inches of plywood and nails lay between us. Then split seconds of silence, till it started again. Dick, so it seemed, must be down! Because now Soc and Ari must have seized this advantage to repay for all grievances past. I could hear them hissing and squealing and bubbling together, like low beasts bent on revenge.

'See, I take this bowl of rice pudding and I stick down his trousers like so!' Ari could hardly get the words out. Soc gave a whoop of pure joy. 'I piss in his ear – no! Yes. I think I do. I think I piss in this filthy pig's ear. He no good. Hold his head – here I go. Look here Auntie – I make pee-pee in dirty Dick's earhole!'

Where was Nutty? Unconscious? Apparently not, he was

speaking in low tones to Auntie. They must have both turned in alarm at Soc's and Ari's intended misdeeds. I could hear Auntie's soft remonstrations. The fact that I could was not simply that now they were clustered so near to the Dumb Waiter, but that quite suddenly there did seem to be over all a calm starting after the storm. But it was a shade too soon to be able to tell whether it was safe for me to emerge. The violence had broken out, that was the strange part, quite independently of me. There was no real way that any of the participants might have linked me with those others involved. The knowledge comforted me. I'd been spared confrontation. It was worth hanging on a bit longer. I drained the Chartreuse, my first drink tonight. I was quite looking forward to another. Brad quite clearly had gone, I'd have known if he hadn't. So had Lionel. Were they fighting it out on the streets, in their vehicles, each racing together crashing through red lights and pedestrian crossings, swerving round corners on kerbs? Zoë's shrill voice was missing, which must mean that Stuffy by now had absented himself.

What of Rufus? Was he there? And if so, did it matter? Might I dare make my presence felt at last?

I scratched like a rat on the side of my cage, trusting someone might hear me. No reply. None at all. 'Vincent,' I wavered. There was silence! Good God! Had they left me?

I thought about Vincent, to subdue my panic. He had been on the point of confession. What could he have done? What might it be that was almost too appalling to tell? We used to, I remembered, play that game as children – would you harbour a criminal? A murderer? A thief? A spy? A spy who had betrayed his own country! That one, I remembered, was considered the worst, the most heinous crime of them all. It was wartime. And a spy, it was pointed out, caused the death of millions whilst a murderer usually only one. Could that be it? Not a spy, not that – I couldn't imagine Vincent diddling MI5. But he might have murdered, in self-defence, any one of the sadistic louts he went round with. And justifiably so. I decided in my mind I'd stand by him. If he ever let me out.

I lifted my arm to strike the Dumb Waiter and opened my mouth in a wail. All the breath left my body as I sharply shot upwards, zooming too swiftly to the surface.

The restaurant, was this it? A landscape of table-legs and stray dishes of cracked crockery and large spoons. And spare bottles – the sort used as weapons. My till hanging loose leaked a littering of silver as limp notes floated down to the floor. Far away near the door a jewelled collection of Bambi splinters glittered and shone.

Vincent bent anxiously, holding his stomach. 'Oh darling – such goings – on! The place is quite wrecked! And I'm feeling so ill. I think I've developed an ulcer!'

'Tell me, Vince.' I spoke slowly. 'Whatever it is, I'll stand by you. You need to know that. You were saying, before, you had something to tell me—'

His answer so filled me with flooding relief, and I found his delivery so tragically funny as he tearfully confessed, that I unfolded myself from the restricting Dumb Waiter and slowly sank to the floor. Poor Vincent thought that I'd fainted.

I was still on my knees, half laughing, half crying and telling Vincent he wasn't to worry, when Rufus arrived. My head rose at the sound of his voice. 'How do I look?' I whispered to Vincent. But Vincent, now with the weight of worry, great worry, lifted it seemed from his life, was still not controlled enough to answer. I left him there at my feet, radiantly weeping.

'Hullo, Rufus – how lovely to see you!' I glanced down at my clothes – remarkably spruce considering all they'd been through. Crease-resistant, quite certainly, Rufus wasn't alone. I was expecting one of the others to walk in behind him, Brad or Lionel, but not this person.

The impression was one of a formal figure, much like Rufus himself, well-suited and smoothly urbane. There was something vaguely familiar there, but I couldn't in this light pin down what it was. Three bulbs had been broken.

'Be careful there, old chap, where you step – hell of a lot of glass!'

Who was he then? Another driver, like Brad – part of the

same mini-cab company? They were eccentric, they employed all sorts from Greek gods such as Brad to defrocked priests, and doctors struck off the register. This one looked too successful though. A professional man. An entrepreneur, but one very far from failure. For some reason, as yet unknown to me then, I guessed his name to be – Guy.

'Guy – let me introduce you,' Rufus was saying even as soon as I'd thought it! But something was occurring downstairs in the kitchen. A rustling and shuffling and the sound of low murmurs. Who was down there – I'd completely forgotten! My mind was momentarily distracted.

My limp fingers fell, reminding me, as they contacted hair, that Vincent lay sprawled at my feet. He lifted a happy, tear-drenched face. 'I love you,' he sang, 'you're the tops—'

'Look here, old girl! What the hell's going on in this hole!' Rufus coloured and blustered. 'Bloody Bedlam broke out a short while ago, whilst I was waiting for Guy here. You missed it, old chap! Just as well you got lost – no driver in his right mind could've kept up with the maniac cabby I had! I shall put in a formal complaint to that company! Funny, I've been using them for years, but lately their drivers have been completely irresponsible. This one tonight coolly entered what was clearly a one-way street off Sloane Avenue – just like that! I cautioned him, and do you know what he had the nerve to claim? That it was much the best short-cut! That's where we lost you – it's a wonder you found this place. Frightfully sorry, old fellow!'

Guy Whatever-his-name took it all in his stride. He'd been studying me closely throughout. Now suddenly he leaned forward.

'Well I'm damned! If it's not you! The adorable one!'

The light caught one cheek, and I knew why I'd thought 'Guy'. He looked like the actor Guy Rolfe, with the same long lean face, lined from cheekbone to chin like dimples stretched out in two skeins. I'd thought it before when I'd seen him in Brighton presenting his lighter to Auntie. He was the one who'd been brisk with the waiter. He needn't start being brisk here. There was no sound at all now from the kitchen, nor any sign of Auntie. I strained my eyes; in the darkest corner there did seem to be something moving. A large shifting shadow made up of more than one person, more than two, I now saw, as three heads sharpened fleetingly in silhouette, Auntie, book-ended by Soc and Ari, melted in one loosely-knit lump. Her voluminous cloak provided a blanket for whatever was occurring beneath. I had a feeling, it made me feel nice, that much stroking was going on in Auntie's cloak. Perhaps Pure Wool led to these things.

Zoë had gone and so had Stuffy, without saying 'Good Night'. I didn't mind, Zoë's face was enough. Her gaiety was almost contagious; to touch her, like a leper, would have been to have caught it. I felt that I wouldn't see them again, either apart or, more likely, together. And now Rufus was speaking of going away! Paying a visit to his wife in Australia!

He told me quickly, whilst Guy – the person called Guy – a past colleague of his at the Bar, whom Rufus now trusted would look after me in his absence – whilst this Guy had returned to his car for cigars. We didn't sell them, not the brand he preferred. Ours were Manikins, hardly the same!

'What do you mean, Rufus – look after me?' The cigar incident, though slight, had ruffled me. As much as the waiter thing in Brighton.

'Legally speaking, in a legal sense. Sorry. Let me say it again. We are amalgamating, he and I. He'll look after your interests in my absence.'

I looked at Rufus. He seemed uncomfortable. There was a familiar bulge in his pocket. 'Is that a gun in your pocket? Or are you just pleased to see me?' A favourite quote from Mae West.

He tugged at the bulge. Was he getting it out! He was. 'A small present. Victorian!' He opened the fine linen, frilled camisole-knickered affair. 'See, quite authentic. Slit from stern to stem. Original Free Traders, one might say. But of course in Victorian times, with a more practical purpose – for pissing through, legs apart, under crinolines. Described in *Walter – My Secret Life*. You remember, I read that bit out. Any chance

217

m'dear?' He grew more agitated as Guy re-entered the door. 'Blasted nuisance, he's dropped in on me tonight. Had it all prepared, you know. Had to cancel a cab that I'd ordered to come here. Guy arrived out of the blue. Ten minutes more and I would have missed him – can't be helped. It's given me the chance to introduce you two. He has restaurants, a whole string of them, in the family. Left by his father – isn't that right, Guy?'

Vince had crept away, he must have crept on all fours. I found a sprinkling of his tears on the floor.

What was happening down below? Was Dick entombed down there with Nutty?

Guy was talking now. 'I seem to have lost your attention!' His tone was so challenging, I chose to ignore it.

Rufus was studying the Menu. He had unfortunately chosen to read one with considerable crossings-out and one with the most bizarre spellings. 'That little son of yours is coming on! Look here, Guy, this child's only two and a half. Amazing, eh, education these days! I know I couldn't have formed capital letters at two. And look, the little chap's managed to state his food preferences—' I didn't enlighten his ignorance. He'd never find out in Australia.

'Might I look at your menu?' What a damnable man this Guy was with his cool, amused air, his expensive cigars and that warmth waiting there in his eyes. Something kindled deep in the bowl of my stomach.

'No. You can't,' I said carelessly. 'We toss them away at the end of each evening. You see, we never have the same thing on twice. That way gives greater variety. No one ever knows what to expect.'

'How original,' he murmured. The dimples deepened as if suppressing a smile. I'd made it sound as if we were producing rare concoctions of culinary art, each dish created, each taste and flavour teased from the ephemeral air. Guy carefully appraised each inch of the decor, and as he did so I saw to my horror that a scarlet gout of that hideous wrecked decor had transferred itself to his suit! Jesus Christ, it had to be him of course!

'You've got paint on yourself.' I got it in first, subtly suggesting that he was at fault.

He glanced down. 'Have I really – how frightfully careless. I apologize for ruining your paintwork. I must have disturbed a surface.' He smiled, all charm. What a clever bugger, what a bastard to be on the wrong side of.

He stood up, he was tall, even taller than me. 'I'd love to look at your kitchen.' He said it ingenuously, like an eager young boy trying to impress his best friend's mother with his manners. It was extremely hard to refuse. Refusal would have appeared not merely churlish, but would have placed him at an advantage, putting me on the defensive. As if I really had something to hide. The loaded silence hung between us. Rufus looked anxiously on, aware of a tension, unhappily knowing he himself was very much outside it.

I was cross with myself and annoyed that the man was undeniably making progress. 'My interest,' he said, as if reading my thoughts, 'is purely professional. I like this small place despite tonight's skirmish, it has an excellent feel. My family's business used to be like this – their very first restaurant, I remember. But then, as happens, they expanded until the whole has now become sadly impersonal. An empire, but lacking what you obviously have here – people who cherish and care.'

I laughed, looking around. It sounded harsh and coarse, rather more than I'd meant.

'Oh, the people here certainly care all right – come Monday we shall be without both a waitress and a chef. I say chef. I actually mean cook – and even cook might be placing too fine a distinction. We use shovels here rather than spoons.'

My honesty must have disarmed him completely, for he threw back his head and laughed loudly. A faint five-o'clock shadow, though it was now well past that, darkened the line of his jaw. Those dimples of his must be devilishly difficult, not to say dangerous, to shave. I stopped myself, this wasn't right. I knew the danger signals, the warning signs that spelt deeper involvement. It always started at just that point of noticing physical landmarks. The lie of an earlobe, the light on a lip, a slight imperfection enough to endear, or a gross one – enough to enslave.

Where was Brad? Where was Lionel? I crossed my fingers mentally now, willing them not to arrive. I could have coped, have managed somehow between Brad and Rufus and Lionel. But things were different now with this Guy.

The telephone rang at precisely that moment, as if to answer my prayer. I picked it up. 'Will you excuse me?' I'd turned my back towards Rufus and Guy and prepared to speak in a low voice to Brad. I rehearsed the words before I said them. I was too tired, was what I'd say. On the point of exhaustion and off home in minutes. I'd see him when I saw him – next week?

A thin high nasal voice spoke my name and asked me to wait. She was putting a Mr Lionel Striving on the line. Thank you, ma'am, my pleasure, I'm sure! I waited in desperation through the pips, which seemed to go on for ever. Then, for no reason at all, they suddenly ceased, the line went completely dead. I turned round. 'It's gone dead,' I foolishly announced for no reason at all. Guy and Rufus were talking together. A cooing and billing, as from contented doves, issued amongst muffled chucklings from the depths of Auntie's dark corner. She'd be pleased to see Guy. She'd said he was lovely. She'd lost the lighter coming back on the train. Had left it, she'd claimed, in the Gentlemen's Toilet. She wouldn't have it that they weren't like that on trains, that the Toilets were neither for Gents nor for Ladies but for both, and for children, even dogs. The phone rang again. I lifted it mechanically, expecting the same harpy. 'Hello, kid! How are you keeping? It's me, Brad – I'm on my way to Bristol, can you believe! I was in your caff – where were you, for Christ's sake? Fuckin' poncey maniacs, trying to kill me! One cunt in particular! And you should have seen the pompous prick who was my fare – but I had to split before I could sort them all out. Sorry kid, I left a bit of a mess. But I had this job to go on to. Just getting on the motorway now – the bloke's paralytic. Too drunk to drive home, got to be in Bristol by the morning. Not a bad old chump – already offered me an enormous whack of money to run his main Massage Parlour! Yes, no kidding! Male-Female Saunas, mixed! Says I'm made to measure for the job – can't get over my beautiful body—'

'Don't boast,' I said. 'None of us can.'

'No, seriously though—' I had been serious, but didn't interrupt any further, not wishing to stem the flow of his sheer youth and vitality. 'I mean to say, he's a nutter but I may give it a whirl. So if you don't hear for a couple of weeks you'll know I'm up there—'

'Pummelling,' I said.

I turned to see first Nutty emerging from downstairs, followed by a dazed, damp, chastened Dick, with Vincent bringing up the rear. The trio looked somehow complete in itself, like a triangle, perfectly met. Each in a way equal, not much on its own, but made by coming together. Dick's cheek was bruised, I could see now quite clearly.

'What happened down there?' I said before I could stop.

Nutty answered. 'Dick fell.' He said it quite simply, but I remembered out of nowhere that, despite Nutty's appearance, he was deceptively strong. Indeed, more than that, he was actually an expert at Judo, even had his Black Belt, I believed. A leap of delight rose in me at the thought of Dick tasting his come-uppance.

'My dear.' Nutty, his swivel-eye steady as a rock, was addressing me, fully in command. 'I thought I'd drive these two fellows down to the country tonight. A spot of fresh air will do them both good, get away from the Smoke for a while. I wondered,' his voice faltered and for an instant he was the old Nutty, 'if you had the keys handy of the Rolls. Be more amusing to take the chaps in that. Dick here, says he's never been in one!'

I looked directly at Dick. I knew his game well. I understood what he was after. If he wanted the Rolls, it was his, I didn't mind. I'd had enough material possessions showered on me to last me a whole lifetime. 'Take it, of course,' I said lightly.

'Look, here are both keys, take the two of them—'

'Oh, no, n-n-n—' Nutty demurred, not completely ready yet to be cast away so brutally. But Dick intervened. 'Thanks, missus.' He stepped forward and took both keys in his hand. 'Case one gets lost, Squire, only sensible.' He'd redressed the balance between them. I wondered, just briefly, where Vincent would fit in. But they needed him there as a buffer, to dilute the violence. I could see it now. He stood there gazing at me. 'Are you sure it's all right, darling? The strain's been so great – I just feel I might die if I don't get away – just for a little while?'

'Do.' I meant it.

'But will you be all right? Will you manage?' Vincent's voice almost broke with emotion. I leant forward and kissed him.

'Haven't I always, Vince? Of course, don't be daft, you go off. I'll let you know, I'll give you a ring. I might not open on Monday.' Or ever again, it occurred to me. That's how it was, to be your own boss, you could do what you liked, when you liked. Or not if you didn't, it was up to you.

The telephone rang, would it ever stop ringing? This time Lionel got through right away. 'God Almighty, you're elusive. I've been trying to reach you for hours – all day! Where the hell have you been? I flew in this morning and came straight to the house – not a sign of life there. I'm only here on a flying visit. Quite literally. I'm ringing from London Airport – they've called my flight – didn't you get my letter? I've got this project, a big one in Pennsylvania – and I've got this cock-rise, just talking to you, already. Three erections I've lost through lack of opportunity! I even came round to that address of your business. By God, but it's rough – do you know what you're at? I couldn't see you, but I didn't dare wait – some bitch heaved a table – split my eyebrow right open. It's lucky I escaped with my sight. No, I beat the hell out of there. I'd already been menaced by a rough-neck cabby who claimed damage whilst driving along – I shall be glad, I can tell you, to get back to the States. At least there you learn to expect violence! The only thing is – my angel, I miss you. God Almighty, this is bursting my breeches! Christ, they're calling my flight again! But my balls are like bullets! Tonight at dinner with this client – I couldn't control it – we were eating oysters – and I kept thinking of your cunt! I'm sure he got wind that something was up when the table-cloth started stirring – dare I wank – no I daren't – and besides there's no time—'

I cut his voice out by the touch of a finger. If I hadn't he could well have missed his flight. And I might find him, if this happened, hot-footing it back. I had other things on my door-step. To make doubly certain that we were indeed cut-off. I kept my finger for a further second on that vital part of the receiver. And then cancelled out all further calls by leaving the thing off the hook.

'Am I to take it that we are at last alone?' I turned round at the sound of Guy's voice. They had all disappeared. Dick, Vince, Nutty had gone. And, mysteriously, Rufus as well – no fond farewells.

'No, we're not. My Auntie's here, somewhere.'

We gazed down together at Soc and Ari. They sprawled, sleeping peacefully, like two satiated cherubs, mouths open, each side of Auntie. Auntie was sleeping, herself, a wide smile on her face. As if she'd slipped from delight into dreaming. There was no reason why she should ever learn that Vincent had taken her money. Taken it as well for the simplest of reasons, not from personal malice or a sense of resentment, but merely to pay off large mounting debts. His sartorial in-terests had led him to financial deep waters, unpaid accounts at places like Mr Fish, for his shirts, and at Turnbull and Asser for silk trifles such as hankies. I'd had to laugh, when all the time I'd been afraid he was under pressure for far more menac-ing reasons.

I could feel Guy beside me; a light spiralling started deep in my stomach. 'It seems a shame to disturb them,' he murmured. His hand brushed my own.

'It does,' I said thickly, my throat had seized up. I passed a small fart in excitement, and prayed that it wouldn't pong. He seemed not to notice, his lips brushed my hair. 'Now would seem a good moment to show me your kitchen—'

We went down. He began to impress me.